BETTING BAD

CATHRYN FOX

COPYRIGHT

Discover other titles by Cathryn Fox at www.cathrynfox.com. Please sign up for Cathryn's Newsletter for freebies, ebooks, news and contests:

https://app.mailerlite.com/webforms/landing/c1f8n1

ISBN Print 978-1-928056-85-0
ISBN ebook 978-1-928056-78-2

TYLER

I might have just spent a long eight years in state prison for gun running, going up against some of the cruelest bastards—lifers with a license to kill and the freedom to use it—but I had no idea what real fear was until this very moment.

I slow my bike, the roar of the engine settling to a soft rumble between my legs as I brace my feet on the cold ground below me and stare down the dark, rain-soaked street of Middletown Chicago. It's late fall, but it's not the damp, frigid night air that's turning the blood in my veins to ice. No, it's the thought of confronting my family again and the girl I left behind. How can I possibly face the deep-seated disappointment in their once proud eyes?

I can guaran-fucking-tee there won't be a single law-abiding citizen in my Westside neighborhood who'll be happy to see known criminal, Tyler Barrett, riding back into town. And the local gang? The Phantoms. Well, they're smart enough not to fuck with someone under the protection of Deacon, the guy who took me under his wing on the inside, and who still runs the streets on the outside.

At least I think they are.

I swallow against the bile punching into my throat, and as my heart thunders in my ears, I steal a glance over my shoulder, take in the long stretch of pavement at my back. A restless energy grips my throat, every instinct I possess urging me to turn my bike around and get the hell out of Dodge.

But I've come too far to turn back now.

I face forward and rev my bike, but not even the sound of the engine splitting the night apart can chip away at the glacier expanding inside me, squeezing the air from my lungs. It guts me, hollows me out inside to know I failed everyone I've ever cared about. That I threw away a college education and lost my football scholarship at Northwestern to a pair of handcuffs and a sunset-orange jumpsuit that paled over the years. I was supposed to make something of myself. Instead I found myself behind bars for eight long years, which makes this dangerous, gang-plagued neighborhood look like a goddamn Disney movie.

But you know what? I'd do it all again. Fuck yeah, I would. If going to state prison and fighting every goddamn day for my life meant protecting my baby brother's future, I'd do it all over in a heartbeat. No questions asked.

My phone pings and I slide my hand into my jacket pocket. I swipe my finger over the screen and read the one-word text from Justin. He's not much of a talker, but when he speaks, we all listen. By *we*, I mean the five of us who banded together for security and protection under the umbrella of Deacon. Even though I grew up in Phantom territory, Deacon took me in. Probably because I got in the way of a lifer ready to take him down. I hadn't realized it at the time. I saw the guy coming at me with a shiv, and fought back. His real target was Deacon, who'd been working out behind me, completely unaware. I'd avoided gangs my whole life, but that was no longer an option on the inside. After that incident,

Deacon took us newbies in, and while he ran the show behind bars and had an army at his back, the five newbies within the group considered ourselves a brotherhood: no judgment, no censure. For the last year we'd all been living in a rundown place in south Illinois, none of us ready to face our demons after doing time. But like an omen with a vengeance, the old house burned to the ground a few weeks back and we knew it was time to return home. Now here I am, my parole over, trying to figure out how to face my family and re-enter a society leery of lawless ruffians.

I glance at the text. *Good?*

I scoff. Isn't that just like Justin? He's the toughest guy I know, yet always has a knack for knowing when there's a shit-storm going on inside of me. But I feel the pain of his return every bit as much as he feels mine. While the five of us were all tight, Justin and I were the closest. Cell mates on the inside. Brothers for life on the outside.

Yeah, you? I text back.

Yeah.

The light dims on my phone and I stare at it until it goes black, much like my mood. I shove it back into my pocket and twist the throttle to set my bike into motion. I pass the familiar sights, the stores with their windows barred, on lock-down for the night. My gaze runs the length of the impene-trable steel. No one gets in. No one gets out. A fine shiver moves through me. Damned if I don't know that feeling all too well.

I peer into the corners and dark alleyways I used to steer clear of in my youth. No way could I risk getting in to trouble. Now, well, none of that shit matters. Why would it? I mean, it's not like any of the motorcycle gangs can take away my future. Nope, I did that all on my own. Well, sort of.

I take a trip down memory lane as I pass through Main Street and turn down the road leading to my childhood home. We might not have had much when growing up, but we always had each other. Dad bailed shortly after my sister was born. Apparently, he couldn't handle having a child who was legally blind. Fucking asshole. I was only ten when I caught the tail end of his car rounding the corner, disappearing from our lives forever.

I might have been the oldest of four, but because I was just a kid, I couldn't help the family out financially. There were times Mom worked up to three jobs to put food on our table and keep us all on the straight and narrow. She scraped and saved to keep us in sports and get my visually impaired kid sister the care she needed.

My fingers take that moment to itch, my mind tripping back to the very specific trade I chose to pursue in prison. I left a nine-year-old little girl at the time of my incarceration, one who needed her big brother, and while learning braille won't make up for the past, I'm hoping it will guide us toward a better future.

I idle down my bike and pull into my driveway, the beating heart of my childhood residence rising up before me. *Home sweet home.* My stomach squeezes when I see the lone light on in the living room. Not much has changed since I left. Yet nothing will ever be the same again. My boots hit the ground with a thud, and I hike up my backpack as I walk quietly to the front door. I knock like a stranger, and the sheer wrongness in that is like a fist to the gut. From behind the once white lace curtain, the frayed edges burnt yellow from the summer sun, I see movement, hear the rustle of slippers on the aged wood floors.

I suck in a quick breath and hold it. I'm the last person my mother expects to find standing on her stoop—of that I'm certain. When I left here all those years ago, I told her not to visit. She had three kids who needed her attention more than me. At least that's what I told her. But the truth was, I couldn't handle the disappointment ghosting her eyes every time she looked at me.

From behind the pane of glass, her blue eyes widen, a mixture of grief, sorrow and happiness playing out like a gut-wrenching slideshow. It wraps around me, squeezes my ribcage like a vice, and all I want to do is lay down in it, curl up in my breathlessness until all the bad memories are nothing but a distant blur.

I freeze at the click of the lock opening, but suck in another fast breath to pull myself together. Fuck man, I need to ground myself in the moment. I'm back home and when that door opens, I'm going to face off against my mother, not some mean, ruthless prison guard who gives all of zero shits about his inmates.

"Mom," I say as the door yawns open, the warmth of the house spilling out into the night but doing little to push back the bone-deep cold inside me.

"Tyler." Tears fill weary eyes as she opens her thin arms to me in a welcoming embrace. I wrap her in a hug, and choke back the pain clutching at my throat. "How...when?" she asks, her shaky voice rumbling against my pounding heart as I hold her tight.

I grit my teeth to keep my shit together and inch back. Since the how and when don't matter, I say, "It's good to see you."

She goes up on her toes to cup my cheeks, the gesture taking me back to my football years, when she used to be proud of me. "It's good to see you, too." We both stand there immobilized, neither knowing what to do, what to say. This moment might have been a year in the coming, but it feels so surreal, like I'm having an out of body experience. I can't help but want to pinch myself to see if I'm dreaming.

Breaking the awkward silence, Mom shakes her head and says, "Come in. Come in." She steps back and the familiar scents of home and hearth hit harder than a guard's baton to the kidneys. I steal a glance around, and my gaze settles on the old chrome table where I used to do my homework. I shrug my backpack from my shoulders and my mother's gaze slides to it.

"Are you…staying?" she asks quietly, like she's battling the emotions inside her.

"Is it okay?" The air feels tight in my lungs as I wait, hating what I'd put her through. If she tells me to leave, walk out the door and never return, I wouldn't blame her.

She blinks up at me, a deep weariness about her. "Of course it is, Tyler. This is your home. It's always been your home."

I exhale the breath I'm holding. "I have a few things stored at a friend's place. I'll have the box shipped here if it's okay." I didn't accumulate much after prison, just enough to help me get by at my job. Justin tossed my things into his truck before I left, and is holding them until I'm settled.

"Yes, have them shipped," Mom says.

I scrub my chin. "How is everyone?" I ask, even though I already know. I might have been locked up, but I always had feelers out, making sure my brother kept good on the promise he made to me the day I stood before the judge. Even from behind bars, I made sure he kept that vow. I might not have been here to give him a personal beatdown if he veered off track, but I had plenty of friends who would step in and do it for me.

Mom takes my hand and guides me to the table. She feels so thin and frail. My heart hitches. She's obviously been working too hard, and I can't forget that my incarceration has taken its toll on the once vibrant woman. No, I can't ever forget that. But I have to somehow find a way to make things right and exist in this world—this family—again.

Mom fills the kettle with water. "Tea?" she asks.

"Sure."

She drops one leafy bag into each mug and takes the seat across from me. We've always been so comfortable with each other. Now, not so much.

"How are you, Mom?"

"I'm fine, Tyler. I'm working down at the Redman's pharmacy, and sometimes I pick up an extra shift here and there at Save Easy Foods. Both are right on the bus route."

"How's everyone else?"

"They're all good kids," she begins, but I get what she's really saying. They don't need my kind of trouble.

I try to ignore the sinking sensation in my chest. "I'm not here to disrupt their lives. I'm just trying to get my life in order."

"I know..." An awkward pause and then, "That's not what I meant." She sucks in a breath and smiles as she lets it out slowly. "Let me try again. Gracie is in her sophomore year of high school. She wants to be a writer. She's such a good student, Tyler, and has an incredible imagination. I'm so proud of her."

"I am, too," I say. "How's Alex?" Alex is the second youngest, and he was only twelve when I left. The tears in his big blue eyes, the way he clung to me and screamed bloody fucking murder when they took me away still haunts me.

"Alex is in his second year of college. Penn State." She frowns and glances down, like what she's about to say next will slay me. "He's on a football scholarship, but he'll be home for Thanksgiving next month."

My heart fills with pride for my baby brother. To know he picked up where I left off and stepped up to be the man the family needed, nearly makes me fucking sob.

"That's great, Mom," I say, and truly mean it. She lifts her eyes, and I take in the fine wrinkles that weren't there years ago. "And Lucas?" I ask. Unlike the rest of us, Lucas never was much of a student. He preferred to use his hands over his brains, and that's all well and fine—except for him, idle hands brew trouble.

"Lucas is working in Mr. Johnson's service bay. He's saving, and hoping to open his own shop someday." The warm smile that comes over her face is enough to wipe away every ounce of pain inflicted on me these last nine years. I did right by Lucas, and that's all I ever wanted.

"Is he helping you out financially?" I blurt out without thinking.

She frowns, and looks down quickly. Fuck. I've insulted her. Mom is a proud woman, and I've been home all of two minutes and managed to make her feel like shit.

"I don't want his money, Tyler. I can take care of my family."

"I know, but he's still living here," I say, changing tactics. "He should at least be paying room and board, right?"

She stands. "Tyler—"

"I'm sorry," I say quickly and stand with her. "You're right. It's none of my business." I shouldn't be walking into my mother's place and trying to step into the big brother role I once had, but truthfully, what Lucas does *is* entirely my business. Except my mother doesn't know that. "I'm just tired. It's been a long day."

The kettle boils and she turns it off. "Why don't you go get some sleep? Your bed is still waiting for you, or you can climb into Alex's old bunk next to Lucas, if you want the company. We can have tea tomorrow."

"Okay." I step back up to my mother, and drop a kiss onto her cheek. I want to talk more, ask about Sara. No matter how long she's been gone from my life, I've never stopped loving her. God, we had such big dreams and hopes. I hope she moved on without me, made a life with someone else. It would have been wrong, selfish of me to ask her to wait. I'm a man with a record now, with little to nothing to offer her. A good girl like her shouldn't be associating with a convict, and I drove that fact home when I pushed her away, refused her visits. She needed to get on with her life as much as I needed her to.

I clamp my mouth shut to prevent myself from asking questions I don't really want the answers to. I'm not sure I'm ready for any more kicks to the nuts tonight. I came back with a plan to work, volunteer, and take care of my family. Associating with a known criminal like me won't do a nice girl like Sara any good, and for me, well, the lost look in her eyes would surely tear my heart clear from my chest. "G'night."

I bend forward a bit, like I'd just taken one too many hard hits from a pissed-off inmate and climb the stairs quietly, my siblings fast asleep this time of night. I make a quick trip to the bathroom, tug off my shirt, and splash water on my face. I find a new toothbrush and claim it as my own, then make my way down the hall.

The floorboards squeak, and I wince. I pass by my room, my steps slowing. The light from the hall slants against the wall, and the sight of my bed, my trophies sparkling on my dresser like a shrine, twists me up inside. Mom left everything like it was, like I would eventually come back and be the same boy who'd left. But I'm not that boy at all. I never will be again.

I walk past the room, not ready to face it, and reach the room Alex always shared with Lucas. I slip inside and kick off my boots. The mattress coils squeak as I crawl into the bed and hunker down for sleep, although I don't expect it to be a restful one. My time in prison still haunts me in my nightmares. Rarely do I wake up without a sweat. I pull the blankets up, and the scent of fabric softener wraps around me. I breathe in the familiar aroma, and my thoughts travel back to the way that smell used to cling to my football jersey when I played in high school. Thinking about high school has my mind going back to Coach Ramsey. Sara's father. While I'm here, I want to give back to the community by putting my football skills to use. But I can't imagine he'd ever let me on his field again. Then again, unless I ask, I'll never know. I came here with a plan, and I have to see it through no matter what roadblocks I might face.

"Ty?" Lucas whispers, the soft rustle of blankets reaching my ears as my brother shifts in his bed.

I flatten myself on the mattress, and put one arm over my forehead. "Yeah, it's me." A pause and then, "You good?" He gets the message behind my words, a message I'd back up with my fists if I don't get the answer I'm looking for.

"I'm good." A moment of silence and then under his breath he says, "You're home," like he's trying to wrap his brain around the fact that his big brother—the guy who got busted caught with a car load of weapons trying to save his punk ass from trouble—is here, in the flesh.

"I'm home," I say, even though I have no idea where or what home is anymore.

2

SARA

I push the stacks of papers and overflowing files to the side and then set my brown bagged lunch on Dad's cluttered desk. I peel back the plastic wrap on my sandwich, and I'm about to take a bite when I catch the peculiar way Dad is frowning, his gaze going from me to my sandwich back to me again.

"What?" I ask. I hold half the sandwich out to him. "Want to share?"

"No, I'm good." He grabs an identical brown paper bag and tosses it onto the playbook he'd been going over. "Your mother made my favorite."

"Roast beef," I say, a statement, not a question.

"What else?"

I bite into my turkey salad and look past my father's shoulders to take in the wide expanse of football field through his office window. Since I work at the bank across the street from Collins High where Dad is the physical education teacher and football coach, I like to pop in every morning to say hello before work, and join him for lunch when I can. As an only child, I've always been Daddy's little girl, and while I enjoy our hour together, I sometimes think it's Dad's way of keeping tabs on me. I moved out of the house last year, much to my parents' dismay, and while I can take care of myself, I get that in his eyes, I'll always be his daughter, someone he needs to protect in a gang-plagued city unkind to those who don't wear colors.

"You know, you're kind of predictable," I say.

He arches a brow. "You say that like it's a bad thing."

I laugh. "It's okay to mix it up once in a while." I wink at him. "Maybe if you didn't hit Lincoln High with the same plays you've been using on them for years, you could walk away with the trophy," I tease. Lincoln is Collins High's rival school, but Dad's team hasn't beat them since...well, since the man I try hard not to think about left for college, then got hauled away to prison.

As if sensing my darkening mood, Dad says, "So now you're a football expert, are you? I think this fancy new position at the bank is going to your head." But there is laughter in his eyes, and I get he's trying to lighten my disposition. "We can beat Lincoln. Just you wait and see."

"I believe you," I say, but deep down I think Tyler's incarceration took something away from my Dad. Tyler was the son he'd always wanted, and without a father of his own, Tyler looked up to Dad. My mom, Mariam, also treated him like the son she never had. When Ty went to prison, he took a piece of us all with him, and Dad doesn't seem to love the game the way he once did.

I try to push all thoughts of Tyler away. I'm not sure why I'm suddenly thinking about him. Heck, who am I kidding? When have I ever stopped thinking about him? After all this time, he still fills my daytime thoughts and my nighttime dreams. But something in the way Dad was looking at me when I first sat down, reminded me of the day Tyler was arrested.

"I don't have the job yet," I say. "I have a few more classes I need first." I bite into my sandwich but it turns to sawdust in my mouth as my stupid mind once again trips back to years ago. Tyler and I had such high hopes. We were both at Northwestern on scholarships, and both taking business classes. I was always hugely into fitness, and the proper nourishment needed for the athlete. The degree was to learn how to run a business, but I also took nutrition courses as my electives. Ty was big into sports, obviously, and took extra courses in kinetics. Our plan was to open our own sports store one day, offer coaching and nutrition clinics, and run the business together. After Ty was arrested, and pushed me from his life, I fell apart, and had to drop out of school. I flailed around for a while, taking on odd jobs until Mr. Fillmore, a friend of Dad's took pity on me and gave me a teller position at the bank, and a few years ago I started taking night classes at the University of Illinois at Chicago, aka UIC.

A noise at the door behind me has my dad lifting his head. I ignore the knocking. Most times we're interrupted by students needing something or other during their lunch break. But when the color drains from Dad's face, unease trickles through my veins. I swallow down the bread stuck in my throat and slowly shift in my seat, but when my gaze meets with a familiar set of eyes, now harder, darker, my limbs freeze and a dull beat begins in my throat and travels all the way to my ears.

Tyler.

I grip the sides of my chair and struggle to keep down the sob threating to break free from my lungs as I gaze at the man eating up the doorway. A man who was just a cub when he left here. But now a wolf stands before me. Big. Bad. Dangerous in so many ways. The years haven't been kind to him, and eyes that were once pure and uncorrupted are a darker shade of blue, harder than I've ever seen them. It's clear he's seen too much, suffered too much.

As everything inside me tightens, my gaze slides downward, over his t-shirt and low-slung jeans. As a quarterback he was always solid, but now he's cut deep with hollowed out grooves—his body all lean lines and thick muscle. There isn't an ounce of softness about him. Tyler might have finally come home, but like those who went off to fight overseas, it's clear he hasn't come back intact either.

His once unflawed face now sports scars. My heart crashes so hard I feel lightheaded as I zero in on the cut that runs from his forehead, through his eyebrow, to his cheekbone. My pulse thuds, and I try to swallow but can't. I can't seem to breathe either. His hands curl at his sides, and he shifts, edgy, restless, a predator ready to pounce.

Truthfully, there is only one word to describe him. Lethal. He's no longer that sweet boy who'd taken my heart and virginity. His betrayal cut deep and there isn't a part of me that hasn't been hurt by him. Which means there's no place for that small burst of happiness, the delirious rush of need zinging through my veins at the sight of him.

I hate how much I want him again, how I never stopped loving him. Heat and longing moves through my body and my nipples tighten, like a testimony of my need. Even though I have no control over that side of me, I know better than to act on my desires. These past years, I've been careful to live a violence-free life, one void of criminal activity. So while Ty and I were once close, what we had is now in the past, and some things are better left there.

As his gaze seeks me out, I sit there, pinned in his crosshairs. Never have I felt so stripped bare, vulnerable, at a complete loss for words as he looks at me, like he can see through my skin, see the pain and suffering, all the bottled up love threatening to tear me wide open and reduce me to a quivering mess.

My father's voice snaps me back to the present, and Tyler squares his shoulders, the muscle along his jaw rippling as he clenches down.

"Tyler," my father says, his voice deeper, harsher than it was earlier. "Rumor had it you were back."

I spin so fast my neck makes a snapping sound. He knew? He knew all this time and didn't tell me? Was that why he was frowning at me earlier? Jesus, he at least should have told me so I could have better prepared myself. Then again, could anything have prepared me for Tyler's return?

"Mr. Ramsey," Tyler says, and then in a softer voice that rumbles through me, he adds, "Hi, Sara."

A sound catches in my throat at the familiar way he says my name, a reminder of the way he used to whisper in my ear when we made love in my dorm room. We were so happy back then. To this day, I still can't understand why he turned to a life of crime. Yes, his family was struggling to make ends meet, but our plan of starting a new business involved them. We talked endlessly about moving them out of Middletown and giving them work in our store. Then one night, just before we were to head back to Northwestern, to begin our junior year, Tyler got caught running guns that were traced back to the local motorcycle gang. I still can't wrap my brain around that.

I shake off that ugly memory and turn my attention to my half-eaten sandwich. I need to get out of here. Now. Feeling completely out of control, my fingers fumble a little as I tug the plastic, and when my brown paper bag falls to the floor, Tyler gets to it first.

I eye his gash, his brutally beautiful face as he drops to his knees, and I hold my breath, frozen in time. His warm, familiar scent wraps around me, and tears prick my eyes for all we've lost. I breathe him in and hold my breath for a long moment as I take in his thick lashes, and remember the way they used to tickle my flesh when he kissed a path down my body. I resist the urge to cry, to curl into him and stay there forever. Instead my gaze meets his and when I find his eyes trained on me, the room compresses and fades to black around the corners.

Jaw locked tightly, he blinks, his lids falling slowly, then opening again. "I got it," he says, his voice so quiet, I almost don't recognize it as he puts the bag on the desktop. Sinewy muscles stretch with his movement and I wait for his t-shirt to tear from the assault. But I forget all about that when his hand grazes mine, skin to skin, and it starts a chain reaction in my body. He inches closer, his warm breath caressing the shell of my ear as he breathes with a calm, steady cadence— far different from the way I'm gulping down air.

Being this close is playing havoc on my body, unnerving me, and urging me to touch him like I used to, to see if beneath that hardness the man I once knew still exists. Unable to help myself, I lightly caress his scar, trace my finger along the swollen purple flesh.

"What happened?" The loaded question spills from my lips before I can stop myself.

His gaze goes arctic as something flickers in his eyes. A memory? There's a war going on inside him, but it passes quickly and his expression shuts down as he shakes his head.

"Nothing."

Message received: it's none of my business. I pull my hand back like it'd just been slapped, turning away from him— again. My gaze flickers to my father, who is watching me with careful concern.

I eye the clock on the wall. "I should get going."

"Don't let me frighten you off," Ty says, his beautiful lips thinning to a flat line in a way I remember so well. I don't even have to try hard to recall how those lips felt on mine, rough with need and hunger one minute, soft and tender the next. "I can come back later, after you finish up lunch with your father."

"You're not frightening me off," I say, trying to pull off polite disinterest, but knowing I'm unsuccessful when he angles his head, his probing gaze moving over my face like he can see right through me. Honest to God, I should have known better than to try and get anything by him. This is Tyler, the man who was once solid and dependable and could light me up with a single look. A man I love so much that just seeing him now sets my chest on fire with heartache. When it came to us, every inch of him, every touch, every whispered word was love.

But I lost the illusion of *us* many years ago.

I take a couple of quick breaths, and my eyes dart to his again. I have to force myself to breathe, speak. "I have some things I need to take care of," I manage to say for good measure. "Go ahead and take care of whatever business it is you have with my father."

I push unsteadily to my feet, and Ty stays close. Too close.

"You okay?" he asks, and for one blistering minute we're back in time and I'm given a brief glimpse of the sweet boy from my youth. His knuckles brush mine, the connection between us as powerful today as it was all those years ago.

"Yeah, fine," I lie.

I force my legs to work and maneuver around him, and when my body brushes his, his soft curses peel back my skin and leave me wide open and vulnerable.

Raw.

"Talk to you later, Dad," I say, doing my best to keep my voice light when all I want to do is go back to my apartment, crawl under the covers and give in to the big ugly cry pulling at me. Sure it will leave my nose red and eyes swollen, but I just want to cry and cry until I have no more tears to shed. Except, when it comes to Tyler, there will always be more tears, more long lonely nights staring at the ceiling wondering why—how could he have been living a life of crime right under my nose? I'm not sure, but what I do know is that Tyler was my whole life, and after he left and shut me out, it took me years to get out from under the darkness.

With tears burning behind my eyes, beating against my lids like thundering hail, I grab my coat and purse, and dart to the door. I need to get away from this man and return to my safe job, my safe apartment, my safe...everything. Tyler doesn't fit into the new world I created for myself, no more than I fit into his.

I step out into the cold and don't bother shrugging back into my coat. I want the cold. I want it to push away the pain and hurt and freeze my bones until I'm numb. I sniff back the tears and step up to the lights, my gaze going to the motorcycle parked in front of the school. It must be Tyler's. There aren't too many high school students riding Harleys.

I keep my head down and hurry to the bank. Needing to be alone, I hurry to the back room, my heels clicking on the tile. When I see Kaitlyn pouring herself a cup of coffee, my feet come to a resounding halt. I love Kaitlyn, I really do. We became instant friends when I first started here a few years back, and we've grown so close, but I'm not sure I can talk to her right now. I'm not sure I can even get my voice to work.

Kaitlyn glances up and smiles, but it quickly dissolves when she takes a good look at me. Her spoon clatters in the steel sink as she drops it and comes toward me.

"Jesus, Sara, are you okay? You look like you've seen a ghost."

I guess in a sense I did. I saw a ghost of my former boyfriend. I force a laugh, try to make light of it, but it comes out as a hollow little sound that has her frown deepening and her eyes narrowing.

She touches my arm and it's all I can do not to fall into her and sob. "Sara, what is it?"

"I...Tyler's back." She doesn't know him personally, but she knows of him, knows what he did to all those who cared about him.

Her green eyes go wide and she pulls me in for a quick hug. "Oh my God. Are you okay?" When I don't answer, she inches back to see me.

I nod, even though I'm not. "I'll be fine. I just wasn't prepared to see him. I didn't even know he was back."

"Did you talk to him?"

"Not really. He stopped in to see my dad."

Her head jerks back. "Really? I wonder what that was all about?"

With shock still racing through me I say, "No idea."

She must see something in my face because her next question is, "How did he look?"

Beautiful is the first word that comes to mind. "Different," I say. "Grown up. Tough."

She gives a nod and says, "Prison will do that to you." Kaitlyn lost a few of her cousins to the system, so she would know. "It changes you. Kill or be killed, right?"

Even though I'm so goddamn angry with him, hurt by his betrayal, my heart pinches, and I feel like I'm going to vomit. I hate the thought of him hurting—of someone hurting him.

"I need to sit."

"Okay." Kaitlyn steps back and I plunk myself down on the sofa below the window.

Kaitlyn sits across from me and eyes me carefully. "You're not still hung up on him, are you?"

"He was my first love, Kaitlyn." I pinch the bridge of my nose. "We had big plans. A girl doesn't get over that so easily."

"It's been a lot of years, you know."

"I know," I say. No need to remind me of that. I felt every one of those years.

"Are you going to try to get back with him?"

My entire body tightens. "Never, not in a million lifetimes," I say adamantly, quickly.

"Well then, there's only one way to get over him and get on with your life."

I know what she's getting at. She's a party girl and for years she's been trying to set me up with one of her guy friends. I've always declined, but now I'm thinking maybe I should have taken her up on her offer. What was I really holding out for? Tyler to return, the same man he was before he left. One look at him today, and it was easy to see that's not the case.

She glances past my shoulder, and a small smile touches her mouth. "Your hot professor is here."

I turn and follow her gaze to see a very familiar man making his way to the front door of the bank. It's my professor, all right. Technically, he's my *former* professor at UIC, but Kaitlyn's statement holds all kinds of sexual undertones.

"You can't deny that he's good looking."

No, she's right, I can't deny that. But he's not Tyler.

"You can't deny that it's timely either, can you?" she asks as her bangles jangle. She's a believer in signs and all things psychic. To her, Caleb suddenly showing up like this means the universe is trying to tell me something.

And what exactly might that be?

Caleb had asked me out for coffee a few times after I finished his course, but I always declined. Why? Oh, I don't know. Maybe somewhere deep inside me I was hanging on to the idea of Tyler and what we had. But honest to God, for the last nine years I haven't been living. I've been existing—barely surviving. Maybe I need to start walking among the living again. If Tyler's return taught me one thing, it's that we're different people now, and I need to find a way to escape what's still between us. Maybe dating someone else is the only way I can get out from beneath his pull, and find some semblance of happiness in this incredibly messed up life I'm faltering through.

3

TYLER

A hot burst of need burns through me, and I try to keep my cool and not run after Sara as she bolts from her father's office. *Sara.* Sweet Sara Ramsey who I'd hurt so deeply, who now looks at me with fear and loathing in her eyes. But underneath that hate, in the darkest depths of her eyes, I spotted need and longing—nine long, hard years in the making.

I fist my hands and clench my jaw hard enough to break bone. I fucking hate myself for the pain I put her through. But I couldn't let Lucas run those guns. He was young and impressionable and likely would have gotten his ass shot off, or find himself in deeper with the Phantoms.

I chose to do it instead. No one held a weapon to my head, forcing me to load my trunk. Nope, I did that all on my own, and was fully prepared to do an out of state delivery. It didn't matter whether I was doing it for my brother, or not once I was caught. I committed a crime and it was my actions that put our future in jeopardy. After my arrest, I hoped that with my impeccable record, I'd never have to do time on the inside. Instead I got fifteen years, out in eight for good behavior, and one spent on parole in South Illinois.

Talk about betting bad.

"What can I do for you, Tyler?" Coach Ramsey asks, the coldness in his tone pulling me back to the present. He gestures for me to sit and I lower myself into the chair Sara just abandoned. The seat feels warm from her body and her scent still hangs in the air. I hadn't expected to walk in on Sara and her father. Then again, maybe I had. Even though I swore to stay away from her, maybe deep down I'm a goddamn masochist.

But now that I've seen her in person, it only made that raw ache of need inside me that much worse. Fuck, man. I hated the wide-open and vulnerable look in those haunted brown eyes of hers. It was all I could do not to pull her into my arms and confess. But if she ever found out the truth, she'd only hate me more.

"Coach," I say, forcing my attention to the matter at hand. Coach scrubs his hand over his chin, his scruff more silver than black now as he waits, somewhat impatiently, to see what I'm doing here. I'm sure I'm the last person he and his daughter wanted or expected to see today. "How's the team?"

His eyes are murderous, his lips compressed as he taps a pen against his playbook. "Been better."

I clear my throat, and chose my next words carefully. "I was wondering if you'd like some help on the field. I'd be happy to volunteer."

He sits forward, braces his elbows on his table. "Is this a part of your rehabilitation program?"

"No, sir."

He angles his head, and I feel like a bug under a microscope. His examination shouldn't bother me so much. Fuck, in prison I'd been stripped bare in more ways than one as guards and psychologists violated every part of me. But I never let them in, never let anyone other than the five of us guys who banded together, get too close.

"After what you did to my daughter, you've got some fucking nerve coming in here and asking for a job."

I didn't just hurt his daughter. I hurt him, too. We both know that. He was the father I never had, and I betrayed his trust. I swallow the bile punching into my throat. On the field Coach can be a real hard-ass, but off the field he's a kind man who cares about others, and would die for his family. There was a point where he cared about me too, and that's why I'm here. He picks up his playbook, rolls it and slaps it against his hand.

"Fucking nerve," he whispers under his breath.

He's right, of course. It took all my nerve to face off against him. But I've faced off against worse and when I came back to town, I wasn't expecting a welcome home parade. It takes a big fucking set of balls to get your life back in order and try to find your way after being incarcerated.

"Yeah, I know. But I wouldn't be here if I wasn't looking to turn my life around. I'm just looking for a chance to prove myself."

"If this has anything to do with Sara—"

"It doesn't." I try not to flinch at the sound of her name. I gesture with a nod to the rolled-up book in his hand. "That looks like the same playbook we used to use back in the day."

His hand stills mid air, and his eyes narrow into a hard glare. "What of it?"

Whoa, I clearly hit a soft spot. Okay, good. Maybe I can use it to my advantage. I shrug. "We could work on some new plays together."

He leans toward me, his eyes hard. "What do you want, Tyler? What exactly are you doing here?"

"I want to give back, sir. I bet the two of us can do great things."

"Are you a betting man?"

I shake my head, my gut twisting. "No, not anymore."

He goes quiet as we glare at each other—like a goddamn Mexican standoff. I've gotten pretty good at this shit over the years, so he's in for one hell of a long staring contest.

Seconds turn into minutes, and I can almost hear the wheels turning in his head. He finally exhales loudly. "You really want to help?"

"Yeah, I do."

"We practice five times a week—"

"I know the drill."

"Only problem is, the school board won't take kindly to a criminal on the field. You'll never pass the background checks."

"I thought about that. I know how to get around it."

He scoffs. "I bet you do."

"If I'm on the field, standing on the sidelines, they can't say much about that right?"

"That's right."

"I mean, it's no different than anyone watching, giving pointers. Parents do it all the time."

He gives a shake of his head and frowns. "That they do."

"I'm sure the parents won't complain. They want to beat Lincoln as much as we do, right?"

He nods, and turns to look out over the field. "They've been giving me hell."

"So do we have a deal?"

He turns back to me and I stand, my arm outstretched. Coach pushes from his chair and eyes me for a minute.

"One condition, Tyler."

"Yeah."

"Stay away from Sara. She's been through enough."

I swallow, and nod. "I have every intention of doing just that," I say.

"Good." He takes my hand in his and gives me a firm shake. "See you tomorrow."

As I leave his office, the school bell rings, the sound taking me back to happier times. Students rush about, heading to their lockers to grab their books for their next class and longing rips though me. I liked being a student. For me, football was just a means to an end.

I step out into the warm afternoon, and look up and down the street, searching for signs of Sara, even though seeing her again will only fillet me. I make my way to my bike, and find a few students admiring it. They back off quickly when I approach, and I take a moment to see me through their eyes. A hardened criminal. Yeah, I'd back the fuck off if I were them too. I throw my leg over my seat, fasten my helmet and pull into traffic.

I cut down the side streets until I come to Mr. Johnson's service bay. My bike rumbles to a stop as I idle it down. I sit there for a moment, and when the rumbling sound of a dozen or so bikes gains my attention, I turn my head toward the sound in time to see the Phantoms drive by. Their clubhouse isn't too far from here, but I don't like they way they're looking at me, sizing me up. I'm sure word has gotten around that I'm back, and while Deacon let me know that if I needed any help on the outside, that he had people poised to help me, when it comes right down to it, if these guys are looking for trouble, there isn't jack-shit Deacon can do to help me, at least not in a timely manner. But I can't imagine any of them want to take on Deacon. He'd take them out in a heartbeat.

They pass by, and I throw my leg over the seat and walk to the shop. The bell over the door jingles as I make my way inside. My boots thud against the floor, and from the bay to the right of the office, I hear, "I'll be right with you."

I glance around at the empty office. Everyone must still be on their lunch break. I follow the sound of my brother's voice and see his legs sticking out from beneath the car he's working on.

When I don't hear noise, I ask, "Are you napping under there?"

I hear a thump—what I can only assume is his head hitting on something solid.

"Fuck," he curses and the wheels on the dolly squeal as he rolls out from beneath the car. I grab his hand to help him up.

"Is that any way to greet your big brother?" I ask.

Lucas stands slowly, his shoulders hunched as he takes a good long time brushing grease-stained hands on his coveralls, like he's stalling, trying to think of where we begin again. He was up and gone from the house before I was out of bed this morning. Had he done that on purpose? So he didn't have to face me?

"Lucas."

"Ty," he says and throws his arms around me. His hug is hard, and tight, and at first I stiffen at the unexpected display of affection. In prison, a guy's first lesson is not to show emotion, but I'm not in prison anymore and this is my brother. I pull him in, fist my hands in his coveralls and hold him harder. "It's good to have you back," he murmurs.

I break the hug, and inch back. He averts his gaze, but I won't have any of that.

"Lucas," I say and his eyes shift. Looking everywhere and anywhere but at me. I harden my voice and say, "What's done is done."

I hear his throat work as he swallows. "I'm sorry, Ty."

"I know." I pull him back in for another hug. I grip his hair and my heart pounds as I hold him. "You good?"

"I'm good."

"Then we're good."

He nods and I say, "Catch a drink tonight?"

"We'll hit Lou's for pool and beer. On me."

"Damn right it's on you," I say and we both laugh, the tension easing around us. In that instant, I know Lucas and I are going to be okay.

He winks. "Maybe I can hook you up with a friend. Get you laid. You look like you could use it."

Yeah, there's no question that I could use a soft body and a hard fuck. I hadn't touched a woman since Sara, and maybe it's damn well time I did. Maybe that will help me get my mind off her and move on.

"You think I need you to get girls for me?" I ask.

Lucas leans against the hood of the car, his boyish smile fading. "Do you have any jobs lined up?" He nods to the office. "I could probably talk to Mr. Johnson."

"Got work lined up at the BSA."

"Blind Service Association? Where Gracie goes?"

"Yeah."

His head rears back. "Really? What can you do there?"

I hold my fingers up. "Braille transcriber. My trade in prison. I'm certified through the Library of Congress."

"No fucking way. That's cool, man." He scrubs his chin, and leaves a streak of grease on his too pretty face. "Have you seen Gracie yet?"

"No, she was gone to school before I was up. I'm heading to see her now."

The bell over the shop door rings, and I push away from Lucas. "I'll let you get back at it. We'll catch up tonight, okay?"

I turn to leave, but stop at the sound of Lucas's voice. "Ty..."

"Yeah."

"I love you, brother."

"Love you too, bro."

I hop back on my bike, and make my way across town, to the private school for the visually impaired. But instead of turning left, I head right, to take the long way. Why? Oh because it leads past the high school again, and there is some part of me hoping to catch another glimpse of Sara, even though it goes against our best interests. Yeah, I'm definitely a fucking masochist.

Across the street from the school, outside the bank, I catch a glimpse of Sara talking to some douchebag in a suit. Normally I'd say he was the kind of guy she should be with, but I instantly dislike him. Sara is gorgeous, easy to look at, but I fucking hate the way he's glaring at her like she's nothing more than a quick lay. I pull over to the curb, idle my bike down and balance the beast between my legs as I flatten my feet on the ground.

I shouldn't be here. I shouldn't be stalking her like this. I should be home suffering in silence—even though I have no idea what or where home is anymore. The truth is, Sara and I have no future, but fuck man, I can't seem to drag my sorry ass away, and if that guy so much as lays a hand on her... She laughs at something douchebag says, and I go battle ready, my entire body tensing, eager to fight for what's mine. But Sara isn't mine, and I swore to her father I'd stay away.

As if sensing my presence, her head turns my way, and her mouth falls open when our eyes clash, hold too long. The man she's with looks over his shoulder to see what, or who, has drawn her focus. She touches his arm to bring his attention back to her, and I take a deep breath to get my shit together, when all I want to do is cross the street and beat the fuck out of the guy. Torn between loyalty and love I sit on my bike and watch from afar, knowing better than to act on the hot burst of possessiveness curdling my blood. Sara doesn't deserve that from me and when it comes right down to it, I'm here to get my life in order, not find myself back behind bars again.

But how the fuck am I ever going to live in a world that Sara isn't a part of?

4

SARA

I've been on edge, completely jittery since running into Tyler at Dad's office last week, and then again later on the sidewalk outside of the bank. God, he looked like he was in attack mode and ready to shred Caleb to pieces simply because he was talking to me. But he has no claims on me, just as I have none on him. After those run-ins, he's been avoiding me, making himself scarce after early morning football practice when I stop in to see Dad before work. And that can only be for the best. Any more time spent around him will be emotional suicide at best.

I check the time and hurry around my apartment. It's not much of a place, just a one-bedroom not too far from work, but it's all I can afford with my current income. Soon enough though, when I finish my education and step into the position of financial analyst, I'm hoping to save enough and purchase one of those cute townhouses I've been eyeing for months. The original plan had been to get out of Middletown altogether, now though, it's apparent I'm setting down roots and settling in for the long haul. Mom and Dad would love to leave here when Dad retires. They always used to talk about getting a big piece of land, and raising chickens. But if I stay here, they'll never leave, and I feel pretty crappy about that, but this is my life now. I've talked to them about moving, and living out their retirement years on a farm, and I'm hoping one day, when they see I'm doing a-okay, they'll follow their dreams. Which makes getting the advance all that much more important to me.

My cell rings, and I nearly jump two feet in the air. Honest to God, Tyler's return has made a complete mess out of me. I shouldn't be so jumpy. I have nothing to fear from him. Heck, how many times can a man break a girl's heart, right? But still the thoughts of him texting me, or running into him again, feels like I'm on a collision course, rushing down the highway at breakneck speed with a severed brake line. When I see it's Dad calling, I slide my finger across the screen.

"Hey Dad," I say, and inject a lightness into my voice that I don't really feel. Tonight I'm going on my first date with Caleb—my first date since Tyler.

"How's my girl?"

"Good, just getting ready. Caleb is going to be picking me up any second now."

I can just visualize the smile on my Dad's face. He worries about me, of that I'm certain, and Caleb is a white-collar professor, which means he's already pre-approved in Dad's book.

"Where is he taking you?"

I hear Mom in the background, saying hello to me.

"Tell Mom I said hi," I say. "And I'm not sure where we're going." I walk into my bedroom, stand before the long swivel mirror and examine the little black dress hugging my curves. It makes me feel a little vulnerable, exposed, like I'm sending a message that I'm ready for this, when I'm not sure I am. But since I had nothing decent for a date, my wardrobe full of yoga pants and pencil skirts, Kaitlyn dragged me out after work and insisted I buy this. Of course, I also can't forget the box of condoms she stuffed into the top drawer of my nightstand.

As Dad says something to Mom, I hold the phone between my ear and shoulder and cup my breasts, readjusting them in my new Victoria's Secret push-up bra, another item Kaitlyn insisted I buy. When it comes to men, she obviously knows what she's doing, seeing as she has a different one in her bed every week.

Will I sleep with Caleb?

My heart speeds up at the thought. The only man I've ever been in bed with was Tyler. He was my first...my everything. But what he *can't* be is my last. I need to move on, and forget about him once and for all. Seeing him last week only cemented that fact. We are different people now, with different lives, and we can never, ever get back what we had.

"Well, have fun," Dad says pulling my thoughts back. "Shoot me a text when you get home."

"Dad," I warn. There is a dangerous motorcycle gang in our neighborhood and I know he worries about me, but I'm a grown up, and can take care of myself.

"Okay, okay fine. Just have fun and stay safe."

"Love you too," I say, knowing that will put the smile back on his face.

Just then my intercom chimes. "Gotta go, Caleb's here." I end the call, give myself one last look in the mirror and practice my yoga breathing exercises as I make my way to the door. I buzz him in and pace restlessly until I hear his knock. I'm on the first floor so it doesn't take him long to reach my apartment. I twist the handle and find a very handsome Caleb, dressed in a suit and tie, impeccable as always, standing in the hall. His gaze darkens as it moves over me appreciatively.

"You look stunning," he says.

"Thank you." I admire his perfectly combed hair, the way his suit hugs his shoulders and tapers to a trim waist. Always so well put together. My gaze returns to his unflawed face. He is good looking in that perfect, magazine cover pretty boy way. Although at thirty, he's not a boy.

He holds his arm out. "Ready?"

I grab my purse, and he guides me outside to his sports car. Clearly we come from different worlds, but I'm not about to judge him because he's a man of entitlement. That doesn't make him any better or worse than me. If there is one thing I've learned, it's that a person can appear as one thing, and end up being something else entirely.

"Nice," I say. He circles the front and I know it's a silly little thing, and so ridiculous I want to roll my eyes at myself —this is the twenty-first century, right?—but when he doesn't open my door for me, disappointment niggles inside me. To this day, Dad still opens the door for both Mom and me. I guess good old-fashioned chivalry is just that...old.

I slide into the car and put my purse on my lap. Cripes, I'm twenty-eight years old. This shouldn't be so hard. I turn to him as he fires the ignition, and smile. He smiles back, and when he showcases perfect teeth and wide dimples, I relax against my seat.

"Do you like Italian?" he asks.

"It's only my favorite."

"I thought we could go to Luigi's."

"Best linguine in town," we both say in unison, then share a laugh. I exhale and my nervousness ebbs as he pulls into traffic and takes us across town to my favorite restaurant.

"So how long have you lived in Middletown?" I ask, curious about him.

He shoots me a quick glance. "What makes you think I'm not from around here?"

I chuckle, because it's pretty damn obvious. "Your accent." I tap my chin, pretending to be in deep thought. "I'd say Boston."

He laughs again and when he takes a turn I lean into him. Our bodies brush, and while I want to feel the rush, the same connection I have with Tyler, it's just out of my reach. Damn you, Tyler.

"And here I thought I'd left it behind," he says.

"It's faint, but every now and then when you say something I can pick up on it."

"Hard to hide anything from you, I guess," he says, the word hard coming out as *hahd*, as he thickens his accent in a teasing manner.

I chuckle at his antics. "So why Middletown?"

He shrugs, but I don't miss the tightening of his jaw. "There was an opening at UIC last January, and I jumped on it."

Why do I get the sense there is more to his story than that. I want to ask, but it's only our first date, so I say, "Have you always wanted to be a professor?"

He angles his head my way. "My dad's a professor at Harvard, mom is in administration. To this day I still can't quite figure out if I became a professor because they wanted it for me, or if I wanted it myself. But at the end of the day, I enjoy what I do." He winks, "I get to meet beautiful women like you."

Something in that statement makes me a bit uncomfortable. Does he treat the classroom like his personal pick up joint? Then again, maybe I'm just looking for flaws. I'm sure that's the case.

He must pick up on my unease, because he says, "Don't worry, Sara. I don't make a habit of dating students, and technically you're not my student anymore, right?"

"Right."

"And the other reason I chose Middletown is because it's a full day's drive from home. Close enough if I have to return in a hurry I can, but far enough that my parents have to call first."

I nod. "Ah, I get it. I have overbearing parents, too."

"Yeah?"

"Oh, yeah, ever since..." My words fall off. What the hell? He does not need to know what happened between Tyler and me—the real reason my parents are so protective. "I mean, ever since I moved out on my own, they worry. It's what parents do, I guess."

"I guess," he says, and when we fall silent, he jacks the tunes. I hum along, and he taps his thumb on the steering wheel. A short while later he pulls into the parking lot of Luigi's and my stomach growls. How embarrassing. I'd been so nervous all day, I'd forgotten to eat. At least the loud music drowned out the sound.

"All set?" he asks as he shuts off his vehicle.

I slide from the passenger seat and Caleb hits the fob to lock the doors. I meet him at the front of the car and he slides his arm around my waist. It feels strange to have his hands on me, but I don't comment on it, or flinch away when he tugs me close in a possessive manner. Inside the restaurant, the hostess leads us to a quiet, intimate table in the back and she fills our water glasses as she takes our drink orders.

Our knees bump under the table as I shift, and place my napkin over my lap. A server comes and delivers our menus, but Caleb doesn't look at his, instead he sets it aside and gazes at me.

"Why now?" he asks. "I've asked you out before, why did you say yes this time?"

I toy with the corners of the cloth napkin. "I figured it was time," I say, not a lie.

"Time?" He angles his head and eyes me, like he's waiting for more of an explanation, but I take a sip of water, then change the subject.

"Have you done a lot of touristy things since being here?"

"A little bit. But it's kind of boring doing those things alone. Maybe we could make a list, see the places together."

I nod. "We can do that," I say, not sure if I'm really ready for that. I've spent the last nine years alone. But seeing Ty after all this time did something to me. Made me realize what was between us really was over, and I needed to start living.

Our wine is delivered, and he takes a sip, and approves it. The server fills our glasses and we both scan the menu.

After we put our order in, and the server disappears, we fall back into conversation.

"So tell me how a beautiful woman like yourself is still single?" he asks.

"I've been busy working, and going to school," I respond, then wanting the conversation off me before I spill the real truth, I say, "I could ask the same about you."

I take a sip of my wine, and he does the same before answering. "Pretty much the same. Busy with school, then pursuing a career. But now that I'm all settled, I have more time on my hands."

I glance up, and a familiar male figure moving across the restaurant catches my attention. I freeze, my lungs squeezing tight. With his broad back to me, and his hand on the shoulder of a young girl, he follows the hostess to a table. Even though I can't see his face, I don't need to. It's the way he carries himself, moves with a quiet confidence. All hard muscle and sinewy strength shifting restlessly beneath a dress shirt constraining to keep his hardness contained. He might have changed, grown up in so many ways over the years, but I'd know that body anywhere.

Caleb looks over his shoulder, and follows my gaze. He turns back to me, his body tense. "Is that the same guy who was watching you on his bike?"

"Yeah," I say, but up until this minute I wasn't sure he was aware that Tyler was watching us that day.

"Who is he?"

Talk about a loaded question?

"An old friend," I say quietly.

Caleb takes a sip of his wine. "He doesn't look like the kind of guy you'd hang around with, Sara."

I shrug. "It was a long time ago. People change."

"It's not my place to say so, but if I were you, I'd stay as far away from him as possible. My guess is he's a gangbanger, and look at the girl he's with. She's barely legal."

"He's not a gangbanger." I defend him quickly. Too quickly, considering the way Caleb is staring at me. "And that young girl is his little sister, Gracie. It's her birthday."

His hand stills mid air, his wine glass poised at his lips "Her birthday? You must know them pretty well then."

"Well enough." Even though Tyler was taken away, I kept in contact with Gracie. It wasn't fair for her to lose both of us, so I made a point to visit her, take her out and do girly things with her. With work and school taking up most of my time lately, it's been a while since we hung out.

"Does he have any reason to do with," he pauses and does air quotes around, "'I figured it was time'?"

"Caleb," I begin, and look back at Tyler. In that instant his head lifts, like he senses me staring at him. Our gazes collide, hold too long. The server brings them their drinks, and Tyler takes a long pull from his beer bottle. He sets it down hard, and I practically jump in my chair.

His murderous gaze leaves me to latch onto the back of

Caleb's head. I look at Caleb as he toys with the stem of his wine glass. He's staring at me, waiting for an answer.

"It was a long time ago," is all I say.

"So you were with that guy?"

"Yes."

"Is it over?"

"Yes," I say again and inject more force into my voice. I'm not sure if it's for Caleb's sake or mine. Just who am I trying to convince here, anyway?

"Okay," he says, and when he looks like he's about to say more, I gesture with a nod to the middle-aged couple two tables over.

"What do you think he's saying to her?" I ask without thinking.

He turns, glances at the couple, then looks back at me. His expression is perplexed. "I have no idea, Sara. What do you think he's saying?"

"Well," I begin, falling back into the silly game Ty and I used to play. "She's leaning toward him, her eyes are wide, very involved in what he's saying. Plus they have a bottle of champagne." They're probably celebrating an anniversary, but I say, "I think he's telling her he just got that big promotion at work, and he's finally going to take her to Paris. She wanted to go there for their honeymoon, but they couldn't afford it." I give a small laugh and unable to help myself, shoot a glance Tyler's way. "It's just a game, Caleb."

He arches a brow. "One you played with him?"

The way Caleb is looking at me makes me feel foolish. I fiddle with the napkin on my lap, and I'm about to answer him when Tyler shifts and climbs to his feet, like he can sense my unease. My heart jumps into my throat as he helps Gracie up and when they come our way, my gaze flickers to Caleb.

"Speaking of *him*, he's on his way over to us."

Caleb stiffens. "Is there going to be trouble?" he asks.

I shake my head hard. Caleb is a big guy, and looks like he can handle himself, but I can't imagine he, or any other guy, would want to go up against Tyler. It's a death wish.

"No. He'd never do anything to you," I say, but now I'm not so sure about that. Kaitlyn said prison changes people, and from the hard look in his eyes, I'm guessing he's not the Tyler I knew and never will be again. Even though I know that the boy I knew is gone, the stupid girlish part of me wonders if I could ever be with this new version of him.

No, never. Get your head on straight, Sara.

I plaster on a smile. "Gracie, happy birthday," I say and climb to my feet to give her a hug. With her cane in one hand, she leans in and wraps her other hand around me. Ty stands close, his big body hovering over his sister like her protector.

"Thanks for the make-up, Sara. I totally love the kit, and I'm going to sign up for the lessons that came with it." She smacks her lips together. "I'm wearing the berry pink right now."

"Oh, I'm so glad, and that looks so pretty on you."

"That was nice of you," Tyler says, his voice deeper, a low cadence that swirls through my blood and settles deep between my legs.

"Every sixteen-year-old girl needs a make-up kit and lesson." Just because she's visually impaired doesn't mean she can't be like other girls her age. I never treated Gracie as less, nor would she want me to. She's as capable as any other girl her age, and it all comes down to sense of touch and lots of practice. Lessons will help her learn how to load her brushes, the strokes, etc. "I'd give the lessons myself, Gracie but I'm not that great at it. I can barely get my own make-up right. Sephora has professionals. They'll do right by you."

"You look beautiful, Sara. With or without make-up," Tyler says. "And that was a very thoughtful gift." He puts his arm around his sister in a protective manner. "Mom was never into make-up and the poor girl got stuck with three brothers. None of us can help her."

I swallow, not knowing how to respond, so I say, "Well, Gracie is the little sister I never had."

"And you're the big sister I always wanted," she says.

Caleb stands, and for a moment I'd forgotten he was even there. "Oh, I'm sorry. Caleb, this is Tyler and Gracie."

The two men stare at each other for a moment, each sizing the other up. Then Caleb holds his hand out. I suck in a breath as Ty stands there, glaring at it like he wants to destroy it. It's not like him to be rude. Well, it's not like the Tyler I knew to be rude. I have no idea what to expect from this new version standing before me. Tyler finally extends an arm and the men nod as they shake.

Caleb turns to Gracie. "Happy birthday, Gracie."

"Thank you," she says, then adds, "You have to stop by the house, Sara. I don't see much of you anymore. I miss your visits at the BSA."

I nod. I feel bad for not volunteering as much as I used to at the Blind Service Association. Gracie used to love it when I spent time reading to her and the others. "I know. I've been taking classes at the university."

"Why don't you come for Thanksgiving? Alex will be home. It will be like old times."

Old times.

Oh God, what I'd do for old times. But those days are gone, and we can never ever get them back.

"Well..." I begin.

The muscles in Tyler's jaw tick as he clenches. "I'm sure Sara already has plans, Gracie."

Gracie shrugs. "I'm sure she does, but if they get canceled or you change your mind, I know Mom would love to see you."

"Okay, we'll see," I say even though I have no intentions of joining the Barrett family for Thanksgiving dinner, this year or...ever.

Ty turns Gracie and they head back to their table. Once seated, he reaches for his beer at the same time as Caleb sips his wine, staring at me over the rim. As I take in the two men, I can't help but think how different they are. If Ty had never gone to prison, would he be sitting across from me dressed in a suit? I quickly shut down that thought. No sense in letting my brain play the 'what if' game, because Ty did go to prison and I'm seated across from a very respected man.

Just then the server comes with our food, and we fall into conversation about work, the tourist attractions he'd like to see, as well as my classes at the university. Over the meal, as hard as I tried not to, my gaze keeps straying to Tyler, only to find him watching me in return.

After the meal, Caleb stands and holds his hand out to me. I reach for it, and in a possessive manner, he pulls me to him, and gives Tyler a nod before leading us back outside. Way to ram home the fact that I'm with him.

I feign a yawn when we reach his vehicle. It's not that I'm tired, I just need to be alone, to work through all these emotions bombarding me. Caleb glances at the clock on his dashboard. "It's still early. Want to catch a movie?"

"No, thanks, though. It's been a long week and I have to get up early to finish my assignment."

He nods. "Damn professors, hey?"

I laugh. "Yeah, I had this one professor. He was a tyrant." I shake my head. "You should have heard the names the students called him."

He grins. "I think I know who you're talking about. Young, smart...totally hot, right?"

I laugh and look him over. "Don't forget modest. He was very, very modest."

Caleb laughs and his hand slides across the seat. He sets it on my thigh and I try not to stiffen. His thumb rubs my leg, and my tight black dress inches up as I shift. He pulls up in front of my apartment and turns to me.

"I want to see you again."

I nod. "I'd like that." He leans in, but I'm not ready to kiss him so I reach for my door handle and practically jump from the car. He meets me at the front of the vehicle.

"Let me walk you to your door."

"Sure," I say, appreciating this display of chivalry. Dad would be pleased.

We walk the cement path leading to my front door, and this is pretty much as far as I want him to go so I stick my key into the lock, and say. "Thanks for a fun night."

He nods. "Okay, good night, Sara."

"Night, Caleb."

I slip inside my building and hurry to my apartment. Once inside, I lean against the door and draw in a huge, refueling breath. Seeing Tyler at the restaurant sucked the oxygen from my lungs and I'd been barely able to fill them since. I push off the door, strip off my dress as I make my way to the shower, wanting to wash away my make-up, as well as the memories of Tyler. I turn the shower on hot, climb in and scrub quickly. When I climb out, I think about texting Kaitlyn to let her how my night went. That thought gives me pause. How did my night go? Well, Caleb was a perfect gentleman, and I agreed to go out with him again, but truthfully, the night was a disaster. After running into Tyler and seeing the murderous gaze in his eyes, everything pretty much went downhill.

A knock sounds at my door and I freeze. Who the heck would be knocking at my door this time of night? Could it be Caleb? How would he have gotten into the building? I grab my robe, slip into it, and knot it at the waist as I pad quietly down the long stretch of hall leading to my door. I go up on my toes, and my heart jumps into my throat as I peek through the peephole.

Oh. My. God.

No.

5

TYLER

I shouldn't be here. I shouldn't be doing this. But goddammit, I seem to be driven by a force I have zero control over. I could try to kid us both and say I'm standing outside her door simply because the protector in me needs to be certain she's okay, unscathed by her date with the DB, aka douchebag. While that's partly true, it's only half of the whole truth. Ever since seeing her at her father's office, I'd been a fucking wreck, thinking about her constantly, even in sleep. I want to see her. *Need* to see her.

Yeah, she's too sweet and kind for a felon like me. Not only do I have nothing to offer her, I told her father I'd stay away. It was part of our agreement. But I'm clearly a selfish prick, because here I am, standing in her hall, unable to keep my distance when it's the best thing for her. She's trying to make something of herself, and the last thing she needs is to be associating with a damn criminal who could ruin her chance of advancement. Then again, I don't want her associating with Caleb, either, a guy her parents would love, no doubt.

For the last week, ever since catching her on the sidewalk

with Caleb, I've been on edge, ready for battle, coiled defensively and waiting for the opportune moment to strike. I'm a pretty good judge of character—one of the many things a guy learns in prison—and it's that instinctual perception that's been driving me to watch over her without her knowledge. I scoff, hardly able to believe I've been reduced to a damn stalker. Just another crime to add to the rap sheet, I suppose. If the DB had been in her apartment, murder might have made the list as well. But he's not inside. I personally watched him drive off, then delivered Gracie back home before making the return trip.

I take in her wide eyes, the circle her mouth is making as she gapes at me. Her hair is wet, her skin damp, and I can only assume she'd just showered. I grip the paint-chipped doorframe over my head, anything to occupy my hands before I pull her to me, press my body to hers, and tell her everything will be okay. But that would be another big fucking lie now wouldn't it, because nothing will ever be okay again. I look her over, study the robe that does little to hide hard nipples—a body in need—and my dick twitches as the sight of her torments my starved body. Christ, what I'd do to strip her of that silk and give her what she craves—what we both crave.

Not going to happen, dude.

I swallow and work to get my shit together as she unhooks the safety chain—a fucking joke of a lock to a guy who's done time. If someone wanted into her apartment, that little piece of metal is going to do jack shit to protect her. The chain rattles as it falls against the wooden doorframe, and I draw a deep breath, let it out slowly.

"Hi, Sara."

"Tyler," Sara whispers as she opens the door a few inches, her body tight, uncertain. "What...what are you doing here?" She glances up and down the hall, her expressive eyes searching, seeking. Who the fuck is she looking for? Her asshole date? Possession I have no right to feel zings through me, and above my head, my fingers curl tighter around the doorframe.

"I just..." I begin, but my thoughts fall off as I lean toward her. I catch her scent, sweet vanilla, and it tears through my blood at breakneck speed, arousing the beast in me with an intensity that frightens me a little. It's been so fucking long since I've held a woman in my arms. I had my pick last week when Lucas and I hit the bar, but it's not just any woman I want. It's Sara. It's always been Sara.

"Just what?"

"Just wanted to make sure you got home okay?"

She squares her shoulders. A change comes over her. A harder edge to her face as shock morphs to anger—my words like tinder to a fire, fuel to her rage. "I've been getting home okay for a long time now," she says through gritted teeth. "I don't need you checking in on me."

Maybe not, but I want to talk to her about the DB. Some woman opens a door down the hall, and stares at me suspiciously as she passes by. "Can I come in?"

"No."

"How well do you know that guy?" I ask, even though the hallway is no place to be having this conversation.

The door widens, and a shadow moves over her face as her eyes shoot daggers. I can't blame her for being angry. I have no right to be standing at her door, asking questions she doesn't need to answer, making demands I have no right to make. But everything about that DB rubs me the wrong way. Call it gut instinct, or prison survival intuition—fuck, call it whatever the hell you want to call it—but he's not a good guy, and she deserves better.

She puts one hand on her hip. "Let's just say I know him about as well as I know you," she says, her words venomous, even though she looks so wounded.

I flinch, her anger and hurt seeping under my skin and twisting me up inside. I try to breathe, but grief presses down on me, fills my lungs and leaves me gasping—like water-boarding torture. I try to speak, only to choke on my reply.

I push off the door and pace, working to get my shit together. After a long moment, I say, "Sara, I don't think you should be seeing him."

Instead of responding, she asks, "How did you get in?"

I shrug. "It was easy. This place isn't that secure." I angle my head. "Hasn't anyone ever told you locks are for honest people?" I give her a wink to lighten things, but it seems to have the opposite effect.

"Ty...ler," she says quietly, her voice cracking and her body shaking as pain and grief overcome her. A sob wracks her body, and I can't even begin to count all the ways I hate myself right now. Painstaking need to hold her pulls at me, but I shouldn't have come. I shouldn't be here starting something we can't finish. Nothing about this is right—our fate was decided the second the wooden gravel hit the desk—but how can I leave now?

I reach for her. "Sara..."

"I can't...you have to go," she says, and presses unsteady hands to her eyes as she wobbles backward. Sorrow batters my pulverized heart, pounds it into my throat until I feel like I'm suffocating, as she shatters before me. I fucking hate seeing her like this. Hate that I'm the reason she's so broken.

Empty, bereft, hollowed out inside, I grip my hair and tug. "I'm so fucking sorry, Sara," I say quickly. Christ, I never meant to hurt anyone, least of all her.

"Ty," she whispers, and the need I hear in her voice explodes through my body. She might be telling me to go away, but her voice and body are telegraphing an entirely different story. She's always been an easy read to me, and despite my promise to her father, the fact that I'm headed down a dangerous path I have no right to negotiate. I step inside, kick the door shut behind me and set the lock. I dip my head, and my heart crashes as I brush my thumb over her warm cheek.

"Sara," I say. She blinks up at me and I'm no longer able to fight the good fight. I give in to my needs and close my mouth over hers.

At first her damp lips are frozen shut, but when I coax them open with my tongue, she closes her eyes and hands herself over to me. A soft mewling sound catches in her throat and I slide my hands around her small body, needing to touch her all over. I kiss her long and deep, and break it only to whisper, "I missed you so fucking much."

I splay my fingers so I don't miss an inch of skin. She goes up on her toes, and her warm palms squeeze my shoulders. A restless ache moves through me, and I breathe past it, wanting to draw this out, and not go at her like a fucking animal—the way my rock-hard dick is urging me to. *Traitorous prick.*

I push my tongue into her mouth, and as it tangles with hers, every old feeling I've kept suppressed for so many years crashes over me like a hammering tsunami. Need unlike anything I've ever felt before grips my balls, and I gather her into my arms, and carry her to her bedroom. She runs her soft hands over my body, our lips still joined as I set her on the edge of the bed. I inch back, sever the intimacy, and try to refill my lungs as she looks up at me with lust-imbued eyes.

"Ty," she murmurs and reaches for me, but I need a minute to just look at her, to steady myself. She hasn't changed much physically in nine years. She's still slim, her big brown eyes stark against her pale skin as they telegraph her need. Her hair is a bit longer, the damp strands soaking her robe. That's what others would see when they look at her, but what I see is a woman who is a shell of her former self. Thanks to me.

"Please," she murmurs and shrugs until her robe slides from her shoulders to expose a stretch of smooth skin. Blood leaves my brain in a whoosh, and my dick grows impossibly harder as I brush the skin with the back of my knuckles. Her gaze drops, rakes down my body and she goes perfectly still when she sees my rock-hard cock struggling against my jeans.

"Please what?" I ask, a desperate ploy to hear her says she needs me. Sorry bastard that I am.

"I need you inside me. I need to feel..."

Christ knows I need to feel too. I've been closed off, my emotions on lockdown for so fucking long, I'm about ready to rupture. Has it been like that for Sara, too? The only way to get through the day was to shut down anything and every-thing that makes you feel?

I rip into my pants, kick them off, and make quick work of my shirt. Sara's eyes go wide as she takes me in, her gaze skating over my scars. As tears well in her eyes, a lump lodges in my throat.

"Sara, don't...please. Don't look at them."

"Ty," she murmurs so low it's hard to hear her. I drop to my knees, spread her legs and slide in between. Her sweet smell washes over me. I breathe her in, fill my lungs until they're fully expanded, ready to explode. It was her scent I'd kept with me all these years, the memory of her—of us—the only thing that got me through some pretty rough nights.

I stand, press my mouth to her neck, and savor her flavor as I lightly run my lips over her quivering flesh. I push her robe down even further as I kiss a path to her shoulder. My hands go to her arms, and I brush them lightly, watching little goose bumps form in my wake.

As I indulge in her body and press open-mouthed kisses to her skin, she unloops the belt and widens her robe to offer her body to me. I could fucking cry as she offers me something so precious after everything I've put her through. She touches me, explores my body, and holds my head as I kiss a path down her curves. I give her a small nudge and she falls back on the bed, her long hair splaying. Beautiful, so damn beautiful and perfect. I climb over her, press her down with my body, keeping her pinned for fear she might come to her senses and flee. I touch her softly, gently, and take one pebbled nipple into my mouth.

"Yes," she moans and arches into me, her nails pulling skin as she rakes them over my back. On fire for her, I clamp my mouth around her hard nub, and she cries out. I break the kiss, her nipple popping free, and I lick the pale nub gently as I shape her curves with my palms.

She writhes beneath me, moving restlessly, her body conveying exactly what she needs. I press my mouth to her stomach, lightly lick her as I move downward, to the spot that's beckoning my touch.

I sink to the floor and grip her thighs, pulling on her until her legs are draped over the bed, and her sex is wide open, mine for the taking. She goes up on her elbows and our gazes meet. The heat in her eyes, the way they turned a darker shade of brown, does the most ridiculous things to me.

"You want me?" I ask.

She nods.

"Say it, Sara. Tell me you want me."

A moment passes as a bevy of heavy emotions flicker over her eyes, and squeezes the air from my lungs. Then she palms my face and whispers, "I've never stopped wanting you, Ty."

Determined to make every minute with her count, I spread her with my fingers, and gaze longingly at her open sex. *Mine.* Her pussy glistens in the lamplight, wet, hot, so eager for me. Her sweet scent fills my senses as I lean in and close my mouth over her soft flesh. Her taste explodes on my tongue and a pleasure so powerful it dims my vision grips me hard. I insert a finger and she's so hot and tight, I can't help but wonder if she's been celibate all these years. I push that thought away. I can't stomach the thought of her with another man.

I crook my finger inside her, never forgetting how she liked to be touched. When she tightens around me, I draw a breath to center myself and keep my own orgasm at bay. I don't want this to be over before it ever gets started.

"Tyler," she cries out, and moves her hips as soft quakes squeeze my finger.

"That's it, Sara. Fuck my finger, take what you need."

I slide another in for a snug fit and she rocks into me, her body trembling almost uncontrollably. I can't believe how close she is. Then again, maybe I can. It's been years for me and the second I put my cock in her, I'm going to lose my shit big time.

I take her clit into my mouth, claim it, own it completely as she rides my fingers. She gives a broken gasp as her hands grip her bedding, tug hard.

"Like that," she says, urgency and emotion in her voice. "Just like that." Her cries grow louder as pleasure centers in her core.

I pull my fingers out and plunge back inside. I swirl my finger around her slick heat, then repeat the motions until she's delirious beneath my ministrations. "That's it, come for me. Let me feel you come all over my fingers."

I lick her clit, and apply more pressure with the tip of my tongue until her head is rolling from side to side. Jesus Christ, I love seeing her like this, so lost in pleasure nothing else matters. My cock throbs, aching to replace my fingers as she breaks, gives in to the need pulling at her. Her hot cum burns my flesh, and I keep my fingers inside her as she rides out the waves. When she finally stops spasming, I spend a few more minutes on my knees, my mouth pressing hungrily, savoring her sweet release and never wanting to leave the comfort I've found between her legs. I lick her, soft gentle strokes to soothe her pussy before I put my cock into her tight sex.

She pants, gasps for breath, as I lap at her. Sexy mewling sounds follow her heavy breaths, and when her breathing levels out, I slowly stand. My hand goes to my cock as I gaze at her, sprawled out on her bed, eager and waiting for me. I pull from the base to the crown, and Sara sits up, her mouth inches from my throbbing dick.

"Sara," I say my voice deep from need as her warm breath fires my blood. She wets her mouth and I brace myself. My cock jumps and my balls tighten as she takes a long time to gaze at my nakedness, like she's committing every inch of me to memory. Impatience thrums though me, pressure brewing in my groin. "Touch me, Sara. Please...touch me."

Her gaze flickers to mine for a second and her mouth curves. "Is this what you need, Ty?" she asks as she takes me into her hands, lightly running her fingers over the long length of me. I tremble. Her soft hands wrap around me like a heated glove and are definitely going to be the death of me.

"Fuck yes," I say, hungry for more, for...everything.

She must sense that in me because she blinks up at me and asks, "What else do you need?"

I touch her face, run the rough pad of my thumb over her kiss swollen bottom lip. "I need you, Sara. I need your mouth on my cock, and then I need to be inside you.

"Fuck," I growl as her hot mouth closes over my crown, her tongue lapping and tasting the pre-cum pearling on the tip. She moans with pleasure, and I touch her hair, move it from her face so I can see her. My heart pinches at the beautiful sight of her, the pleasure she's so willing to give me after all the hurt. But I don't want to think about the hurt. I can't think about that right now.

She stretches her lips around me, taking me impossibly deeper, the warmth of her mouth driving back the cold that resides within me. She makes a noise, a soft purring sound, and it vibrates around my aching dick. Hunger and need consume me, take control. I shake with blinding pleasure, and my breath comes in a ragged burst. She cups my balls, massages them gently, and rocks into me. Seeing my cock slide in and out of her sweet mouth just about does me in. I clench down, eager to hang on. There are so many more things I need to do with her tonight.

"Jesus, Sara," I growl and push her damp hair off her forehead, her bobbing head dragging my focus. I'm so goddamn hard, haven't felt anything soft on my dick for a long ass time that I'm right there, ready to explode in her mouth. But I'm not nearly ready for this to be over. I want to savor tonight, because there won't be any more. The urgency in her body tells me she knows that too.

She greedily sucks me in, then pulls out, only to take me back in again. My hips jerk forward, as lust explodes in me, and I need this to stop almost as much as I need it to continue. I suck in a quick breath, and step back. My cock plops from her mouth and she whimpers in disappointment.

"Come here," I say, and lift her to her feet. I pull her against me, run my hands down her back, over the lush curve of her ass. Her skin is hot against mine, burning through my flesh and into my soul. "I need my cock in you," I say and she visibly quivers. I pick her up easily and position her in the center of the bed. I climb over her, my dick throbbing against her thigh. My mouth finds hers again, and her hands race over my body, palm my muscles as we exchange hot, hungry kisses.

She widens her legs and puts them around my back, a familiar move, and my crown probes her entrance. "Shit," I say, and inch back. "I don't have a condom."

"Top drawer, nightstand," she says quickly. When we were

together I always took care of protection, and as I reach into the drawer, I don't want to think too much about why she has condoms. I shut that from my mind and bite into the foil wrapper.

Her chest is rising and falling as I quickly sheathe myself. She gives me a smile, sweet and slow, as I fall back over her, my lips finding hers again. I kiss her long and deep, and she once again wraps her legs around me. I reach between our bodies, brush my crown over her clit, then position it at her opening.

"Yes, Please..." she whimpers, lifting her hips to force me inside, but I want to go slow, draw this out. "Ty, fuck me."

Her words prompt me into action, and in one quick thrust I power home. *Home.* Inside Sara, where I was always meant to be. My senses explode as our bodies meld, and I could fucking weep with pleasure. Her wet heat, her moans of satisfaction, and the need gripping my balls, complicate my mission to go slow. I pull out and power back in again. Her thighs squeeze my sides, and I push her damp hair from her face. Our eyes lock, and the air around us changes, charges, becomes so volatile and explosive I'm sure we could light up her entire apartment building in a blackout—for a month.

"Sara...fuck, Sara. I missed you."

"I missed you too, Ty," she says, and our lips meet.

Our bodies rock together. Just like old times. For a fleeting minute I pretend we're back in her college dorm room, the future wide open, with nothing or no one able to come between us. I bask in that for a moment, curl up in it and let it live inside me, thinking about nothing but the hot pulse of need beating at me like a baton.

In no time at all, my brain shuts down, my body taking over. I hammer into her at a maddening pace. Gentleness gone, I fuck like a man deprived for nine long years. *Savage.* Hot need drives my thrusts, and Sara opens to me, taking everything I'm giving her. I sink into her warmth, revel in it, lose myself to her completely as I go impossibly deeper.

"Oh, God, yes, Tyler." Her nails dig, her hips rise to meet each hard thrust, and I bend to swipe my tongue over her sensitive nipple. She cries out, and her sex clamps around my dick.

"Fuck, Sara, I'm not going to last."

"I want you to take what you need, Ty. Take everything."

I swallow hard, because I want what she can't give me— the trust I once stole from her. If I took it again, it would leave her flayed, hollowed out and lost, far more than she already is.

I reach between us, press my thumb to her clit, and she clings to me as soft gasps tear from her lungs. Her body clenches down on my cock, her hot cum coating me, dripping over my drawn up balls, and in that moment I know I'm a goner.

I continue to pound into her, my body seeking more... something other than just release. On the brink of orgasm, a growl rips from my lungs. One hand crushes in her hair and I hold her close, yet can't seem to get her close enough. Her hands race over me, edgy, out of control, pulling, pushing, and I feel a possessive tug on my emotions. Ruthless, my hands move to her hips and dig in as I let go, and pleasure burns raw and deep as I explode inside her, giving her a part of me...all of me.

I collapse on top of her, and we're both panting, gasping for breath. Her hands move slower over my back, urgency gone as she reacquaints herself with my body. I shiver under her soft touch, and she chuckles, the sound like music to my ears.

Tenderness moves through me, and a need I can't assuage —will never be able to assuage when it comes to Sara—pulls at me, as I roll to the side and drag her with me. I hold her tight, her little wisps of breath tickling my skin. As I come back down to earth and stare at her ceiling, a car backfires on the street. My ears ring at what sounds like a gunshot and my brain makes the leap to nine years ago, when a dozen cop cars closed in on me. Do I wish I'd done things differently? Hell, yeah. But I'd committed a crime—made a split-second decision that ruined our future—and I can't change that now.

As reality comes crashing over me like a cold shower, it pushes back my post-orgasm bliss. Regret inches its way into my gut, and I feel a fresh flash of panic. What the fuck have I done? I tense and sit up. Sara sits up beside me, her eyes wide, stark, conflicted as she looks at me.

As my bliss dissolves, I shake my head. "Sara..."

"I know," she says, but she doesn't know. She doesn't know the truth about everything, and when it comes right down to it, I was caught with a shit-load of illegal guns. The fact that I did it to save Lucas doesn't matter. My actions cost us our future. "We shouldn't have done this," she whispers. I turn to see the tears forming in her wounded eyes, her body shaking all over.

"Fuck." I put my arm around her, drag the blankets up to keep her warm, and hold her to me. I press a kiss to her forehead, and put her head on my shoulder. "I shouldn't have come here tonight."

"Why did you?" she asks, and inches away from me to pull her knees to her chest—a defensive move.

Because I fucking love you.

"It's Caleb," I say instead. "I don't like him."

"You don't know him."

"Neither do you."

She makes a sound, a half laugh, half cry. "You're right, and I guess you never really know anyone, do you?"

As her words hit like a slap, and a new kind of tension in the air, I say, "What's his last name?"

"What does it matter?"

"I want to know."

"Why, so you can check up on him?"

"Yes."

"Tyler. Stop."

"You can tell me, or I'll find it out on my own, either way..."

"It's Douglas, okay. Caleb Douglas."

I lock that away.

"I don't know why you're making such a big deal out of this. Is it just him or is it any guy I want to date?"

"It's him," I say. At least I think it is. He rubs me the wrong way, but more importantly, he looks at her the wrong way. "I don't want you to date him."

She goes quiet for a moment, and tightens her hands around her legs. "I *have* to date him, Tyler. Don't you see? I have to. I have to close my heart to you. It's the only way I can get past us." She sniffs and shakes her head, and her hair falls over her shoulders. "I should have done it a long time ago. I don't know what I was holding out for."

I sit there for a moment, and try to wrap my brain around what she's saying. "You've not been with anyone?"

"No," she says.

"The condoms?" A tear clings to her lashes and I gently wipe it away.

She chokes out a strangled laugh, even though there is nothing funny about this situation. "Kaitlyn gave them to me."

I scrub my hand through my hair, and hate how happy that makes me. I want Sara happy. Want her with a man who will do right by her. Caleb isn't him. Neither am I. "Anyone but him, Sara."

She regards me with wide eyes, open, vulnerable, hurt in far too many ways. "Why?"

"He's not the guy for you."

"Then who is, Tyler? You?" she shoots back, her bliss long gone as hurt turns to anger.

I grit my teeth. I want to be the guy for her, but she deserves someone better. Someone who isn't going to tear apart what they have, without her ever really knowing why.

"I don't trust him, okay," I say so harshly, her head rears back.

She takes a quick moment to compose herself, then glares at me. "What do you know about trust, Tyler?" she asks, her voice tight, accusing, indignation sweeping through her.

Everything.

I shake my head. So this is it. This is how it begins and ends. "Nothing," is all I say as I climb from the bed. "Nothing at all."

Saturday passed in a blur, literally. Tears clouded my eyes for the better part of the day, dripping onto my textbook and making studying impossible. Here I thought Ty couldn't break my heart any more than he did. Boy, was I wrong. Watching him walk out on me, seeing his scarred and battered body retreat after making sweet beautiful love to me, picked away at the already tattered threads, undoing the work I put into stitching my heart together over the last nine years. But the responsibility lies with me, too. I gave myself over to the things I was feeling. When it comes to him, I simply have no strength to resist the pull between us. All the more reason to avoid him and get back into the dating scene.

My phone pings, and from my comfy seat on the sofa, I turn toward the kitchen. My damn phone has been going off all day, but I haven't answered it. I'm not in the mood to talk to anyone. Then again, I suppose if it's Mom or Dad I should check, otherwise they'll be pounding on my door to make sure I got home safely from my date last night. In much the same way Tyler had.

I drop the carton of ice cream I'd been picking at for breakfast, lunch, and dinner, and pad to the kitchen, where my phone is sitting on the counter. I glance at the screen and see I have messages from Caleb, Kaitlyn, and...nothing from Tyler.

My heart goes into my throat. When he left here last night, I never expected to hear from him again. So why am I so disappointed that he hadn't called? Jesus, I'm such a mess. I slide my finger across the screen, and read Kaitlyn's message.

So, how did it go? Did you have some straight up awesome sex with Caleb?

Oh, I had some straight up awesome sex, but it wasn't with Caleb.

I don't kiss and tell, I text back.

Ohmigod, you did. I want deets, girl. Spill.

I set the phone down, walk to the fridge and open it. My stomach growls. Other than a bottle of wine, a carton of milk, and some eggs and cheese, it's pretty much empty. I shut the fridge and think about making a grocery store run when my phone rings. I nearly jump two feet in the air. I check the display before answering. It's Kaitlyn, no doubt wanting all the dirty details. What will I tell her?

I slide my finger across the screen. "What's up?" I say and try to inject a lightness into my tone. Even I know I've failed miserably.

"Um, I think I should be asking you that question."

God, I really need to stop wearing my emotions on my sleeve. "I'm okay," I say, and feel the tears threatening again. "How are you?" I deflect. "Did you go out last night with Dave?"

"You're not okay."

"Kait—"

"What did he do? He didn't hurt you did he? So help me, I'll feed him his balls if he did."

"No. He didn't. He was a perfect gentleman."

"Then why are you crying?"

Frustration builds inside me. "I...just am."

"I'm coming over," Kaitlyn says.

I shake my head even though she can't see me, and walk into my bedroom. I glance at myself in the mirror, take in my beautifully bruised body, a reminder of all the ways Ty touched me last night. "No, it's okay. I'm okay," I say, even though I know it's futile. When Kaitlyn sets her mind to something, nothing can stop her. "I'm just studying," I fib.

"You are not okay. Have you eaten?" Clearly she knows me well, and the concern in her voice warms me. I used to get annoyed when she tried to set me up, but deep inside I know she's doing it because she cares and wants to see me walking among the living again.

"No." I glance at the clock. "Don't you have a date tonight? With Jack, right?" Sometimes I can never keep her men straight.

"I'll break it."

"Kaitlyn—"

"I'll grab us a pizza and be there within the hour."

I want to protest I'm so not in the mood for company, but she hangs up. I stare at my phone, but before I power down, I check Caleb's message.

Had a great time last night. Are you up for seeing the sights tonight?

I swallow, Ty's words of warning filling me with a measure of unease. Is there really something wrong with Caleb or is it just Tyler being overprotective of me, not wanting me with anyone but him? But I can't be with him. I was lost in a pit of darkness and despair when he went to prison and it took me years to crawl out of that fiery hell. I refuse to go back. I can't go back.

I run my fingers over the phone and text Caleb back. *Rain check? I have to study*.

His text comes back fast. *Professors!*

I laugh at that and some of the tension eases out of me. I set my phone on the counter, and pad down the hall. I jump in the shower, needing to wash the scent of Tyler's skin from my body. If only I could wash the memories away from my brain so easily. I scrub my skin until it's almost raw, and wrap a soft cotton towel around me to ease the sting.

God, if Mom or Dad knew what I'd done, well, I shiver to think about it. They were the ones who were left with the broken pieces of me after Tyler left. I do know one thing for certain. Dad would never let Tyler back on his field. That would be a shame, because I think it's something they both need.

I dress and dry my hair as I wait for Kaitlyn, and when I hear a knock on the door, I rush to it. My steps slow as something niggles in the back of my mind. How could Kaitlyn have gotten in? She didn't buzz me to let me know she was here, and she doesn't have a key. My heart jumps into my throat, because there's only one person I know who isn't deterred by a lock.

I look through the peephole and my legs go weak. I stand there, shocked, but ripples of bliss dance over my skin, so goddamn happy to see Tyler outside my door, it horrifies me. A lot. There is no room in my life for this kind of need. I breathe deep, and as I let the air out slowly I decide not to open it. I can pretend I'm not here. It's not like he's follows my every move right?

"Open the door, Sara."

His deep voice curls around me, seeps under my skin, fills me with a longing so powerful it physically hurts. My body shakes, uncontrollably. I wrap my arms around myself and hug tight as I work to recover. No way can I open that door. I *won't* open that door. Deciding to wait it out, wait for him to give up, I inch back, afraid he can hear my heart crashing against my chest.

"I know you're in there."

Damn him.

I wait another moment, and glare at the door, willing him to go away. But this is Ty, and he's going to stand there until I finally give in. The fight goes out of me. God, I am so pathetic. With a miserable groan, I close my hand around the knob. Ty holds silent as I unlock the door and inch it open. I make the mistake of looking at him, catching the heat back-lighting his eyes as he gazes at me. My heart flutters like a silly schoolgirl with an impracticable crush on someone she can never have. But scarred and all, he's still the handsomest man I know.

"Hi, Sara," he says.

God, when he says that to me, in that low sexy voice, it temps me in far too many ways. My chest clenches and I pinch the bridge of my nose to keep from touching him, hurtling myself at him and begging him to take me again.

I harden myself, and my voice holds all kinds of accusations when I ask, "How did you know I was home?"

He stiffens, his body looking bigger and tougher than when he walked out on me last night. "I just did." His gaze rakes over me, a hot caress, and I become acutely aware of my yoga pants and t-shirt, the state my hair is in, and the red puffiness around my eyes. But what do I care how I look? I'm not trying to impress him.

"Tyler, if you're—"

"Can I come in?"

I hold the door tight. Not that I think he'll push his way in, I don't. But if I let it go, I think my wobbly knees might go out from underneath me. "I think we said everything we needed to say to each other."

"I'm not here to talk, Sara. I can't find my wallet. I think it must have fallen out of my pocket when..."

He lets his voice fall off, like he can't bring himself to say, *when we were making love.* "Oh," I say, and inch the door open. "Come in, then."

He steps into my small apartment, his big body eating up the space and overwhelming me. "I'll go look." I try to sound calm, even though my heart is racing.

I turn, and his warm breath is hot on my neck, fanning the need inside me when he says, "I'll help you." He stands close, so close the hairs on my nape tingle with excitement.

Get it together, Sara.

I hesitate for a moment. Tyler in my bedroom again. I can see all kinds of wrong with that scenario. "Okay," is all I manage to get out, as heat vibrates through me.

He follows me down the hall and when I enter the bedroom, see the mussed sheets, warm memories of last night wash over me. I hear his throat work as he swallows, and can only imagine he's reliving the night too.

I glance around, looking everywhere for his wallet, a desperate need to focus on something other than the big man looming behind me. "Maybe it fell under the bed." I drop to my knees, go down on my arms and glance under the bed. A dark tortured noise cuts thought the air, and my pulse leaps.

"Sara, get up."

Instantly realizing my mistake, I grab his wallet, brush the dust off it, and jump to my feet. Heat burns along my neck and moves into my face as he grips his hair and tugs like he's in total agony.

"I found it," I say quickly, berating myself for sticking my ass in the air like that. He takes it from me and shoves it into his pocket. But he doesn't move. He just stands there, dominating my bedroom as his blue eyes burn through me, strip me bare, and leave me quivering like a leaf in a windstorm. My composure slips a little and I suck in a breath, trying not to feel so vulnerable and exposed beneath his dark stare.

"I guess that's it then," I say.

He looks tense, poised for a fight—or something else—as he takes a measured step toward me. Honest to God, if he touches me again, I'll fall apart, cave, go down for the count. No way can I let myself get lost on that dark path. I'll never find my way out of it this time. Never. Pain burns though me, scratching my throat raw and I try to swallow past it.

"Ty," I croak out, but he stops when we hear a noise at my door.

Kaitlyn!

"I'm guessing these flowers are from Caleb," Kaitlyn says, her voice trailing down the hall. "I know you said he was a gentleman, but he must have done something bad. You're crying and he's sending flowers." A pause and then, "Never mind him. Tonight we'll hit Studio Paris and we'll find you a real man. One who won't make you cry."

I stare at the man who I've shed years of tears over and he freezes as Kaitlyn comes barreling into my apartment. The smell of pizza hits, followed by that of roses.

Had Caleb sent roses?

"Hey wait, why is your door open?" Kaitlyn asks, panic in her voice. A pause and then, "Sara, where are you?"

"In here," I say, eyes still locked on Ty.

"I should go," he says and I wait for him to make a move. When he doesn't, I slide past him, and he sucks in a breath as my body brushes his. I leave the room and his boots thud on the floor as he follows me, closing the gap until I can feel heat emanating from his hard body.

"Are you okay?" Kaitlyn asks, her voice getting closer.

She rounds the corner to the hall and comes to an abrupt

halt when she sees me coming toward her, Ty so tight on my heels I can feel his hot breath on the back of my neck.

"I'll just get out of here," he says.

Kaitlyn's head rears back and from the look on her face, Tyler was the last person she expected to find coming out of my bedroom. I was pretty adamant when I told her it was over between us.

"Wait. Are you...Tyler?" she asks.

"Yeah." He runs his hand through his hair, his gaze shifting, like a wild wolf needing to break free. Kaitlyn holds her hand out. "I'm Kaitlyn. I've heard a lot about you."

A sound catches in his throat, a humorless laugh. "I can imagine," he says, then gives her hand a quick shake. "Nice to meet you, Kaitlyn." He turns to me. "I'll see you around, Sara," he says, his words dark, pained.

I walk him to the door, and I'm about to shut it behind him when he turns. His lids drop, then slowly open. "Sara, I wanted to say thank you for taking care of Gracie when I was gone. She told me all the things you used to do with her." He pauses, takes a hard breath and adds, "Please don't stop coming around because of me. She needs you."

"I won't," I say.

I stare at his back as he walks down the hall and turns the corner. When he's out of my line of vision, I close the door carefully, and turn. I sag against it, and find Kaitlyn staring at me, mouth agape. Oh, God this is bad, so freaking bad.

"What the hell was that?" she asks.

She still has a dozen red roses in her hand. "Who are those from?" I ask.

"Caleb," she says. "I caught the delivery guy at the front door, and your neighbor let me in as he was leaving. When I talked to you earlier and you sounded upset, I thought the date went bad, and figured that's why he sent you flowers."

"The date didn't go bad. It was perfectly fine, actually."

She stares at me for a moment. "Then what was Tyler doing here?"

I walk to the living room, sink down onto the sofa and press my palms to my forehead. "He forgot his wallet."

"Holy shit." She sets the bouquet down, and plunks herself onto the coffee table in front of me. "Back up. Start from the beginning."

"I ran into him and his sister at the restaurant last night, and then he showed up at my door shortly after Caleb dropped me off." Her eyes go wide as I fill her in, and when I'm done, she lets loose a long, slow whistle.

"Okay, well, first let me say, he's hot as hell and no wonder you fell into bed with him, and second let me say, ohmigod."

I shake my head. "Yeah, I know."

"Come on. Let's eat and then get our asses to Studio Paris."

Hitting the most popular club in town is the last thing I feel like doing. "I'm not in the mood."

"I don't care. We're going and you're not leaving there until we find you a man."

7

TYLER

Exhausted from my workout with the punching bag, I lean into it, rest my forehead against the hot leather and take deep breaths. It's late and the gym is closed, but an old football buddy of mine owns it now and gave me a key to use at my leisure. I take a few deep breaths and let them out slowly. I shouldn't be so pissed that Caleb sent Sara flowers, or that she's going clubbing tonight with her friend. It's not my business.

Then why the fuck did I spend the entire day doing a return trip from here to the prison—a place I swore never to step foot in again—just to talk to Deacon? After an online search of Caleb, and finding nothing but a long list of accomplishments and awards to his name, I should leave it at that, right? I want to think I'm wrong about him, but my fucking gut won't let it go. A guy learns that kind of shit inside, and if anyone can find dirt on him, Deacon can, even from behind bars.

"Are you working out or trying to get a date?" Lucas asks as he towel-dries the sweat from his forehead.

I angle my head to see my brother smirking at me. "You ever heard of Studio Paris?"

"Yeah. It's a new place over by the college. Why?"

"Get showered. We're going."

Lucas tosses the towel over his shoulder and leans against the closed door separating the gym from the showers, crooking his knee and pressing the sole of his foot to the panel. "I don't really think it's your scene, bro."

I release the wrap around my hands, and bend to untie my shoes. "No, why not?"

"It has a dress code and has overpriced drinks. Lots of stuck-up college girls. Wouldn't you rather go to Lou's? You can get some nice pussy at Lou's and won't have to spend a fortune on drinks to get it." My head snaps up and I glare at my brother. He grips the edge of the towel and says, "What? You don't like pussy now?"

The tendons on my neck tighten. "Have some fucking respect."

"Jesus, Ty." He pushes off the door, and straightens, but he knows better than to get up in my face. "What the fuck?"

I glare at him for a moment longer, to let his punk ass know I'm serious. There were enough guys in prison who talked smack about women. I'm not going to hear it from my brother too. Finally, I break the tension and ask, "What's the dress code?"

He looks at me for a moment, like he doesn't know whether to let it go or not, but then says, "Dress shirt. I think jeans are okay."

I have plenty of dress shirts. After prison, I had to clean up and apply for jobs, all part of my release program, and at BSA, I always wore collared shirts and dress pants. I'm just lucky Claudine, my boss, took a liking to me and made some calls to get me transferred to the offices here. My gaze rolls over my brother's frame. He's about the same size as me. The few shirts I managed to salvage from the fire would likely fit him.

"You have a dress shirt?" I ask.

"Yeah. Don't have much use for it at the garage, but I bought one last year for cousin Jimmy's funeral."

I nod. Jimmy was a good kid growing up, but after I went to prison, he got mixed up with the wrong crowd and ended up getting himself killed during a gang initiation. Stupid fucker held up a corner store and the owner pulled a shotgun and blew his head off. I heard the news in jail, and it tore me up inside not being able to go to the funeral and pay my respects. I make a mental note to head to the gravesite soon as unease rips through me. His death was so fucking senseless. But when it came to the local gang, nothing made sense and nine years ago, I took the job because I feared it would be the death of my brother.

There is a part of me that understands why Lucas chose to run guns. Expenses for Gracie were piling up, but I was sending money home from my cafeteria job on campus. For some reason Lucas took our family finances upon himself, thinking he was the man of the house while I was away. Dumb kid was doing all the wrong things for the right reasons. I grab the punching bag to keep myself upright as memories flood me.

"You good, bro?" he asks, his voice pulling me back.

I snap out of it. "Yeah."

"Maybe we can go another night. I kinda had some plans tonight." He shifts and for some reason I get the sense he's hiding something.

"Yeah, what?"

"Was going to meet up with some buddies."

I stare at him, long and hard. "Who?"

"Just some guys. You wouldn't know them. We were going to work on some cars."

I relax. "Can you reschedule?" I give him a nudge on the chin. "I need my wing man tonight."

A moment of hesitation, then, "Yeah, sure."

"Thanks."

I push past my brother and step into the locker room. I grab my soap and as I make my way to the shower, I try to talk myself out of going to the club. But my efforts prove futile. Sara is there, and I have to see her, have to make sure she's safe. By rights she should tell me to fuck off. She's been taking care of herself for a long time now. But now that I'm back, I fucking want that role again, and there's nothing I can to do change that.

I shower quickly, meet Lucas outside and we make the short trek home so we can get out of our sweats and into something decent for the club. The door is locked and Lucas pulls a key. I stand back as he opens the door, and a tightness in my chest squeezes the air from my lungs. Mom hasn't given me a key, and I haven't asked for one. An oversight on her part I'm sure, but not on mine. I still feel like a stranger inside these walls.

Mom shuffles to the kitchen when she hears us. Dressed in her familiar floor-length flannel robe, tied tight at the waist, she smiles when her gaze lands on Lucas. "How was the workout?" she asks

"Good," he says and drops a kiss onto her cheek.

"You boys hungry?"

"Yeah," Lucas says, then darts up the stairs to his room, leaving Mom and me alone. Fuck, I hate the awkwardness between us. I search my brain for something to say, but come up empty.

Mom gives me a smile, the shuffles to the fridge. I reach out, put my hand on her shoulder and stop her, when what I really want to do is punch Lucas in the face and tell him to make his own goddamn food. "It's okay, Mom," I say. "You don't have to wait on us. I can heat up some pizza."

"Nonsense," she says. "Have a seat, I'll fix you both a sandwich."

I hold my ground for a moment, but then soften when she smiles at me, a genuine smile that helps push back some of the cold. She's the one who held this family together after Dad left, after I left. It's not my place to come in and change things. Besides, I think she needs to feel wanted. It gives her purpose.

"Ham and cheese. Your favorite."

It touches me that she remembers. "Thanks, Mom," I say. "I'll be right back." I go up the stairs quietly, not wanting to wake Gracie. I pass by my old room, still unable to venture inside, and find Lucas pulling a dress shirt from his closet. The box I had packed up and shipped here had arrived the other day, and I tear into it. My buddies pass through my mind as I pull the clothes out, some of their jeans and shirts mixed in with mine. We all wore each other's clothes, shared everything and I miss the fuck out of them. I pull my phone from my back pocket and think about texting Justin. I know he's dealing with some pretty rough shit himself as he tries to assimilate back into society—the family and friends he left behind. Fuck, we all are.

Lucas pulls on his shirt, and his dimples flash as he buttons it up. "I clean up good, huh?"

"Yeah," I say and grab a plain blue shirt. I want to blend into the crowd tonight. I'm not even sure I want Sara to know I'm there. She's trying to get her life together and doesn't need the complication of me. But I just need to make sure she's okay. At least that's what I keep telling myself when I get downstairs. Mom has the sandwiches on the table. "Looks great," Lucas says, and Mom beams at him. He sits and scarfs two down in record time.

Mom looks like she has something on her mind as she sits next to me, touches my arm gingerly. "Gracie said you guys ran into Sara at the restaurant last night."

The bread lodges in my throat and I work to swallow. "Yeah, we did," I say and get up to get a glass of water. I run the water until it's cold, take a long drink, but don't turn just yet. I don't want to talk about Sara. I don't want to hear what Mom has to say—what I need to hear.

"Gracie said she invited her over for Thanksgiving dinner."

"I know."

"That was thoughtful of her, but I work at the pharmacy that day. I plan to have the turkey on Sunday and I'm not sure—"

"Don't worry," I say as I turn slowly and walk back to the table. Lucas is eyeing me, his gaze stricken as he searches my face. But I keep my jaw locked, hard. He's suffering enough as it is and doesn't need to know my fucking heart is in two pieces, that seeing Sara again and not being able to make her mine is harder than any prison sentence. I clear my throat. "She's too busy and won't be able to make it."

"Yes, she is very busy, isn't she? When I ran into her father the other day, he said she was taking night classes and working her way up through the bank and will soon be stepping foot into a senior analyst position. Isn't that exciting? She's doing very well for herself, Tyler." I nod, because it's what she's not saying that is clawing at my insides like a fucking rat digging it's way out of a trap.

Stay away from her.

I shove the sandwich into my mouth, and nod my head. "Yeah," I say but it comes out like a hollow little sound that fills the room with tension and takes me inside myself, where I weep for my lost youth, the loss of Sara.

"Well, we should get going, bro," Lucas says, before we all get too caught up in the unease filling the air, taking up space.

"Yeah." I shove the last bite into my mouth and stand. Mom reaches for my plate, but I grab mine and Lucas' and take them to the sink.

"You boys be careful out there."

"We will," Lucas says, and we step outside. The lock clicks in place behind us, but it's not the sound of metal on metal that's sending cold shivers along my vertebra. No, it's the string of bikes riding by my house, slowing down as the drivers take in me and my brother. I stand straight, hard, letting them know I'm not intimidated. These aren't Deacon's men, but I'm pretty damn sure they're not going to fuck with a guy under his protection, inside the prison or out. That's what I'm betting on. Then again, I'm no longer a betting man.

They pass and I turn to my brother, who's gone stiff behind me. "What's that all about?"

He shrugs. "Beats me."

"Lucas."

"I don't know, Ty. I guess they're letting you know they run this town."

"As long as they're not running you."

He gives a quick shake of his head, too quick, and my nerves fire. "If you're in any kind of trouble, you need to tell me right now."

"No trouble," he says, and hurries down the three steps. "Are we clubbing or not?"

I stand there for a moment. The Phantoms are the last people my little brother should be fucking with. If I ever find out he's mixed up with those bastards again, I'll fucking give him a beatdown that'll do permanent damage to his pretty face.

I climb onto my bike, and tug on my helmet as my

brother jumps on his Harley beside me. I nod for him to lead the way, and follow him out of the driveway. The air is cool tonight and soon I'm going to have to store the bike for the long-ass winter and find myself an old car to use. I'm sure my kid brother will be able to hook me up with one, seeing as how he loves to work on cars, even during his off hours.

It's nearing midnight by the time we hit the club. The big motherfucker of a bouncer gives me a once over as we step up to the front of the line.

"You in the right place?" he asks, and I resist the urge to punch him in the face just for assuming I'm here looking for trouble.

Lucas is about to say something, but I stop him and calm myself. When it comes right down to it, the guy is just doing his job, and I don't fit the mold of the regular clientele. "Yeah, I'm in the right place."

"We don't want no trouble."

"Not looking for it."

We square off for a moment, stand eye to eye then he nods and allows us through. We pay a ridiculously high cover charge and make our way inside. I cringe at the loud music and bodies jammed together. Lucas was right. I would rather go to Lou's for beer and pool. Fuck, when did I get so old?

A few girls grab at my shirt and gyrate against me, and the smell of perfume mingling with sweat nearly gags me as I look for Sara. I'm a good head taller than most, but can barely get through the crowd. I lose Lucas in seconds, and when I turn back to find him, he's got a harem of women attacking him. The boy's got a pretty face and definitely cleans up nice.

"Want to get a drink?" a girl asks loud enough to be heard over the pounding beat as she puts her hand on my chest and curls it in my shirt.

I'm sure the only way I'll get through this crowd is by pushing people out of my way, or letting her lead me. Since the first will only end up getting me kicked out, and she seems to know what she's doing, I nod. She slides her hand into mine and gives a tug. We weave through the throng, the music deafening as she finds two stools at the bar. I sit and instead of taking the seat beside me, she settles between my open legs.

"I'll have a rum and coke," she says loudly.

I hold up two fingers, and the bartender nods.

"I'm Candy," she says, and coils long blond curls around her finger.

Of course she is.

When I don't say anything she asks, "And you are?"

Not into Candy.

"Tyler," I say.

She purses he lips, and looks me over. "You're not from around here are you? Are you just passing through?"

"Something like that."

I scan the crowd, then look back at Candy as she blinks up at me, her gaze going over my scars, intrigue dancing in her eyes. Is this what she likes, what she gets off on? Does the good girl want to play with the bad boy? I scoff.

"What?" she asks, and pouts at me.

"Nothing." I look past her head, search the sea of people for Sara, and when I find her alone at a corner table, tucked in against the wall, uncomfortable as some drunk jackass comes on to her, every muscle in my body clenches. The bartender brings our drinks. I toss some bills on the counter, and take a drink. I stare at Sara as the amber liquid burns down my throat. Jesus, she sure has a knack for picking the wrong kind of guys.

"What's wrong?" the girl asks as she takes a sip and puts her hand on my thigh. She shimmies in closer until her hot center is pressed against my crotch. She frowns, like she's disappointed that I don't have a hard on for her.

"I have to go. Enjoy your drink."

A loud noise climbs out of her throat, and then she says, "Jerk."

"Yeah, I know," I say and push through the crowd with a little more force this time. I walk past the guy making his play on Sara, and put my body between theirs. She smiles at me, and relief mingles with surprise when our eyes meet.

"There you are?" I say, and bend down and press my lips to hers. It was only supposed to be a quick kiss, but the second I feel her lips on mine, I linger a moment longer, breathe in her sweet aroma and let it block all the other overpowering scents of the club. When I break the kiss, she seems a bit breathless. I inch back, take in her smudged lipstick and wipe my finger over my bottom lip.

"What...what took you so long?" she asks breathlessly, so in sync with what I'm doing she doesn't miss a beat. Nine years might have passed, but we can read each other today as well as we could back then.

I angle my head in time to see a drunk college boy, dressed in a sweater, khakis and some kind of expensive-looking shoes, slip and grab the chair to right himself. The beer in his glass sloshes over the edge.

"Who the fuck are you?" he slurs.

Keep it together, dude.

I turn toward him, and fold my arms over my chest. Since Sara isn't prone to violence and does not need to see the guy I've become behind bars, I say, "I'm her boyfriend. Who are you?"

His head rears back and he gives me the once over. "You?" He points to Sara. "*Her* boyfriend."

"Yeah, that's right." I turn my head slowly until my eyes on locked on Sara's. "Isn't that right, Sara?"

"That's right," she says. "And we were just leaving." She scoots out from behind the table and when she comes up to me, I cup her face, and plant another soft kiss on her mouth, simply because I want to this time. I break it, and stand back. That's when I see the skintight, knee length little black dress she's wearing. Shit, she looks gorgeous, and I can't fucking stand the idea of any other man gawking at her.

"What the fuck?" the guy says. "I never took you for the kind of girl who likes to go slumming." I stiffen, and Sara puts her hand on my arm and gives it a squeeze. I nod, and relax. The guy is drunk, and really, Sara is slumming when she could do so much better than me.

I point to the bar, toward Candy. "That's Candy," I say. "She likes rum and coke."

His head bobbles and he zeros in on a pissed off Candy, who is glaring at us. "Yeah?" he asks. "She ask about me, or something?"

Or something...

"You two will be perfect for each other."

He pats me on the back. "Hey, thanks man. You're not so bad."

"Yeah." I put my hand around Sara's waist to guide her outside, but she hesitates. "What?" I ask.

"Thanks for helping me out, but why are you here?"

I look through the crowd. "Grabbing a drink with Lucas." It doesn't really answer her question, but she nods. "Saw you were in a bit of trouble and thought I'd help out."

She crinkles her nose. "This really isn't my scene."

"Want to get out of here?"

"I came here with Kaitlyn. I can't just bail." Dark lashes blink fast over darting eyes. "We look out for each other."

I turn back toward the crowd. "Let's go get her."

Sara shakes her head. "No, she won't want to leave."

"Are you saying you want to stay? If so, then we'll stay."

"No, I don't want to. I don't really like it here."

I stand still and wait to see what it is she wants to do. She bites her lips and shifts from foot to foot. "Sara, we can't just stand here and take up space. We either get a table and stay or we go. It's your call. Either way, I'm not going anywhere without you."

"Let me go find her and see what she wants to do."

I hang back and watch Sara get lost in the crowd. My gaze slides to the drunk college boy and Candy, who seem to be hitting it off at the bar. I grab my phone and shoot a text off to my brother. I hate leaving him, after practically dragging him here, but I need to get Sara out of here. He'll understand. Besides, he's pretty busy with his harem. Sara finally comes back, breathless after fighting through the people. "She's hooking up. So I'm good to go."

I dip my head, take in her big brown eyes. Her hair is long and loose tonight, her face full of make-up. She barely wore make-up when we were together. I know we've changed a lot over the years, in so many ways, but I don't get the sense that this is the Sara she's become.

"How did you get here?" I ask

"Kaitlyn drove."

"Is she okay to drive?"

"Yeah, she lives around the corner and barely drinks anyway."

"Okay." I capture her hand and I'm about to turn when something catches my eye. I still, and stare toward the long hall leading to the bathroom. I could have sworn I just saw Caleb. Must be my imagination. What would a douchebag professor be doing hanging at a club where his students party? That has to be a conflict of interest, right, going against school policy? Forgetting about him, we make our way out into the cool night and Sara shivers.

I look her over and frown when I realize she's in nothing but that short dress. "Where's your coat?

"Kaitlyn's car. We didn't want to coat check them. Takes too long."

I glance around the full parking lot, even though I have no idea which car is Kaitlyn's. "Can you get it?"

"Her car is locked. I'll get it tomorrow."

"I'm on my bike, Sara, you'll freeze."

"Okay, I'll go get the keys." She makes a move to go, but I stop her. "Here. Wear this. I don't want you going back in there." Especially if my mind wasn't playing tricks, and Caleb is on the prowl. I shrug out of my leather coat and put it around her.

She tries to shrug out of it. "I can't take this. You'll freeze."

I tug it back over her shoulders, bend forward, and zip it up until it's around her neck. "I'll be fine."

"Ty—"

"I'll be fine, Sara." I guide her to my bike, grab my spare helmet and put it on her head. My fingers brush her warm skin as I clasp it. I take in her tight skirt. "Um, how are we going to do this?"

"Not easily," she says, and I laugh, but it turns to a garbled moan when she inches her skirt up to get her leg over the bike. How the fuck am I supposed to ride with her body exposed like that—pressing in to me?

Motherfucker.

"Yeah, okay, that will work," I say, hoping she can't hear the want in my voice, but this is Sara and I doubt I can get anything by her. I just hope it doesn't scare her off. I tug on my own helmet and throw my leg over the seat and nearly bite off my fucking tongue when she shimmies close, the heat of her sex seeping under my skin and aiming straight for my cock. I clear my throat. "You good back there?"

Her thighs squeeze around my hips and my cock grows another inch. Great. Just fucking great.

"I'm good." I'm about to start the bike when she puts her mouth near my ear and says, "Thank you for what you did in there, Tyler. The guy just wouldn't take no for an answer. I was about to introduce his groin to my knee when you came along. Saved me the trouble."

I put my hand on her thigh and give it a squeeze. "I know you can take care of yourself, Sara," I say. "I was just in the right place at the right time, and thought we could end it without a scene."

"I've taken self defense lessons," she says, almost indignantly.

"Good." I feel a measure of relief to know she can defend herself against unwanted touches as I back out of the parking spot, and ease into traffic. She hangs on quietly as I drive, the bitter wind biting at my flesh. Her hands come around my body, close over my chest and bring warmth with them. I touch her hand with mine, hold it for a moment, then put it back on the handle bars. I make my way to her place, but I'm not quite ready for this night to end. I drive past it, and she taps my shoulder. I ignore it for a moment, the take the corner until we're in the parking lot of Lou's. I shut the bike of, and she taps my shoulder again.

"What are we doing here?"

I slide from the seat and help her off, then set the kick-stand. "I thought we'd hang out, have a game of pool. Grab a beer. You got all dressed up to go out tonight, and I hate to see you just go back to your apartment." I pull my helmet off, then reach for hers. Beneath the glare of the parking light, our eyes meet, and the worry on her face is like a gut punch. "Just like old times," I say and when she frowns, I instantly regret it. Who wants to remember what we can never have again? I sure as fuck don't. "Just friends, Sara. I thought you might enjoy a game and a drink without some drunk college boy drooling all over you."

She goes quiet for a moment, looks down at her feet, like the gravel holds all the answers in the universe. Okay, she doesn't want to be here with me, even as friends, and I don't blame her. I need to take her home. I open my mouth, but close it when she lifts her head.

"Okay, a game of pool and a beer."

I guide her inside and a few heads lift, give a nod and then go back to doing whatever it was they were doing. None of the regulars are surprised to see me. I've been stopping in for a drink every night since I've gotten home and we've gotten the small talk out of the way. A few brows did lift when they see who I'm with, though. We walk to the back, and grab one of the free pool tables. Penny, an old friend from high school, steps up to us, tray in hand.

"What can I get for you tonight, Tyler?" she asks. The music is lower so we don't have to scream to be heard.

"Hey Penny, you remember Sara." I gesture with a nod to Sara, who is looking over the pool cues.

Penny turns toward her, and her eyes widen. "Sara, I didn't realize that was you." Her gaze rakes over Sara's face, then takes in her too tight mid-thigh black dress. "You look...different."

"Hair and make-up. New dress," Sara says, shifting from foot to foot, a familiar habit.

Penny clucks her tongue. "You look super hot."

Sara's gaze cuts to me, a light pink color crawling up her neck as she reaches for a pool cue. "Thanks, and you always look nice, Penny."

"Aw, you're too sweet."

"We'll have two beers," I say.

Penny disappears with her tray and I step up to Sara. My chest presses against her back, and her quiver goes right through me. I touch her shoulder lightly, run my finger down her arm, and it takes every fucking ounce of strength I have to keep my lips off her. I promised her friendship only, and I won't do anything to break it.

"You okay?" I ask.

Her knuckles turn white as she clutches the stick. "I'm fine," she says but I can read her well enough to know she's not. Fuck, man, I'm not going to keep her here for my own selfish reasons. Yeah, I didn't want to take her home when she'd gotten all dressed up for a night out. While that was partly true, I also wanted to spend more time with her.

"Look, if you want to get out of here—"

She turns to face me, and shrugs out of the oversized coat. "Let's have one game and a beer. It's not that often I get dressed up and go out. I shouldn't waste that."

I set the balls, and we flip a coin to see who breaks first. Sara wins and cracks the balls and sinks two high balls.

"Nice." I grin at her. "I'm impressed."

"You should be."

"Been practicing?"

"No, but it's like riding a bike." She walks around the table and I scrub my chin working to keep my eyes off her ass, and the way her dress hugs it so nicely. Penny comes back with our drinks and I take a huge gulp, but it does nothing to douse the heat building inside me.

Sara takes a sip, sets it on the side of the pool table, and bends forward to take a shot. I nearly bite my fucking tongue off. She glances at me.

"You okay?"

I lift my glass. "Yeah, fine," I say and take another drink. For a second, I wonder if she's fucking with me on purpose, but maybe that's just wishful thinking. She takes the shot and misses and I push off the wall. She backs up as I make my way around the table and when I glance over my shoulder at her, I find her staring at my ass. Her gaze lifts slowly, and heat moves into her cheeks. She might not be trying to tease me, but I see the need backlighting her eyes, feel it in her body. I take my shot and sink the ball.

"Nice. I'm impressed."

"You should be," I say.

She grins, like she's really enjoying herself, and it's so fucking adorable, I have to fight the urge to go claim that mouth of hers. We each take a few more shots, and by this time, I'm winning.

"We should have put down a bet." I wink and add, "I might have if I didn't think you were hustling me."

She arches a brow, her mood a bit playful, and I fucking love seeing this side of her. "You think I'm hustling you?"

Not really, but I say, "Maybe a little."

"Yeah, what would you have bet, Ty?" she asks, and grabs the chalk.

"You really want to know?" Unable to help myself, I step up to her, brush the back of my hand over her warm cheek. Do I dare tell her what I would have laid on the table?

"Yes, I really want to know," she whispered.

"I would have laid it all on the line, Sara. Winner takes all."

"Define all."

"You, in my bed."

She inches back and if I could kick my own ass I would. I shouldn't have said it. What the fuck was I thinking? "Sara, I'm sorry—"

"I want to go."

I nod and put my cue back on the rack. "I'll take you home."

"It's just around the corner, I'll walk."

I shake my head and drive my hands into my pockets. "No way, Sara. Not happening."

"I need the fresh air."

"Then I'll walk with you."

She puts her hand on my chest, and my heart crashes as she blinks thick lashes up at me. "You can't be seen walking into my place with me, Tyler." She glances around. "We actually shouldn't even have been seen here together. If my father ever found out, he'd kick you off his field, and I can't even imagine what he'd do to me. I can't put him through any more. Plus, I work at a bank..." She lets her words fall off. No need to say what were both already thinking. I'm a goddamn criminal.

I step back from her. "I understand."

"So you agree you won't walk with me back to my place?"

I grit my teeth. "I won't." But that doesn't mean I won't follow.

Her chin shoots up, like she's challenging me. "But you're going to follow, aren't you?"

"Yeah."

A small laugh escapes her throat as she puts her cue away, and turns back to me. "Honesty. It's a great trait, Tyler." She cocks her head to the side, and silence falls as her gaze rakes over my face, a slow careful assessment. I can almost hear the wheels spinning as she studies me. What is going through her mind? "Okay, just so you know, once I'm inside, the security door will lock behind me, but that shouldn't be an issue for you, right?"

My heart goes into my throat as my gaze searches hers. Is she saying what I think she's saying? "Sara—"

She puts her hand back on my chest, the same hand that touched me so greedily last night, and my heart pounds against her palm as heaviness settles over us. "I can't fight it, Tyler. I just can't." She looks broken, shattered, her expression hollow and haunted, and so help me God, there is nothing in the world I want more than to be the guy to put her back together again. "But what I can do is try to get you out of my system. We both need this. This is the only way I know how. But before we go down this road, we need to establish some ground rules."

I nod, but I'm not entirely sure what I'm agreeing to. Not that it matters, if it's what Sara wants, then it's what Sara gets.

8

SARA

It was his steely determination that did me in, the way he stood next to me, intimidated by no one, as he peacefully sent the drunk college boy packing. Everything in the way he so easily read my body language at the club, and had came to my rescue without causing a scene, washed away every reason I had for keeping my distance.

Truthfully, I shouldn't be with him. I'm smart enough to know that. But despite it all, despite everything he put us all through, I can't resist him. Not then. Not now. I'm helpless to my need as everything about him strips me bare and undermines my willpower to walk away and never look back. We can't have a committed relationship, and now, all I can hope for is that after enough sex and time I'll get him out of my system once and for all. It's a gamble, a foolish one at that, but I have no choice but to take the risk, because we can't keep going on like this. It's insanity at best.

In the distance, I hear his boots breaking the quiet of the night, save for the squealing tires and cop sirens a few blocks away. My stomach clenches, and tingles race down my spine. Arousal and need swamp me and I pick up my pace. I cut across the dimly lit street, duck between two parked cars, and make my way to my building. I climb the steps and steal a glance over my shoulder. In the dark corner, masked by shadows, I spot Tyler. My protector in the night. The same guy who completely destroyed me by breaking every promise he'd ever made to me.

I fish my keys from my purse, enter my building and hurry to my apartment. I let myself in, and set the lock, my heart racing a million miles an hour. Will Tyler break into my building and come for me, or will he be the sensible one and realize the huge mistake we're making?

Which do I want more?

I shrug from his jacket, and his scent curls around me. Silence falls over my apartment as I wait to hear his boots, his rap at my door. I back up, on edge, not knowing what to do with myself. Butterflies whirl in my stomach as the minutes stretch on. I turn to see my clock, now convinced he's not coming.

Liquor. That's what I need. Lots of liquor.

I turn and head to the fridge where I have a bottle of white wine, but stop when a knock on my door vibrates through me. I straighten to recover my composure and walk slowly across the room. Habit has me peeking through the peep hole, and I know I was just with him, and that we'd already had sex, but my heart jumps in my chest because this feels like the first time.

I open the door, and he stands there for a minute, like he's unsure of what comes next. That makes two of us. I wave my hand and step back.

"Come in."

He walks past me and I catch his scent. I suck in a breath, close the door and lock it behind me. I turn slowly, and my knees nearly give way when I find Tyler standing there, dominating the space. Head bent, his eyes burn through me, sear my flesh from my bones and leave me wide open.

Now that the moment is here—a decision made—nervousness rakes across my skin, gathers low in my belly. "Drink?" I ask. I don't wait for an answer. Instead I dart past him, grab the bottle from the fridge and pour two glasses. I don't need to turn to know he's in the kitchen. I can feel him standing behind me, watching me carefully. Anxiety rolls off me in waves and I'm sure he must feel it.

"Sara," he murmurs and goose bumps break out over my flesh as he whispers my name. I gather my bravado, turn, and plaster on a smile as I hand him a glass. He takes it, but doesn't drink. "What are we doing?" he asks, his voice somber.

"We're doing this, Ty." I take a big gulp of wine, set it on the counter, and reach for his pants. I push the button through the hole and add, "For however long it takes. Okay?"

"Okay." He pulls me into the crook of his am and presses a kiss to the top of my head. I lean against him, unable to get close enough. God, how many times have we touched like this? "You talked about ground rules, Sara. I need to set one, too."

I inch back to see him, but instantly miss his warmth and the way it curls around me and makes me feel safe, even though when it comes to Tyler, I'm anything but. This man is a danger to me in far too many ways.

"What's that?" I ask.

"Just us." Tortured eyes meet mine, and my body thrums for his touch. "No one else while we're together? Or I can't do this."

I know he's asking about Caleb. I'm not the kind of girl to sleep with two men at the same time. Heck, up until his return, I wasn't even the type of girl to sleep with one man. As for Caleb, I only went out with him because I thought I needed to walk among the living again, and he'd been showing interest. I thought it would help me move past Tyler. It didn't and this is my last resort.

"No one else," I say. Caleb shouldn't be too difficult to deal with. We'd only been on one date. But he had sent those flowers and I did tell him I'd show him around the city. I'll text him and ask if I can have a talk with him on Monday after my class.

"What are your terms?" Tyler asks, pulling me back.

"No one can ever know. We keep this a secret."

He nods. "I'd never do anything to jeopardize your relationship with your family or your chances of promotion at the bank, Sara," he says.

"Thank you." He drops a kiss onto my forehead and my head swims, wondering where we go from here. When his stomach makes a noise, I ask, "Hungry?"

"Yeah, starving," he says, and scoops me up. I give a little yelp as he carries me to the bathroom. His lips brush my ear and my whole body trembles.

"What are you doing?" I ask.

"That asshole touched you tonight and the only scent I want on your skin is mine." His eyes darken, and in a move that has possession written all over it, he takes my mouth with his, his hands cupping the back of my neck to hold me in place, like he fears I'll flee. But this was my idea, and I'm not going anywhere until we're finally done with each other. Sated. Spent. Completed.

He sets me on the counter top, opens the frosted sliding door, and turns on the shower. I blatantly stare at his ass, and a grin creeps in around the corners of his mouth when he turns back to me. My insides warm. I haven't seen him smile —really smile— since he's been back.

"Stare much?" he asks his voice like a rough caress.

I laugh, some of the tension easing from my body. "I stare when I like what I see."

His eyes roam over my body. "Yeah, me too." He tugs his shirt off, and this time I try not to focus on the scars. I crook my finger and he comes toward me. I look him over, and his hair falls forward as he lets out a hard breath.

"Touch me, Sara. Please…"

I place my hand on his chest, feel his thundering heart-beat, and widen my fingers. He hisses in air, his muscles rippling beneath my palms. "You got hard," I say as I trace the deep groves and high ridges.

"I'm hard all right. Everywhere," he teases, a twinkle in his eyes. "Slide your hand lower and you'll see."

I know he's trying to change the subject, but my stomach coils tight when I think about what he endured in prison. "Did you…work out a lot?"

He shakes his head, like he doesn't want to talk about it. When I blink up at him, he says, "Sara, don't."

Letting it go, my fingers slide lower over his exposed flesh, and he holds his breath when I cup his cock through his jeans. "You're right," I say, to let him know I won't bring up prison again. "You are hard everywhere." With my eyes lowered, he leans in and presses his mouth to my head, peppering me with hot, kisses. My heart squeezes painfully, his actions so damn familiar. I unzip his pants, and slide my hand inside. His cock is hard, like rock hard—steel—as it pulses against my palm. Moisture floods between my legs and dampens my panties.

"We need this, Tyler," I say. I'm not sure why I keep repeating that or who I'm trying to convince more. I close my eyes as I touch him. Even though he hurt me, left me heart-broken, I missed him, missed this.

His throat works as he swallows. For a beat he says nothing. Then he whispers, "I know." He rocks into me, and I stroke his long length. My body burns up, my sex clenching in anticipation of things to come.

He grips the hem of my dress and tugs it over my thighs. His fingers brush my inner legs and I widen for him, greedy for his touch.

"Sara," he murmurs, and presses his head to my forehead. We stay like that, breathe together for a long time. "Sara," he says again, like he loves the way my name sounds on his tongue. Missed having it there for so long.

"I know, Ty. I know," I finally say.

His lips find mine again, and he kisses me, gentle at first, but then it expands, deepens, until we're lost in each other. He picks me up from the counter and unzips my dress. I shake my shoulders and it slides to my feet. His eyes dim with desire as he takes me in.

"Much better," he says, his voice a deep husky rumble. "More like the real you."

He reaches behind me and unhooks my bra. It too falls into the heap on the floor. He places warm hands on my sides, a soft slide over my skin, and toys with the elastic on my panties. He tugs a little, then his fingers sink into my curves, bruising my delicate flesh enough to let me know he's claiming me, leaving his mark. I push against him and he sinks to his knees and presses his mouth to my sex. Even through my lace panties, his hot breath scorches my skin. I tremble, and he puts one arm around me to hold me tight.

He rubs his mouth over me, and I grip his hair, tug a little. My nipples swell, ache for the heat of his mouth. He nips at my panties, tugs them from my hips with his teeth, and an exited shiver runs through me.

He drags my panties down, and my belly tightens as his calluses rake over my skin. He reaches my ankles and I lift my feet one at a time so he can remove the scrap of material. I wait for him to stand, take me into the shower, but instead he parts my folds with his fingers and goes back on his heels, just looking at me standing there, spread open for him.

"Ty," I murmur, my voice hoarse and uneven. I don't even sound like myself.

He leans in, licks me from bottom to top and his touch zaps though me like I've just been hit with a high voltage wire. A cry catches in my throat. "I need to spend some time here, Sara," he murmurs and opens his mouth wide to eat at me. His tongue slides over my hard clit, swirls around it until I'm taking deep gulping breaths. I rake my hands through his hair and hold him to me, because I too need him to spend some time between my legs. Tears prick my eyes as I stand there, paralyzed by his mouth, so desperate for his touch yet terrified by it just the same.

My breasts grow heavy, achy as he presses a finger into me, a deft finger that has touched every inch of my body and knows just what I need to take me over the edge. His tongue slides, his mouth eats, and his fingers slick in and out of me, slow at first, but now reaching a faster pace. I undulate my hips, crash against his mouth as he destroys me.

My breath comes in fast, short, choppy gasps as he rolls his tongue over my clit, then applies the perfect amount of pressure. Wild, needy, I cry out his name, mindless of anything but this man and what he's doing to me.

My body flexes, pulses, lets go and gives in to the throbbing desire between my legs. Air evacuates my lungs and the room whirls around me. I shake, stop breathing, and stand there mindless, a quivering mess until there is nothing left of me. Ty slides up my body, grips the back of my neck, and puts his mouth close to my ear.

"Breathe, Sara."

I suck in a quick breath, feel his rigid length on my

stomach as he backs me up and guides me under the hot spray. His mouth claims mine again, a deep sensuous kiss that arouses me all over again. It's frightening how much I want him again. He grabs my loofa, squirts my vanilla-scented liquid soap onto it, and rubs it over my body. A new ache builds inside me, spreads rapidly through my body and I gyrate my hips to let him know.

He backs me up, presses me to the tile, his muscled arms on either side of my head, like two barricades locking me in. His mouth falls over mine, and his kisses are slow, tempered, a captive animal about to be released. His kiss deepens until he's devouring me, a man driven by need and hunger. I touch his arms, as he bends and presses his mouth to my neck, consuming every inch of me. I quake, loving that I can touch him like this again.

His tongue skates over my quivering flesh, and I slide one hand down his body to capture his hard cock. I take him into my hand and his groan falls heavy, a deep-rooted animal sound that coils through me. I stroke him, weigh his thickness in my hand, and wet my mouth, wanting to taste him again. But he seems to have other ideas because in a fast move, he turns me around, takes my hands and places them on the tile wall.

"Stay like that, Sara."

He inches away, and I miss his heat. I glance over my shoulder to find him watching me, his face twisted, tortured, and my heart crashes harder. The years have been so goddamn hard on him.

"Take me, please..."

His hot palm rakes down my back, tracing my vertebra, until he reaches the swell of my ass. He takes my cheek into his hand and squeezes, then brushes lower, between my legs.

"Widen for me," he whispers into my ear.

I spread my legs, and he hooks one muscled arm around

my waist to hold me, the move so familiar my heart pinches. He bends over me, his mouth on my back. "I want to fuck you like this, Sara."

"Yes, please," I say, knowing how much he's always liked this position. I wiggle my ass and he groans as his crown slips between my legs. I move and twist and try to force him inside, but then he goes completely still. My heart stops pumping. Has he come to his senses, realized we shouldn't be doing this because it comes with an expiration date and somewhere in the back of both our minds we know this can only lead to more heartache?

"Condom," he says roughly.

I shake my head so hard my wet hair whips around my face. "No, Tyler. Like this."

The way we used to...

"Sara—"

"Like before, Tyler. Skin on skin. Nothing separating us. Not this time. Just you and me, no barriers." It will strip me bare, leave me raw, and completely destroy me. But so help me, God, I can't help it. Maybe I need to be totally broken, hit rock bottom before I can start to rebuild again. "It's the only way."

He swallows hard. "Are you on the pill?" he asks softly.

"Yes. I'm on it to regulate my cycle."

"Sara..." His voice falls off, giving me the sense that what he's about to say next is almost too painful to put into words.

I breathe in and brace myself. "Yeah."

"I need you to know that I've not been with anyone since you," he says, his voice so ragged with emotion, I worry he's drowning in grief.

A peach-sized lump clogs my throat and I try to talk, want to ask him what happened to him in prison, the abuse he endured, but can't for so many reasons. I make a small tortured noise, and when my knees give, I lean against the wall for support.

As if reading my mind, he says, "I was never raped in prison." He brushes my hair from my shoulder and I'm almost glad he's telling me this when I have my back to him. I'm not sure I could survive seeing the pain in his eyes.

He clears his throat and whispers, "I know you must have been wondering about that."

I breathe deeply, my heart bleeding, as I absorb and assimilate his words. "Okay," I finally manage to say as his hands slide to my hips.

"I came close to it once, and fought back. That's when Deacon took me under his care." I have no idea who Deacon is, but I remain quiet. "I guess I proved myself worthy of him or something." A long painful pause and then, "What I'm trying to tell you is, I'm clean."

"Me too."

"I know," he whispers, his breath falling over me as his crown breaches my opening. He opens his mouth like he wants to say more, but I'm not sure I can take it.

As my heart rattles against my ribcage, I say, "Tyler..."

"Yeah."

"Make love to me."

He slides into me, and I hold my breath. He thrusts gently, filling me. *Intimate.* I close my eyes as we become one, and revel in the closeness, yet at the same time, I can't seem to get close enough. Heat builds inside me and I move against him, ground into him, needing every inch of his hardness. He growls and powers into me, harder this time, more demanding.

I rock backward and meet his every fierce thrust, familiar want burning through me. His touch brings me back to life, and my senses feel sharper, the smell of him, the feel, even the taste. His cock is relentless, driving into me with hard blunt strokes, rough and fast...so good. He always was a great lover. His hands race over me, swift, feverish as he impales me. He cups my breasts, pinches my nipples, then he slides his fingers between my legs to pluck my inflamed clit.

I cry out as he fills me, a low keening sound that seems to make him wilder. He ravages me, savage thrusts that take me to the edge and push me over. I let myself soar, free-fall without a safety net and shatter around his cock, my release so hard and primal, I tremble from head to toe. He groans, a deep vicious sound of need as I come around his cock, and keep coming, and coming. I blink and gasp, unable to believe how much cum he wrung from me.

"Fuck, yes," Ty growls, holds my hips for leverage and stills inside me. I feel him pumping his seed into me, and I squeeze my muscles, wanting all of him, every ounce that I've been denied for nine long years. When he stops spasming, he falls over me, his arms wrapped so tightly around my body, I can't breathe. I let him hold me, until I need air, then I shift.

"Tyler," I whisper, but he doesn't let me go. He stays wrapped around me, as unraveled as I am. He stands, still holding me, and pulls me under the warm spray. It washes over us and hides the tears pricking my eyes. I swallow as he holds me tight, and he turns me. I take in his brutally beautiful face, his scars, and settle my head against his chest and listen as our erratic heartbeats even out.

With our bodies temporarily sated, he slides open the frosted door and he guides me out. I stand on the mat, and neither of us speak as he grabs a big fluffy towel and pats it against my body, going to his knees so he can dry me from head to toe, and turning me around to do the same to my back. Once done, he tosses another towel over his shoulder and wraps me in mine.

His eyes are intense, haunted as he carries me to the bed, and gently sets me down, in-between the sheets. He towel-dries quickly, then slides in beside me. The bed dips as he rolls toward me, caging my body. His mouth finds mine and this time our kisses are soft, gentle, a mournful exchange of a lifetime of lost.

I love him.

I wish I didn't. Lord knows I wish I didn't love a man who shattered me, a man I can no longer trust to return to crime. He's changed in so many ways since leaving here, but I can't deny that I saw glimpses of *my* sweet Tyler—the boy from my youth—as he made love to me. Tears fill my eyes, and he breaks the kiss to see me. Sadness washes over his face as my tears fall. He brushes them away, only for more to follow. He gathers me carefully, places my head on his chest and holds me to him, cocooning me in his arms and warmth and stroking me tenderly as we both cry ourselves to sleep.

9

TYLER

The morning air is crisp and my breath turns to fog in front of my face and I yell out drills to the guys. Dressed in my jersey and pads, I'd been going through the exercises with them—so much for hanging out on the sidelines—but now I'm standing back to look for weaknesses and strengths in the line. I get that Coach is taking a big risk, and his ass will be on the line if anyone files an official complaint, so I'm doing my best to make his team great again, and keep as low of a profile as I can. I owe him that.

From the sideline, Coach is watching us, and a measure of guilt twists me up inside. Yeah, I told him I'd stay away from Sara, swore to it actually, and I'm going against my word. I fucking hate that. A man's word is everything. What is he without it? But this is what Sara needs. What she asked me for. I wish I could say I was doing it solely for her, but that would be a big fucking lie, now wouldn't it. I can't stay away from her any more than she can stay way from me, and it's not just Coach that wants me to keep my distance. My mother, in not so many words, said the same thing to me the other night.

Do I think this plan of hers will work? Do I think after time in her bed, it will help her get me out of her system? I can't speak for her, but I know walking away from her again will be the fucking death of me. But I hope it's what she needs, because the truth is, I want Sara to be happy. I want her to get everything in life she deserves. For as long as I've known her, she wanted out of Middletown, and it fucking slays me that she seems to be settling in for the long haul. I'd do just about anything to help her move to a better neighborhood. Is moving up in the bank what she really wants? I somehow doubt that, but it's none of my business to bring it up.

I blow the whistle and call the captain over. He tugs off his helmet, and rakes his hair from his face as he runs toward me. In that moment, my gut twists. The kid reminds me so much of myself back in the day.

"Hey, Tyler. What's up?" he says.

"I want to run some new plays tomorrow. Last night I worked on a few, cleared them with Coach, and I want to go over with the team tomorrow."

He spits. "Fuck, I'm glad to hear that. I'm sick of running these same plays. If we want to beat Lincoln, the old man needs to get up to speed already."

I glare at him. I'm not much older than these guys, but if I want their respect I have to show them I'm the assistant coach, not their friend. "Coach doesn't like swearing on the field, Jackson," I say, my voice harder. "And he's your coach, not an old man, got it?"

He straightens. "Right, sorry."

"Go," I say. "Tell the guys we'll be meeting in the locker room tomorrow morning. Have a chalkboard there for me."

"You got it, Coach," he says, and darts down the field.

I pick my helmet up from the ground and head toward Coach Ramsey, who'd just called Tanner off the field. He's the team's wide receiver, and with a little help could be the best kicker too. From my distance, I can't hear the conversation, but from the way Tanner is staring at his feet, his shoulders hunched, I'm guessing it's not a happy conversation.

I make my way toward them. "Tyler," Coach says, and from the familiar look on his face, it's easy to see he's playing hard-ass right now.

"Everything okay?" My gaze goes from Coach to Tanner, who keeps pinching the bridge of his nose, like he's trying to fight back tears.

"Report cards just came out. If Tanner can't get his math grade up, he'll be off the team." He turns back to Tanner. "Can you ask Mr. Phillips for extra help after class?"

He shakes his head. "Mr. Phillips is the problem. He doesn't explain things right. He just ends up confusing me more." He shakes his head. "Come on, Coach. There must be something you can do. Football is my life." He pauses and says, "My father will kill me if I get kicked off the team."

I nod without thinking. I had Mr. Phillips for math back in the day. The man is brilliant, and should be teaching at a university level. He can't relate to teens, or teach at their level. Everyone knows it, even Coach. Tanner is a sophomore with mad skills on the field. If we can get this team performing again, he has a real shot at a scholarship, but if he can't get his math up, that could fuck him over.

"What about a tutor? Do you know anyone who can help you?"

"I can't...I don't..." I know he's trying to say he can't afford it, but is too embarrassed to get the words past his tongue. It was never easy for me to admit those things either. I clear my throat to cut the tension.

Coach folds his arms and rocks on his feet. "You got something to say, Tyler?"

"Yeah. I'll tutor you, Tanner."

Tanner's head lifts, and his eyes go wide. "It's math," he says, like I'm an uneducated dickless felon who can't add two and two.

I stand eye to eye with him. "Your point."

"I...uh..." He cocks his head, and scrubs his hand over his chin. "You any good in math?"

I scoff at the hit on my intelligence, but I'd taken worse, and really, can I blame the kid? "Hey, it's no sweat off my balls. Take the offer or don't. I'm not the one who is about to be kicked off the field and never get a chance at a scholarship."

I'm about to leave when he says, "You think I can get a scholarship?"

The hope in his voice makes me smile. I keep my back to him so he can't see it. "That's up to you."

"When can we start?" he says quickly before I can leave.

I turn back. "Tonight I'll be at the library at UIC. You got wheels?"

"Bus pass."

"Good. Be there for seven and bring copies of all your tests. Oh, and Tanner, we're going to work on your kicks too."

I angle my head and nod to Coach, who's just standing there glaring at me, arms across his barrel chest. He nods back and I tuck my helmet under my arm.

"Tyler," Tanner says.

"Yeah."

"Thanks, man, and I uh...didn't mean to—"

"Tonight, seven sharp. If you're one minute late, it's off." Yeah, I'm playing hardball, but sometimes that's what these kids need. It was Coach's firmness with me on the field that kept me working hard in the class. If I hadn't kept my grades up, I would have been off the team and no way would I have gotten a scholarship.

I walk off the field, and make my way inside the school. It's nearing eight and kids are just starting to file in. I walk to Coach's office, and tug off my dirty jersey. I need to hit the showers and get to work by nine. I'm looking forward to reading to the kids at the blind school, and putting my translator skills to work.

I grab my backpack from the floor and when I stand back up, and see Sara watching me from the doorway, her gaze raking over me like a hot caress, I go perfectly still.

"Hey," she says, and my body fires at the softness in her words.

We hadn't seen each other since Sunday morning, when we made love in her bed and had breakfast together before I snuck out and went home to spend time with my family. Gracie wanted me to take her to the library that afternoon, and I wouldn't miss that time with her for the world. I have so much time to make up for with her, with everyone. She was beyond excited to help me pick out books for translation. If only she hadn't picked all those New Adult romance novels. How was I going to keep a straight face reading Pride's Run— the first in a three-book series she's anxious for me to read, is beyond me. The book is about an eighteen-year-old girl who's a werewolf—used as an assassin by a drug lord—and her big escape from the compound with a boy she falls in love with. I groan inwardly at the thoughts of it.

"Hey yourself," I say. Jesus, she looks so good, and soft in her professional skirt that showcases long legs I can't wait to feel wrapped around me again. Fuck man, I need to think about something else before I get a damn hard-on and bend her over this desk and show her just how much I missed her yesterday.

She leans against the doorjamb, and crosses her legs at the

ankle. It draws my focus and my blood roars, my mind tripping back to Saturday, to when I spread her wide open and
pushed my tongue high inside her.

*Jesus, get it together, dude. This is neither the time nor place for
those kinds of thoughts.*

"I talked to Gracie last night." Sara has a grin on her face
that is so fucking adorable it's all I can do not to cross the
room and kiss it off. As I hunger for her, my mind takes that
second to remind me of her father, and my heart races a little
faster. I steal a quick glance over my shoulder.

"Christ."

"Don't worry," she says. "Dad is still on the field. I can see
him from here."

"He wouldn't like us in here alone like this."

"I know. You should go." She angles her body to let me
through the doorway. I make my way toward her and that
grin returns. "I know how anxious you must be to get to
those romance books."

"Fuck," I say and we both laugh. I stand over her, feel her
heat reaching out to me. I stifle a groan and say, "Did you
have something to do with that?"

She blinks innocently and puts her hand on her chest. My
gaze drops to it for a second, and my cock twitches as her
fingers splay over her breasts.

"Me? What would make you even ask such a thing?"

I pitch my voice low, and put one hand on the door beside
her head. I step close, crowd her, and a breathy little sound
escapes her lips. "You're going to pay for this, Sara."

"While I like the sound of that, I really didn't have
anything to do with it. Your sister is a sixteen-year-old girl.
Sixteen-year-old girls are thinking about sixteen-year-old
boys, Tyler. Whether you like it or not, Gracie is growing up."

"No guy is getting near her," I growl. "He'll have to go
through my brothers and me first."

Sara laughs. "Oh, that poor girl. Three overprotective brothers." She shakes her head and her long hair falls over her shoulders. Unable to help myself, I reach out, coil a strand around my fingers. Her sweet vanilla scent fills the air, and I burn with the need to taste her again. "She's going to need me around and on her side more than I thought," Sara says.

I need her more than she thinks.

Boots echoing in the hall heralds someone's approach and I jump back just as Coach rounds the corner. He pauses for a moment, takes in the two of us standing there. Fuck, talking to Sara like this is risky. I'd vowed to her father to stay away from her, and I promised her I'd keep what we're doing a secret. It's a promise I plan to keep. Which means, we can't ever do this again, no matter what. If I see her here, I need to run the other way.

"Don't you have somewhere to be, Tyler?" he asks in a hard voice as he delivers a cutting glare.

As he watches me with narrow eyes, I say, "Yes, Coach. I was just getting my bag when Sara showed up." I nod to Sara. "Nice to see you again, Sara."

"You too," she says, and I push past her, my body rubbing hers in a promise of things to come.

"Hey Tyler," Coach says, and I freeze with my back to him. Fuck. Fuck. Fuck.

"Yeah"

"What you did on the field with Tanner."

"What about it?"

"Thanks for that."

"Not a problem, Coach," I say and expel a heavy breath as I walk away. I hear Sara asking what I did as I escape, but her father changes the subject and asks about her date with Caleb. Blood roars through my insides at the sound of his name, but it gives me a measure of comfort to know Sara won't be seeing him again.

With that last thought making me happy, I round the corner and hurry to the showers. Once I reach the locker room, I strip off the rest of my gear and rinse off quickly. Today is my first official day of work, and I don't want to be late. I pull out my dress shirt and pants, tug on my brown leather shoes, and make my way outside, steering clear of Coach's office—of Sara.

I shoulder my bag and ease my bike into traffic. The air bites at my bare hands and as much as I hate the idea, it's time to put my ride away for the winter. I pull into the parking lot and take in the big brick building before me as I shut off my bike. I'd been here before with Gracie. Sara and I both have, actually. It was here my kid sister found friends, fit it, learned to live with her disability.

I take off my helmet, smooth my hand over my clothes and walk toward the doors. I'm not sure how the staff feels about having a convicted felon working among them. Will they hide their purses, lock away their valuables? I'm not here looking to make friends, but it would be nice to have a good relationship with the staff. I pull open the heavy door and step up to the front desk. I introduce myself to the middle-aged lady tapping away on a keyboard behind the counter. She stops when she sees me, and after I tell her who I am, she directs me to the third floor.

"Thanks," I say and tap the counter.

She gives me a big, welcoming smile. "You have a great day, now."

"You too."

I pass the elevator and take the stairs instead. I'm not all that fond of enclosed spaces anymore. My legs eat up the stairs two at a time, and I push through the door to see my new workspace. Similar to a library, books line the shelves, and there are round tables set up, a few chairs occupied by a young child, a woman who appears to be her mother, and a man I'm guessing is her father. They're talking quietly and give me a nod as I pass. At the other end of the room, I spot an employee. She has her back to me, but she's wearing a vest identifying her as staff.

"Excuse me," I say and she spins, her long blond hair falling over her shoulders. She's young, a little bit younger than me, and looks somewhat familiar. She blinks up at me, her gaze zeroing in on my scar. It doesn't bother me that she's staring. I'm used to the reaction by now. "I'm Tyler Barrett. You must be Cassie."

"I am," she says, still blinking at me. I'm good at reading people, but I can't quite figure out her reaction. Is it that she can't place me, or is it that she knows me? I'm not sure, but the one thing I do know is that I'm throwing her off her game. Maybe she wasn't expecting a six-foot cut up man to check in for his first day of work. Or maybe she was.

"Claudine arranged—"

"Yes, yes of course," she says, my words pulling her out of her trance-like state. She glances at her watch. "You took me by surprise, is all. I wasn't expecting you so early."

"I like to make a good impression on the first day," I say and flash her a grin.

"That you did," she says quietly, and holds her hand out. "It's nice to meet you, Tyler. Like I said on the phone, you'll be shadowing me for the next week, and then we'll get you set up at your own workstation." She shrugs. "I know you've done this job before, but it's protocol."

"It's okay by me."

She gestures with a nod toward the hall. "How about a tour of the facility first?"

"I'd love that." I shrug out of my backpack.

"Here let me take that for you. We have lockers." Before I can stop her, she reaches for my bag, and it sinks to the floor like a rock, heavy in her small hands.

"What do you have in here, a dead body?" she asks, then stiffens. "I mean—"

"Football practice," I say, coming to her rescue. I don't want tension between us. "I'm helping Coach Ramsey out with the team over at Collins High."

"Oh really. That's where I used to go."

"I thought you looked familiar."

She shakes her head. "No, you wouldn't remember me. I was a freshman and you were a senior." Her face lights up as she smiles. "Star of the football team. I went to all your games."

"That was a long time ago," I say and before things get awkward again, I say, "How about that tour?" I bend to take my bag from her and when our hands connect she sucks in a little breath. Shit. I lift my head quickly and she averts her gaze, but I don't miss the pink in her cheeks. One of two things is happening here. She's either still infatuated with that young boy from high school—who is long gone—or is now frightened by me. Neither of which bode well for this situation.

I follow her to the locker and shove my bag inside, then she gives me a tour of our floor. I meet Josh, who is also one of the transcribers. He's a middle-aged man, and seems friendly enough. My workstation is next to his, with all the technical and computer equipment I need to put books into braille.

After a tour of our floor, we take the stairs, and she shows me the classrooms where activities such as artistic expression take place.

"Last month we had a Japanese Origami class."

"Cool," I say.

"Outside of artistic expressions, we also have guide dog user meetings here."

"Very similar to the set-up where I was."

We go down the hall and she opens the door to a computer lab. "In here we have computer training and private computer sessions. You're familiar with the adaptive software Jaws, ZoomText, and MaGic?"

"I am," I say.

She arches a brow and coils her hair around her finger. "You might be interested in doing some work in here as well. You can also make extra money private tutoring."

"I'm open for anything."

She pulls her bottom lip between her teeth, and turns from me. "Claudine told me you volunteered with the book clubs."

"I enjoy reading to the kids." I ignore the knot tightening in my gut. I missed a lot of time with my little sister, and while reading to the young ones won't give me my years back with her, it helps make me feel a little less guilty. "Wait, you know Gracie, my sister, right?"

"Yes, she's a sweet girl."

We walk toward the stairs, and I open the door and gesture for her to go first. "She asked me to pick out some books for the club."

She nods. "They have to be approved first."

The door closes with a bang, and I follow her down the next flight of stairs. With any luck, they'll veto them, and I won't have to read romance out loud to a bunch of girls.

"She's in later today after school," I say. "I'm sure she'll bring them with her and submit for approval."

She shows me around the administrative offices, and our final stop is the kitchen. I'll have to run out at lunch and grab a bite, since I didn't pack anything.

"Coffee?"

"Yeah, for sure."

"Coffee is free here, and we have water and soda in the

fridge. All provided, so help yourself." She drops a pod into the Keurig machine, and goes to the fridge for milk.

"Black for me," I say.

When the machine gurgles to a stop, she removes the pod and puts a fresh one in for herself. I take a sip, and savor the flavor.

After her coffee is done, we head back upstairs and she shows me around the library before we make our way to her desk. She grabs a chair and places it beside hers and I sit.

"Any questions?" she asks.

"No, pretty much the same set-up as it was before."

"This isn't exciting work, but I'm organizing the annual Light The Way Benefit. We have a silent and live auction to raise money for youth programs." She passes me a sheet. "We're reaching out to companies to see if they want to donate, or put an ad in the program book. Here is the list we reach out to. I'll take the top half if you want to take the bottom." As soon as the words leave her mouth, she swallows, like she said something wrong...or something sexual.

I look over the list, grab a pen and draw a line to separate the top half from the bottom. "Do we phone or email?" I ask.

"There are different contacts for different companies," she explains. "Also, if you know of any companies that might like to donate, we can add to the list and reach out."

"Okay," I say. "I'll start with the ones who want to be called first."

I reach for the phone and make my way through the list. The morning passes quickly, and I have to say, while I'm not in to marketing, I was able to secure quite a few donations and ads. By the time lunch rolls around, I stretch and stand, my stomach taking that moment to grumble.

"Is lunch an hour?"

"Yes," Cassie says as she stands with me. "Did you pack? If not, I can share."

"That's really nice of you, but I'm just going to grab something. I have to stop in to see my brother. Maybe you know him. He was a few grades behind me. Lucas Barrett."

She nods. "I remember Lucas. He works at Mr. Johnson's service bay, right?"

"Yeah." I make my way to the locker, and she follows along. "If you ever need any work done on your car, he's your guy."

"I'll remember that."

I reach for my bag, shoulder it, and grab my helmet, then take the three flights down the stairs. I step outside and the early morning clouds have parted to give way to a warm fall day. I walk to my bike and an uneasy feeling moves over me. It's a feeling I know well, and never ignored in prison. I walk slowly, and casually glance over my shoulder and scan the street. People mill about, but a punk-ass kid in baggy clothes and a ball cap leaning against the side of a store building, head down texting, catches my eye. I watch him as I climb on my bike, and he only looks up when I ease into traffic.

Fuck man, it better not be one of the Phantoms watching me, wanting to get me away from Deacon and into their club —or worse. I make my way to my brother's service bay and slow when I see one of the Phantoms peel out of the lot. What the fuck? Once he disappears, I park my bike just as one of the service bay doors open.

An SUV backs out, and I take in the stick figures on the back, that of a man, woman, son, daughter and two dogs. I swallow down the thickness in my throat. That's the kind of family Sara and I talked about. Right down to the two dogs. Is this the universe's way of mocking me? Well fuck you.

I make my way inside, to find my baby brother at the counter, scribbling something onto a piece of paper. His eyes go wide when he sees me.

"What's up, bro?" he asks.

I glare at him. "What was a Phantom doing here?"

He flinches, and the move doesn't go unnoticed by me. "Just looking to get some bike work done."

"You work on their bikes?"

"Sometimes."

"Jesus, fuck, Lucas."

"Look, this isn't my business. I work for Mr. Johnson. I do what I'm told to do."

I pace, and my boots scrape on the floor. I exhale slowly and walk back up to my brother, meeting his gaze straight on. "I don't like this."

"It's always been this way, Ty. Nothing I can do about it."

"Just stay the fuck away from them outside of here, got it?"

"Yeah, I got it." He looks past my shoulders, then turns his attention to the cash. "Aren't you supposed to be at work?"

"Lunch break. Wanted to check in with you to see if you have any leads on a good car for the winter."

"Yeah, sure. I know a guy who's selling his old Ford Focus. Lots of miles, but it's a good car." He reaches for the phone. "Let me call him."

I turn, and walk toward the window. From the other side of the street I see movement. I shade the sun from my eyes, and every nerve I have goes on high alert.

Why the fuck is that punk-ass kid following me?

With the nights getting darker earlier, dusk falls over the city as I hop off the bus, UIC's campus rising up in the distance before me. Students mill about as I zip up my coat, and hurry my steps, the cooler air wrapping around me and bringing on a chill. I was late getting away from work this afternoon, and have been rushing around ever since. Class doesn't start until seven, but Ty said he would be at the library, going over books for braille before he had to tutor Tanner and wanted to see me before class. No way did I want to miss seeing him.

I'm not sure if he chose the UIC campus to tutor because it was convenient, or if it was because I'd be in class tonight. Either way, I can't deny the bubble of excitement building inside me at the thought of seeing him again. Sneaking around is ridiculous, I know. I'm a grown adult, but I have a lot at stake. My family would disown me, and I work in a bank, for God's sake. I can't imagine my boss would be thrilled to find out I've fallen into bed with a convicted gunrunner. And then there's Tyler. He's here trying to get his life back in order by working and helping my dad out on the field. I know he loves the game, and is trying to right some wrongs. I commend him for that, and I don't want him to disappoint Dad again. Being back on the field has been good for both of them. I can already see Tyler's idea breathing new life into my father. He's smiling more, seems more alive on the field.

I peel off my heavy jacket as I step in through the front doors of the library and the familiar smells of old books fall over me. I go through security, and make my way toward the rows and rows of books shelved at the back. It's quiet, and a few people are studying at the tables, or punching away on their laptops. The rush whipping through my blood, knowing I'm seconds away from seeing Tyler again, is insane and my stomach squeezes, the hamburger I scarfed down before running to catch the bus currently doing flip flops. As excitement wells, I press my hand over my belly to quiet the rush, but then another thought darkens my mood. Tonight I need to talk to Caleb, break this thing off between us before it gets started.

I pass rows and rows of shelving and when I spct Tyler, plunked down on the floor, cross-legged, looking so damn boyish—the teen I knew from my youth—as he flips through a book, my heart stalls. I fight the urge to rush to him, throw my arms around him, and hold him to me, forever. As I stare at him, lost in the book he's reading, my pulse jumps in my throat, and warning bells jingle in the back of my brain.

Is what I'm doing here smart?

No, it's not, but I'm at a loss, such a goddamn heartbreaking loss I'm going against everything my head is telling me to do and letting my stupid emotions rule again. I stand at the end of the aisle, and grip the side of the shelving cabinet to keep myself upright. The man before me is all muscle and power, a hard body carved from stone, with fists that fought for survival, yet the way he touched me the other night, softly, gently, like I was a delicate flower that could be broken, had me coming apart. I'd toughened up considerably after he left, but maybe when it comes to Ty I'll always be that delicate flower who wilts without his love and affection.

As though sensing my presence, his head lifts and a heady rush of bliss burns through my blood when a smile splits his lips—lips that kissed and explored every part of my body so thoroughly. Heat moves through me and no doubt my cheeks have turned a light shade of pink.

"Hey," he says quietly, and makes a move to stand, but I shake my head to stop him, just wanting to see him sit there a little longer. I like the way it makes me feel, like we're kids again, stealing kisses in the campus library before rushing off to our next class.

He gives me a perplexed frown and looks past my shoulders. "Everything okay?"

Of course not.

"Everything is fine," I say and walk toward him. I sit down, and mimic his position. "I was just standing there, wondering what you were thinking," I say, reminding him of the game we used to play. The one I foolishly tried to play with Caleb, like he could somehow step into Tyler's shoes. Our eyes meet, lock, and I reach out and touch his face. My fingers rasp over the day's growth, and he leans into my hand.

"I missed you," he says, his voice deep, tortured.

"I missed you, too."

"But that wasn't what I was thinking."

He gives a devilish grin, and reaches for the hem of my sweater, rubs it through his fingers, and the backs of his knuckles brush my flesh. I shiver, and pull in a ragged breath.

"No, then what were you thinking?"

"I'd rather show you."

"I'd rather like that," I say.

His eyes go back to mine, and the smile falls from his

face. "You didn't get into any trouble with your dad this morning, did you?"

I shake my head. "No. He might not trust you, but I think he trusts me to make the right decisions." God, he's so wrong about that.

He shakes his head and exhales loudly. "Sara, I'm sorry, I'd never—"

"This isn't on you, Tyler. I'm the one who invited you into my bed. I'm the one who told you I needed this, for however long it takes," I say and lean toward him to seal his apology with a kiss. Our lips touch, graze softly, then he angles his head and deepens it. He parts my lips, taking his time with me, even though time isn't something we have, and his tongue sweeps inside. My entire body softens, as I taste mint and coffee on his tongue. I kiss him back, the familiarity in what we're doing wrapping around me like a blanket, cocooning me in warmth and comfort. I wrap my hands around his neck and he pulls at me until I'm on his lap, my legs slide around his waist. His hands splay over my back, and I absorb his heat, let it curl through me and push back the cold in my bones.

He's wearing a big smile when we break apart, but then he glances behind me and he goes stiff, like he's suddenly spooked.

"What?" I ask, and glance over my shoulder, expecting my father to be standing over us.

"I think someone was watching us."

I scan the library. I only see students milling about, but what we're doing is risky and inappropriate. "Then we'd better get out of here."

He taps my ass. "You go. I'm tutoring Tanner," he pauses to glance at this watch. "In about fifteen minutes."

"Okay. I'd better get to class." I stand, and he picks my backpack up and puts it over my shoulders, then he hands me my coat. The warmth and heat between us is so powerful my chest is heavy, the air almost hard to breathe. It's a wonder everyone in the library can't feel it. Then again, maybe they can.

"When can I see you again?" he asks quietly, touching a strand of my hair. His fingers brush my neck and I quiver.

"This weekend?" I pose it as a question, because I honestly have no idea what his plans are and don't want to sound as anxious as I feel. Truthfully I'd like to see him tonight, but he has early morning football practice and I won't be home until late. Of course, I can't forget I have to stay after class to talk to Caleb.

"Okay. You go first," he says, then adjusts his pants. "I need a minute." I chuckle slightly as I walk away from him, but putting distance between us is as hard today as it was all those years ago. I make my way to the front of the library when I see Tanner rushing in, his gaze going left and right, like he's worried he missed Tyler. I'm about to tell him he didn't, but then think better of it. No way do I want this to get back to my father.

I glance over my shoulder to catch one last glimpse of the man I should be staying away from, and freeze when I see him talking to some guy with baggy clothes and a ball cap pulled down low on his head to conceal his identity. He's leaning in to Tyler conspiratorially, and as I take in the vision, warning bells ring loudly in my brain. I suck in air, and grip my coat tighter against the stabbing pain in my chest as old hurts and betrayals squeeze the air from my lungs. The room darkens around me, and I get a sinking feeling deep in my core, snaking into the most cut-up and carved out pieces of my heart.

Tyler's eyes snap to mine, like he feels me watching. His eyes are hard, dark—a stranger to me. The Tyler from prison. He doesn't make a move toward me, to tell me it's not what I think, and there is nothing in his body language to suggest this encounter is innocent, coincidental. I quickly tear my gaze away and hurry through the doors. I try to process what I saw as I practically run down the hall to class. The kid isn't wearing a cut on his jacket, identifying himself as a Phantom, but if he's not, and he's in Phantom territory, he might be concealing his colors to protect himself. But everything about him says he's a gangbanger. Which begs the question, what is he doing here, and what business does he have with Tyler?

I can barely catch my breath by the time I round the corner and take my usual seat at the front of the class. How I'm supposed to concentrate on advanced finance is beyond me. Derek, a man who works at a different branch of our bank, sits beside me. I've gotten to know him over the last few months, and he likes to tease that we're competitors going for the same job. But we're at different branches, on opposite sides of the city, so I don't really get that. I plaster on a smile and brush my hair from my face, hoping he can't see my anxiety.

"How did you make out on last week's assignment?" he asks. He shakes his head. "It was the toughest one yet."

"It was hard," I say, but dammit I sound as breathless as I feel. "Took me hours to finish it."

He angles his head and I pray he doesn't ask me if I'm okay. I might just burst into tears. Before he can speak, the professor walks in, a few students filing in behind him. Grateful for the interruption, I face the front of the class and open my laptop as the door shuts and class begins. The prof begins to ask about last week's assignment and I pinch my eyes shut, forcing myself to concentrate. But can't seem to do it. Goddammit, I need to get my mind on school and off Tyler and his extracurricular activities if I want this promotion. I can't let him derail me again. I just can't. There is too much at stake.

The next couple of hours drag on, and I take notes,

hoping they'll make sense to me later. I glance at my phone in my bag, and consider texting Ty. Do I come right out and ask who that guy was? Do I even have a right to? I asked for a sexual affair to get him out of my system. What he does on his own time doesn't concern me, right?

Then why do I feel like it does?

Class finally ends and I power down my laptop. I grab my phone, toy with it in my hand when it beeps. I nearly jump out of my chair. The text is from Caleb, asking me to stop by his classroom. Once again, an uneasy feeling closes in on me. I'm not one to hurt anyone's feelings, but it's best to end this now, before he gets the wrong idea.

Derek is saying something to me, as I pack up. "I'm sorry, what was that?"

He angles his head again. "Are you okay? You seemed a little distracted tonight."

"Perfectly fine," I say. I'm not about to spill my life to this guy, even though he seems genuinely nice. "Just have a lot to do." I give him a big smile and hurry from the classroom. I pass students leaving Caleb's class as I make my way down the hall. My steps slow as I approach the door. He has his back to me and is doing something at his desk. I knock softly, and he turns.

"Glad you could come." He looks past me. "Would you mind shutting the door?"

At first I'm a bit reluctant, I'd rather just say what I have to say, and get out of there. If I'm lucky, I can still catch the bus, and not have to wait a half hour in the cold and dark for the next one, but I do as he asks because I am breaking things off with him, and I owe him that much. Plus, the last thing I want is for any of his students or fellow professors to overhear our conversation. Professors aren't supposed to date students, right? Then again, I'm not his student anymore. Still I wouldn't want him to get in any kind of trouble or to be dragged in to it myself. I do everything I can to avoid trouble, or draw negative attention to myself.

"I haven't heard from you lately." He straightens to his full height, and there is a strange sort of tension about him.

I take a step toward him. "Sorry about that. I've been so busy," I say. "Professors, right?" I add to lighten the mood. As I approach, the hairs on the back of my neck tingle. This is the same Caleb I've known for a long time now, but there is something very different about him tonight.

"Busy, huh?"

I begin to inch backward, flinching at the hardness in his tone as I take a look over my shoulder to see where I'm going. "Yeah. Work, school. I'm sure you know—"

"And busy with your gangbanger." Our gazes collide when I turn back to him, and he glares at me. "You can't forget your gangbanger."

My limbs freeze, his words like a sucker punch to the gut. "What?" I ask, pinned beneath his scrutiny, his judgment, a look I'm so damn familiar with. When Tyler was taken away, all eyes turned to me. Was I too, a criminal? I heard the hateful words, the allegations.

"Come on, Sara." He smiles but it holds no humor. "I saw you two at the club Saturday night. I saw you leave with him. Why did you lie to me and tell me there was nothing between you?"

"I didn't..." Flustered at his accusations, and the way this is all going down, I set my backpack down, and pull in a flustered breath. "This has nothing to do with Tyler," I say, and it's a half-truth. Caleb and I hadn't connected the way I wanted us too. There was no spark, no little flutterings of the heart or little explosions that made my pulse beat faster. Those things only materialized when around Tyler. "But I came here tonight to talk about us."

He steps up to me, and grabs me by the arm, hard. My

entire body tightens, and I try to pull away, but his grip is tight, his fingers biting into my skin hard enough to leave bruises. He twists my arm, and I struggle. I've taken self-defense lessons, but from the way he's holding me, it's clear he knows plenty of moves himself. Underneath his impeccable suit, he's a fighter.

"Let go," I say, my voice firm, the way I was taught in self-defense class. What the hell does he think he's doing? I struggle against him, but my efforts prove futile.

"Us, huh? What exactly is it you want to say about us?" he demands, and squeezes harder, everything about him radiating danger.

I take a quick, fueling breath as he towers over me, six feet of intimating male. I might have taken self-defense classes, but Caleb is strong, and he's got a good solid hold on me, so I don't want to make any rash movements. My heart is pounding so hard in my ears, I'm sure he can hear it, but I calm myself, biding my time. Since I don't want this to turn violent, my first instinct is to talk myself out of the situation so I chose my words carefully. "I don't think I'm the right girl for you. I'm just not ready for anything serious, or any kind of relationship."

He makes a sound, a half laugh, half snort. His once soft eyes turn hard, almost menacing, and his mouth thins, his lips a milky shade of white as he stands over me, his nostrils flaring. My mind races back to Tyler's warnings, and every instinct in my gut is screaming at me to get out of there, but he won't let me go. I decide to change tactics.

"It's not you, Caleb. You seem like you're ready to settle down, and I'm just not ready for that."

"Oh it's me, all right. Here I thought you were a nice girl." A dark threatening laugh rumbles from the depths of his throat. "You sure had me fooled." He holds me pinned in his crosshairs as my mind races, searching for a way out of this.

"You should have told me you liked it rough and dirty with convicted felons," he says, his breath hot and sour as his ugly words fall over me. "Yeah, that's right. I asked around about him." A pause and then, "I can give you rough, and dirty, Sara. Oh, believe me, I can give you that, and then some."

He grabs my shoulders, and shoves me against the wall, then pushes his pelvis against me. I feel his arousal, and a sound catches in my throat. His eyes, black as the night sky, compliments of dilated pupils, narrow to thin slits, something dark and deadly seething beneath the surface.

With my back poker straight, and my skin prickling in warning, I steel myself against the threat. How could I have not seen this side of him? Tyler had, though. He'd warned me.

It takes a criminal to know one.

"Is this how your gangbanger treats you? Like you're one of his old ladies he can fuck when he wants, how he wants, and wherever the fuck he wants?" The look in his eyes is beyond frightening, but I try to keep the situation under control.

"Caleb. Tyler and I are friends." My insides twist, all hope of ending this without violence sinking inside me. "It's not like that."

"Friends who fuck." His words are soft, but the anger behind them is most obvious. He drags the back of his hand down my cheek until he reaches my neck. His fingers curl around my throat and when they tighten, my stomach recoils.

"Let me go, Caleb," I say as calmly as possible, when I'm so close to breaking down in front of him, but I don't want him to see that. I don't want to give him the satisfaction. "We'll just forget we ever knew each other, and this didn't happen."

"Nah, I'd rather fuck you."

Fear clogs my throat, making it hard to talk. "Caleb—"

"Come on." He pushes his pelvis against me again and

when he tears at my sweater, I swallow a cry. "Stop pretending that you don't want this."

As the situation escalates, my self-preservation instincts kick in. His grip is so tight, flight is out of the question, which means the only way I'm going to get out of this class-room with my life is to fight.

But how can I possibly win?

TYLER

Where the hell is Sara?

I sit on my bike and watch the bus she usually takes stop, pick up a few passengers, and take off again. What the hell is taking her so long? I crinkle the note in my hand and glance at the front doors of the main campus for the millionth time, waiting for her to come out. Had her class run late? I steal a glance around, and another minute ticks by.

Okay, fuck this.

I climb off my bike, and hurry across the street. I take the stairs two at a time. I have no idea where her classroom is. I only know it's in the main campus building where the library is housed. I wander the quiet halls on the first floor, my heavy bike boots echoing around me. I need to explain to her what she saw tonight. When she took off, she had a look of horror on her face. I'd wanted to go after her, but I needed to hear what Deacon's man, the punk-ass kid who'd been following me—to ensure he was giving the right man the information— had to say.

I continue down the hall and, through the little door

window, peer into the classrooms. The lights are out in most and the doors are locked. I continue down and when I reach the end, I go up to the second floor. The heavy stairwell door slams behind me, but the sound is soon drowned out by a woman's scream.

Sara.

I hear a loud growl, following by a hard bang, and my steps turn into a full on run.

Motherfucker.

I see a light on in a classroom, and look through the window, and my heart jumps into my throat at the sight before me. I practically kick open the door and rush inside. "Sara," I say and bolt to her, my breath coming in ragged bursts as her sweater hangs open, her bra exposed.

"Tyler," she cries out and sags forward, bracing her hands on her knees as she takes deep gulping breaths. "Thank God you're here," she chokes out.

I look her over quickly. "Are you hurt?"

She shakes her head no, but it's a lie. She's convulsing, heaving, like she's going to be sick. I pull her away from the wall, tuck her safely behind me and glare at the man writhing in agony on the floor, cupping his balls like they'd just been kicked into his mouth. It takes everything I have not to finish the job, but Sara is shaking and that's not what she needs from me right now. I give a silent prayer of thanks that the self-defense lessons paid off.

"I didn't know," she says, her voice trembling, her breaths coming in hard, ragged gasps. "I didn't know," she keeps repeating.

With Caleb no longer a threat, I turn to her. "You couldn't have known," I say, and her frightened look rakes over me, leaves me raw, icy inside.

Her cold, shaky hands dip under my jacket, curl in my t-shirt. "Tyler," she says, a deep gulping cry catching in her throat.

"It's okay, Sara. I'm here. He's not going to hurt you. Ever again."

"I want to go."

I open my jacket and tuck her inside. Her head lies against my chest, and her tears fall harder, soaking through my shirt. "We can't go. We have to call the police."

She gives a hard shake of her head, and glances up at me, her eyes wide. "No. I...this isn't my life, Tyler. I don't talk to the police."

"Sara, please." I reach into my pocket, pull out the crinkled piece of paper and smooth it out. "I dug up information on Caleb. It's all here. I never trusted the guy and there's good reason for that."

She inches back a bit, and looks over the paper. Her eyes widen as she reads about the complaints filed against him while teaching at Harvard. From what Deacon's source dug up, the douchebag's parents had a lot of pull, and hushed everything up. Then they had him transferred to UIC, where he was supposed to become an upstanding citizen and keep his hands off his students.

Well, fuck that. This time his victim isn't some young girl who can be paid off or hushed. I'll personally see to it.

"I didn't know," she murmurs again.

"The information was buried, Sara." Jesus fuck, I hate seeing her like this. I glance over my shoulder and see Caleb making his way to his knees. My hands are shaking with the need to punch the fuck out of him. But I resist. My main priority right now is to get Sara to safety and call the police. "There was no way you could know." I walk her toward the door, and guide her into the hall. I use my body to block the entrance because no fucking way is Caleb going anywhere—unless he's in handcuffs.

"You did, though, Tyler. You knew." Her eyes are as big as peaches as she looks up at me, and she doesn't need to speak for me to know what she's thinking—I knew Caleb was a danger because I'm a convicted felon. What is that old saying? It takes a thief to catch a thief. Yeah, that's the one.

"Wait, if the information was buried, how did you get it?" she asks.

"Sara," I say, and pull her against me as Caleb mumbles curses behind me. "It doesn't matter."

"You got it illegally," she says quietly, under her breath. "That boy in the library, that's what the meeting was all about wasn't it?"

"Deacon had some of his guys do a little digging."

"Deacon?"

"A guy who kept me alive in prison." With Caleb moving, I grab my phone and force the issue. "We need to call the police."

"Tyler, I can't."

"Sara, I understand. Believe me. But we can't let this douchebag get away with this. Not again. We can't let him hurt someone else." She goes silent, like she's mulling it over.

"I don't want the attention. My parents...the publicity. Not again, Tyler."

"Don't worry. I'll protect you from it."

"What about you, your job? Could this affect—"

"This isn't about me, it's about you and I won't let anything happen to you." I run my hands through her hair and hold her to me, but my heart is racing as Caleb pulls himself together behind us. Jesus, she must have given him one good hard kick to the nut sack for him to be down so long.

"Okay," she says quietly, putting her trust in me when I have no right to ask for it. But the truth is, I'd give my life to protect those I love. I'd fucking kill for Sara.

I slide my finger across my phone and punch in 911 as I hold her to me. The dispatcher answers, and I give her the details and our location. When I'm done, the sound of Caleb's shoes on the floor gains my attention.

"Get the fuck out of my way," Caleb says from behind me and when I angle my head to see him, Sara stiffens in my arms. Caleb takes a step toward me, his actions threatening.

"Cops are on the way," I say, turning to him fully as I keep my voice low, controlled, intimidating. "And you're fucking lucky that you're dealing with them and not me."

He glances around the room like he's searching for a way out. But the only way out is through me or the window. He'd have more chances of surviving the two-story fall.

When he realizes he has nowhere to go, he hardens himself, and says, "Oh yeah and what are you going to do?"

I secure Sara behind me, and turn to face him straight on. I can be an intimidating fucker when I want. I glare at him, and he falters a little under my stare. For eight long years, violence had been my life. This little douchebag doesn't faze me at all. I'll snap him like a fucking twig, then light him on fire.

I calm myself before my anger takes over. Fighting isn't conducive to my plan to keep out of prison, and if I'm locked away again, I can't be here for Sara. "Another place, another time, and you won't get off so easily."

He scoffs, but from his body language, it's clear he understands my threat is real.

"It's not what you think," he says.

"It's exactly what I think. Now shut the fuck up before I shut your mouth for you."

He rakes his hands through his hair and paces, making his way to the window and back to his desk. "Look," he begins again.

"I'm not interested in what you have to say, asshole. Tell it
to the cops."

The shrill of sirens puncture the night, and Sara hugs me
tighter. I back her away from the door when boots herald the
arrival of two officers, a male and female, their faces stern,
emotionless. They look us both over, take in Sara's ripped
shirt. I cover her up and gesture with a nod to the classroom.

"He attacked her," I say to the guy.

The cop nods and steps into the classroom while the
woman stays outside with us.

"I want to leave," Sara says.

"I can take your statement here, or downtown," the
female officer says, her voice softening as she takes in the
situation.

"I think I just need to get her out of this building," I say,
and the cop nods like she fully understands. I nod toward the
classroom again. "Would you mind grabbing her coat and
bag." I don't want to leave her alone and I don't want her
stepping foot in the classroom again.

The officer grabs Sara's things, and I help her into her
coat, then gather her into my arms. The cop follows us as I
lead Sara to the stairwell. She sags against me as I hold her
tight and guide her down and out into the night. She folds
her arms around herself to ward off the chill and I zip her
coat up.

The officer begins to ask questions, and hot rage rockets
through me as Sara answers, her voice shaking. It takes everything in me not to go back up those stairs and beat the living
fuck out of that asshole. As we stand there, the rumble of
bikes reach my ears and I turn toward the sound as the Phantoms slowly make their way down the street toward us. I
glare, and they glare back.

"You know those guys?" the cops asks, deep suspicion in
her voice.

"No," I say, but get the feeling that I'm going to know them, real soon. I'm suspecting all these coincidental drive-bys are anything but coincidental.

"Then you should probably stop glaring at them like that." It's good advice and I should take it, but I don't want the fuckers to think they can intimidate me or my family in my own neighborhood. I'm not that innocent nineteen-year-old who walked a mile the other way to avoid a run-in with them.

The cop comes out with Caleb, who has his hands cuffed. Good. The leader of the Phantoms slows on the street right in front of us, braces his boots on the ground, and folds his arms across his barrel chest as he takes in the incident, unafraid of the cops.

Sara moves in closer to me as Caleb is led to the police cruiser and put in the back. I tuck her against me so she doesn't have to look at him, then tell the officer what I learned about Caleb's time at Harvard. Once our statements are taken, the female officer joins her partner in the car and flick their lights back on. The Phantoms' leader revs his bike and takes off, his gangbangers following close behind, their eyes all on us. The fucker better not start anything with my family or me. I'm here to get my life together and stay out of trouble, but I'm suspecting that's going to be harder than I thought.

By the time everyone is gone, and we're alone in the night, she's so shaken up, I don't want to leave her, but it's cold out and I'm not so sure the back of my bike is the right place for her right now. I zip her coat up to her chin, and lift her collar.

"Do you want me to grab you an Uber, or do you want to ride on the back with me?"

She grips my coat like she's afraid to be away from me. "I want to ride with you."

"Okay." I guide her to my bike and I'm about to fit her

with my spare helmet when she holds her hand out to stop me. "Second thoughts?"

"I think I need to call home. Word travels fast in this town, and I don't want my parents to find out about this from someone else."

I nod, and she reaches into her bag to produce her phone. She sniffs as she calls, and her eyes meet mine and hold as she waits for someone to pick up. I can only imagine how shaken up this is going to make her parents. They wanted her out of this city as much as I did. The only reason she's still here is because of me and the guilt from that eats at me like a thousand angry ants.

"Hey kiddo," her father says when he answers. The volume is up high, allowing me to hear both ends of the conversation.

"Dad," she says, her voice shaky.

"What is it, Sara?" he asks, alarm in his voice.

She glances at me, and I stiffen, waiting for the shit storm about to hit when her father finds out she's with me.

"I'm okay," she says quietly.

A pause and then, "Where are you?"

"I'm...I'm outside of the campus. There was an incident."

"I'll be right there."

She shakes her head and her hair falls over her shoulder. "I'm okay. I'm with Tyler."

"Jesus, Sara. If he—"

"No Dad, it's not like that. You remember Caleb."

"Yeah, the nice professor. What's going on, Sara?"

"Turns out he's not so nice. Tyler warned me about him, but I..." Her voice falls off, and she takes a gulping breath.

"What did he do?"

"He attacked me." Her face pales as she speaks the horror. "But I'm okay. I fought him off, and then Tyler showed up."

Her father curses, and my heart trips up. If I had a daughter, I wouldn't want her on these streets either. But it wasn't the streets where she was attacked; it was on campus, where she's supposed to be safe. Nowhere is fucking safe anymore.

"I need to see you," her father says.

"No, Dad. I'm okay," she says alarm in her tone. "I gave my statement to the police, and Tyler is taking me home."

"What is Tyler doing there anyway?" I hear the worry, the accusation in his tone.

"He was tutoring a student."

"Tanner, that's right."

"He came across me fighting Caleb off in the classroom. If he hadn't shown up..."

"Sara—"

"I'm okay, Dad."

"Okay, get yourself home. I'll look into the situation tomorrow."

"I'll stop in to see you before work, okay? Give Mom a kiss and let her know I'm fine."

"Just shoot me a text when you're home safe okay?"

"I will."

She ends the call and her breath is fog in front of her face as she exhales.

I touch her cheek, run my thumb over her chilled flesh. "You know you had the situation under control, right? I didn't save you, Sara. You saved yourself."

"I'm not so sure about that. My legs were so rubbery, I wasn't even sure I could make it to the door."

I fist my hand and lightly nudge her chin. "You did good, kid."

She attempts a smile, but she is still trembling. She glances down at her feet. "I want to take some more self-defense lessons."

My heart aches, hating that I was gone all these years and wasn't able to protect her. That I hadn't gotten to her faster, to stop any of this before it started. I mentally kick myself. I had the fucking information on the douchebag, and sat on it, waiting for her to come out so we could talk. I hadn't expected them to be together tonight, for him to try to... Fuck, I can even bring myself to think of the ugly word.

"I can teach you some moves," I say. "If there's one thing I'm good at, it's fighting."

"You can teach me to fight?"

She blinks, and I catch the tears pooling on her lashes. I brush them away. "Yeah," I say. "My buddy gave me a key to his gym, and I go there after hours. If you want, you can come with me."

"I'd like that."

"Okay, let's get you home, and we can talk more about this once you're warmed up."

I help her onto the bike and climb on front. Her hands slide around me and hold on tight as I drive her home. I don't park on her street. Instead, I move on to the next. No way do I want anyone seeing my bike outside her place. I help her off, and we walk through the dark night until we reach her building. She fishes they key from her pocket and I make an attempt at humor.

"If you can't find it..."

She grins, produces the key and waves it in front of my face. "I don't even want to know what it is you do to get in here."

She opens the door and I hold it for her to enter. I stay close to her as we walk to her apartment, and she drags in a deep breath, like she can finally breathe again when we step inside. I understand the feeling. Now that I have her safe in her home, my chest loosens, allowing me to draw in air again, too. She's still shaking, and I guide her to her sofa. I help her out of her coat and she fires off a text to her father as I grab the throw blanket to wrap it around her.

Once she's all tucked in, I go to the kitchen, grab the bottle of wine from the fridge and pour her a glass. Her hand quivers when she takes it from me.

"Drink up," I say.

She nods, takes a sip and I start to walk away again.

"Where are you going?" she asks, a measure of panic in her voice.

"Run the bath."

"Okay." She takes another sip of wine as I step into the bathroom, and drop to one knee to turn on the water. I adjust the temperature, pour some of her vanilla scented body wash into the tub and make my way back into the room. Her wine is almost gone, so I remove the glass from her hand, set it on the coffee table, and pull her to her feet.

"Let's get you warmed up." I hold her hand and guide her to the bathroom. She reaches for her torn sweater, and I help her remove it, then I unhook her bra and toss it aside. I look over her body to check for bruises, then make quick work of her pants. I drop to my knees, and tap her legs one at a time. "Lift."

Once I have her stripped bare, I sit on the edge of the tub and help her in. Water splashes over the sides, soaking me as she settles into the sudsy water and I turn off the tap. I drop to the floor and lean against the wall, my mind going over the night and how much worse it could have ended. I need to stop the direction of my thoughts, or I'm going to have to break something.

I reach into the tub and take her hand in mine. "I'm sorry I wasn't there for you, Sara."

Water splashes as she sits up straighter. "Tyler, don't, you—"

My throat is aching when I say, "For the last nine years, I'm sorry I wasn't there for you."

"Ty," she says and cups my cheeks. There are tears in her

eyes as she looks at me. I lean into her, and when her lips touch mine in a soft kiss, and I finally come down from my adrenaline rush, I shake all over. "Are you okay?" she asks.

"No, Sara," I say, my voice deceptively calm when all I want to do is hit something. "Not even a little."

12

—

SARA

Early morning sunshine slants against the wall, pulling me from my sleep. I jackknife up in the bed and grip at my throat to loosen the noose cutting off my air supply, but as my nails scratch skin and the world around me materializes, I realize it was just a bad dream. I'm not up against a wall, Caleb's rough fingers tightening around my throat, his foul breath spilling over me as he tells me all the ways he's going to hurt me. I'm home in my bed, safe for the time being. I gasp in relief, but it comes out sounding more like a cry.

"Sara," Tyler whispers, his voice hoarse from sleep as he reaches for me. His hand snakes across the mattress, and he touches me in a comforting way. But my heart is crashing so hard against my chest I think it might break a rib. "Come here."

The roughness in his voice gives way to softness as he pulls me to him, and I melt against his body. He surrounds me with his heat and strength and the anxiety ebbs away when I find myself within the safety of his arms—a temporary calm in the storm my life has become. When Tyler holds me like this, I can't help but think the image on the outside—tough and scarred—doesn't fit with the man on the inside. Much like Caleb. A man who was wealthy, educated, always so well put together, but on the inside he was ugly and flawed. The signs were there now that I think about it, but I'd been so driven to get over Tyler, I'd missed them. I just hope it's the last we see of him around here.

Tyler broke your heart, Sara. Is he really who you think he is on the inside?

No, he's not, and I'd be wise to remember that as we play out this thing between us. But no one has ever evoked a need in me the way he does—which is why we need to ride this thing out, let it burn bright until it all fades away.

With my face to Tyler's bare chest, I breathe him in, let his warm scent fill my lungs as he brushes my damp hair from my face. A moment later, he inches back and deep worried eyes search mine.

"You were having a nightmare," he says. "I suspect you will for a while." He goes quiet, his eyes dark and tortured—sorrowful—as they look past my shoulders.

"What?" I ask, and trail my finger over his chest and his muscles bunch beneath my touch.

His throat works as he swallows hard, then he asks, "Do you think maybe you should get some counseling?"

I shake my head. "No, I'm okay. It was just a bad dream."

"I don't think you should go in to work today. I'll call in too, and stay with you."

I touch his face, warmed by the sweet gesture. "No, Ty. If I do that, then it gives Caleb power over me. I won't do that. What happened, happened. We can't change that, but we both need to move past it."

"Together," he whispers. "Like old times, when we could get through anything together. Remember?"

"I remember. Like old times," I say, even though we can

never recapture what we'd lost. He touches my arm, and a shudder vibrates through me. The air around us changes, charges, and I'm certain that I'd never needed Tyler more than I do this very second. I lift my chin, and close my eyes, offering him my lips and my body—but not my heart. Never again. That still doesn't stop everything inside me from craving to feel the warmth only this man can give me. When the kisses don't come, my lids flicker open to find tortured eyes staring back. "Kiss me, Tyler," I say and put my hand on his shoulder.

He runs his thumb over my cheek, a feathery light caress that brings on a quiver as his eyes fixate on my mouth. "Are you sure?"

I take in the uncertainty in his eyes, and I understand where he's coming from, but I refuse to let Caleb come between what we're trying to do here, or hold any kind of power over me. I've had worse things happen in my life—things that I didn't walk away from unscathed. Tyler and I don't have forever, we only have today, with no guarantee of a tomorrow or a tomorrow after that. I need to make the most of every second, and pray it helps us break this insane connection gripping us both so we can move on with our respective lives.

"I've never been more sure of anything," I say, arousal edging my voice. "I need you to touch me. I need your hands on my body." Only Tyler's tender hands can wash away Caleb's crude contact, and help me forget and move past last night.

I roll onto my back, and pull Tyler with me. His hard body settles over mine, presses me into the mattress, and sheaths me in a bubble safety. His lips find mine and as we exchange soft kisses, I put last night's situation out of my brain. Now is not the time to ask why the Phantoms were watching him. Although I can't help but wonder if they're trying to initiate him—now that he's a criminal and all. Or is he in some kind of danger? While Ty was busy talking to the officers, the eye contact made between Caleb and the gang leader as he was being led to the police cruiser hadn't gone unnoticed by me. Caleb comes from a privileged background and might be a lot of things, but in no way do I think he's mixed up with a gang as dangerous as the Phantoms. Maybe he was just staring in shock, the same way I was. Either way, I have more important things to thing to think about right now, mainly the way Tyler is breaking the kiss, our breaths hot on each other's skin as our heart rates kick up a notch.

Big fingers idly stroke my hair. "I love kissing you," he murmurs, his soft words and the need behind them stripping me bare. "I'd spend the rest of the day in this bed just kissing you if you'd let me. Then again," he says, grinning. "There are other things I need to do to you." We breathe together and he puts his lips back on mine, a slight caress, then begins kissing a hot path down my neck. I sigh, astonished at the tenderness in his touch, the slow way he's seducing my body, when he's so clearly as needy as I am. The trembling of his muscles, the impatience in his body, and the way his breathing has changed, becoming labored, is a testament to his current state of restraint.

I move beneath him, rake my hands through his hair as he lifts the t-shirt covering my body, a t-shirt he dug out of my drawer and pulled over my head after carrying me from the tub to bed last night—where he tucked me in and held me until I fell asleep.

His big warm palm cups my breast in an achingly familiar way, and he kneads slightly as his tongue languidly slides over my pert nipple, a slow unhurried taste I can feel all the way to the hungry spot between my legs. He treats my other breast to the same pleasure as his erection throbs against my leg, and my hips lift as I shudder involuntarily.

He pulls his mouth from me, and inches back. The rush

of cool morning air kisses my damp nipples, and a noise catches in my throat. The hot-cold combination is most erotic and we're suddenly nineteen again, making out in my dorm room. But it's not that boy I invited back into my bed, it's the man he's become. The two aren't the same and I can't ever forget that. Nor can I ever forget how frightening it is that I want him, either way.

Deft fingers grip my thighs and widen them. He glances up at me, a quick check in behind heavy lidded eyes. I smile, letting him know I want this. The rough pads of his warm fingers dig in deeper as he spreads my thighs and bends my knees until they're by my sides.

"I like you wide open like this for me," he says, the heat in his voice enough to make me orgasm without ever having been touched. "Stay just like this for me."

He goes back on his heels, and I capture my knees in my hands to hold the position. My gaze rakes over the pleasure sliding across his face. Seeing him so happy, catching the waves of contentment radiating from his body, does the most ridiculous things to my insides. His burning eyes leave mine slowly and track down my body. He touches my inner thigh, and with the lightest of touches, he circles his finger over my quivering flesh. I shut my eyes against the beautifully broken man with the deep scars, lost in the way he's touching me.

"Look at me, Sara," he whispers, and my lids flicker open at the vulnerability in his tone. "Do you need my cock in here?" He brushes his knuckle over my sex, nudging my swollen clit.

"Yes," I cry out as pleasure consumes me.

"You need me to fill you up and make you feel good?" The hunger in his voice lights up every dancing nerve inside me, and I open my mouth to speak, to beg him to make me feel good, but the only sound that comes out is a shattered cry.

"Yeah, you do need me, don't you?" I take in his eyes, dark, intense...unguarded, as they caress me with sultry heat.

Since my voice has failed me, I nod, and it brings a slow smile to his face. He pushes on my hands and my knees drop toward the bed, leaving me so wide open and exposed it might have frightened me if it was anyone else but Tyler in my bed.

"I need my mouth on you first."

Yes, please...

He bends, and parts my folds with the soft blade of his tongue and I expel a heavy breath. So good, so damn good. He gives me a long, slow lick and I shut my eyes against the pleasure—the soft, slow seduction driving every sane thought from my passion-rattled brain. He pulls back and I cry out from the loss. My gaze flies to his, and he's brushing his tongue over his bottom lip.

"Fuck, I love the taste of you," he murmurs, like he's completely savoring my flavor. My pulse kicks up a notch, as everything inside me blossoms from the way he's treasuring me...us.

He bends forward to bury his face between my legs again, and I go up on my arms, hypnotized as I watch him swirl his tongue over my sex. It has to be one of the most erotic things I've ever seen.

Dizzy with longing, and a throat that is far too tight with emotions as this man pleasures me, I move against him. "Ty, that feels so good," I finally manage to say. My gaze drops to his hard cock, and I know it's taking all his effort to go slow. I wet my mouth, wanting it on him. He glances up at me, and when our eyes meet, it's clear he knows what I'm thinking.

"You want your mouth on my cock?" he asks.

"Yes, I want you to come down my throat."

"Sweet fuck," he curses and it brings a smile to my face to know I can reduce this rock of a man to a quivering mess.

"If I do that, I'll never get inside you." He pushes two thick fingers into me. "So hot, wet and tight. My cock is dying to slide in here and fuck you long and hard." He moves his fingers, stroking the sensitive bundle of nerves inside. "But I can't say no to you, Sara. If you want my cock in your mouth, that's what you get."

"I'll tell you what. Since you're letting me call the shots, how about tonight I'm all yours, anything you like. You can even tie my hands to the bedpost." I smile at him, my mind taking me back to all the fun things Tyler liked to do in bed.

As I offer him a measure of trust with my body, I catch the play of emotions on his face, the pain in his gaze, and my stomach twists, knowing how haunted he is by past incidents.

"You'd...you'd let me do that?" he asks, a hitch in his voice.

"Maybe on my way home I'll also stop at that little sex boutique at the mall."

"Maybe I'd like that," he says, and giving me his full attention, pumps a little faster. One big, callused hand slides up my body to pinch my nipples, and I moan against the erotic assault.

"I'm going to be hard all day thinking about the things I'm going to do to you," he grunts out.

Desire races through me as I envision it, but my mind goes to the points of pleasure between my legs. Breath shallow, I curl into him, wrap my entire body around his penetrating fingers as he slides his thumb along my sex, and drags it over my clit. Heat sparks inside me, lighting behind my eyes, until my vision fades and the only thing I can do is feel —every delicious touch of this man's hands and mouth.

My body thrums with excitement as he applies pressure, the perfect amount of friction to take me to the edge and leave me hovering. He laps at me, his hot tongue searing my flesh and I want to let go, freefall over the cliff as much as I want to hang on, suspended on the precipice a little longer.

His fingers pump, his thumb sweeps and his mouth feasts, the perfect trifecta to deliver a mind-numbing orgasm. My body swells, a beautiful feeling of fullness building as he plunges deeper harder, blunt strokes that prolong the pleasure. I move against him, my body hot, flushed, as he eats at me like a man starved. His fingers shift, rotate, and desire twists inside me. No longer able to hold off, I give in to the hot release of pressure.

"Yes," I cry out and grip the bed sheets as my senses explode. I close my eyes against the flood of heat as Ty kisses me hungrily, drinking in every last drop as I come and come and come, my entire body a quivering mess, every muscle clenching as he laps at me. He moans from between my legs, and pulls his fingers out when I stop spasming. He goes back on his heels, and puts his fingers into his mouth. A shiver wracks my body and I nearly tumble into another orgasm. When I stop quaking, he slides up my body and moans against my throat. The vibrations go right through me. His cock settles against my thigh, rock hard and ready.

He brushes my hair from my face. "While we're working on getting past us, I'm going to make you come like that every day, Sara. Every single day."

He's not asking, he's telling me, but I'm so far gone, lost in pleasure right now, I'm sure I'd agree to just about anything. I reach for him, pull him closer. His mouth lands on mine and I taste my sweetness on his tongue as it slides between my lips.

"Mmm," I moan and the sound seems to do something to him. His mood changes, a new urgency about him as his cock grows impossibly thicker against my thigh. I give him a little shove until he's flat out on the bed beside me. I stare at his hard cock as it clamors for my attention, unable to take my eyes off his beautiful length and girth as I settled between his legs.

"Sara," he says softly as I bend forward. His fingers curl through my hair and pull it to the side to watch as I take him deeply. I want him to come in my throat. I want every drop of him inside my body where I can keep it forever. I take him to the back of my throat and close my hand over the rest of his shaft, barely able to get my palm around it.

He growls, and powers upward into my mouth as I rock back and forth. I lick his pre-cum and our moans mingle. His fingers tighten in my hair, grip a little harder and I like the feel of it. I whimper, and work my mouth and hand along the length of him as he mumbles and curses beneath me. I glance up at him, catch the heat in his eyes and my sex comes to life again with a hard clench. Ribbons of moisture drip down my leg and tickle my inner thighs. I squirm, and needing the intimate contact, I straddle one of his legs. My wet sex presses against his thigh, and I grind down, rubbing my aching clit all over him.

"Motherfucker," he moans.

I caress my clit as his body tenses, his cock thickening as hot blood races through his veins. I hold him in my mouth, moving only slightly as I wait for his release.

"Sara," he growls, his body letting go and filling my throat with his warmth. Like me, he comes and comes, and I drink him all in until he's flat out on the bed, trembling, spent, lost to everything except us.

I inch back, and crawl up his body. He tangles his hands in my hair, and we hold on to each other like our lives depend on it. In some way, I think they do. As the world settles around me, I glance at the clock. I don't want to move. I want to stay here in Tyler's arms for the rest of the day, but we can't do that. We have responsibilities, and we both need to get moving if we want to make it to work on time. Plus, I have to stop by Dad's office. He's expecting me. Even more so after last night.

"We need to move," I say.

"I don't want to."

"Me neither. But if I'm late seeing Dad, I don't know what he'll do." A pause and then, "Ty?"

"Yeah?"

"He can't know you stayed here."

"He won't."

Ty drops a soft, affectionate kiss onto my forehead, and my insides twist at the tender way he cares for me. "Why don't you go shower and I'll make us something to eat."

"My fridge is pretty empty. I do have cereal."

"Captain Crunch?" he says his eyes so big, I can't help but laugh.

"We're not twelve anymore."

"I know, but dammit I used to crave Captain Crunch when I was..." He stops speaking like he can't use the term incarcerated around me.

"It's okay to say it, Tyler. I know where you were."

"I know, I just... I don't want to talk about it."

Wanting to lighten his mood, I say, "Tell you what. On the way home from work, I'll pick up a few boxes of Captain Crunch for you. I need to get some groceries anyway."

He runs his fingers down my arm, the heat in his eyes holding all sorts of promise. "If you want me to stay over again, all you have to do is ask. You don't need to ply me with sugary cereal."

I laugh, pick up the pillow and hit him with it. He ducks and grabs it from me. He's about to hit me back with it, but stops when he sees the smile is gone from my face.

"What?" he asks.

"You staying here last night. It was probably a bad decision."

He drops the pillow and climbs from the bed. He exhales heavily and I take in his long hard body, mesmerized by the changes in it as he stands before me completely naked.

"Yeah, well, we've been making a lot of bad decisions lately haven't we," he says. "We can add it to the list."

I pause for a brief moment, my mind going back to the Phantoms. I pluck at the sheets, pull away an imaginary piece of lint. Is one of his bad decisions getting mixed up with the local gangs? I want to ask, I really do, but I'm too afraid of the answer. He's changed so much since I knew him, and he's just trying to find a way to survive in his new world.

"What about your mother? She's going to want to know where you were."

"I'll tell her I stayed at a friends." He shrugs. "It's not a lie. We are friends, aren't we?"

"We are," I say.

"Sara," he says and crosses around the bed. The mattress dips when he sits next to me and takes his hand in mine. "I don't want you staying here alone."

"Caleb's in custody. He isn't going to cause me any more trouble."

"Here's how it's going to go down. He'll go to his hearing before the judge today, pay his bond, and be back on the streets until he gets a court date. You'll have to go and testify at that time."

My stomach lurches. "But he won't be allowed back on the campus, right?"

"Probably not, but I plan to go with you every night, and keep you by my side. He'll most likely be charged with battery, and I'm sure an order of protection will be a condition of his bond, meaning he won't be able to have any contact with you."

"You know a lot about this," I say, and swallow, hard, understanding, and hating why he's so familiar with the judicial system.

"Yeah," he says quietly then adds, "I'm driving you back and forth. I'm not asking, Sara."

"Tyler, I have to work and so do you. You can't be with me twenty-four seven."

"I'm not saying I'll be by your side twenty-four seven. Just school nights, and well, nights in general." I open my mouth to protest, but he puts a finger to my lip and adds, "Your building is easy to get into, Sara." He pokes the bed. "This is where I want to be every night. Holding you in my arms." His muscles flex as he rakes his hair from his face. "Tell me you want that too?"

I do. I want that so damn much, but it's impossible.

"We can't," I say. "I can't even be seen with you. If my father...my boss..."

He frowns intently, and I can almost hear the wheels spinning as he wages an internal war. My intercom beeps and I practically jump in the bed. "Who could that be?" I slide from the bed, throw my robe around her shoulders and hurries to the other room. I press the intercom. "Who is it?"

"It's your father, Sara. Open up."

13

TYLER

With October bleeding into November, the morning air is cooler and seeps into my bones as I quietly slide Sara's bedroom window shut behind me, and hurry from her apartment building. I shrug into my coat and glance over my shoulder to take in the strange looks a few people are giving me, but I smile and nod and just keep on my way. Most people in this city mind their own business and keep to themselves, so I'm pretty sure the cops aren't going to be called. No one wants to get involved in anyone else's problems.

I round the corner and breathe again, thankful that Coach Ramsey hadn't caught me inside or seen me leaving. Sneaking around like this is total bullshit, but I made a promise to Sara and one to her father. Opposing promises. Honest to fuck, I shouldn't be with Sara to begin with. But she asked for this, and after everything I put her through, I owe her that much, right?

Except leaving her when she's done with me is going to snap the last filaments holding my fucked-up heart together. I pull my coat across my chest to ward off the chill as I hurry down the street, my mind mentally cataloguing Sara's apartment to ensure I left no evidence of my presence behind.

I squeeze between two parked vehicles and cut across the street, and a car hits the horn as it bears down on me. Ignoring the man giving me the finger, I take the corner to where I parked my bike last night. At least I did one fucking thing right by hiding it from plain sight of Sara's apartment.

I stop dead in my tracks, as my heart thuds faster. What the ever-loving fuck? I glance up and down the street, and when my bike is nowhere to be found, I nearly fucking lose it.

"Jesus fucking Christ," I curse under my breath, and fist my hands, ready to punch someone or something. Who the fuck stole my bike? I reach for my phone, hesitate for a second. Who the hell am I going to call? There's always Lucas, but what would he know about my missing bike? Fuck me. The only call I can make is to the cops, and that doesn't give me a warm fuzzy feeling. The less I deal with them the better. Shit. But what choice do I have? I need to report the crime. I slide my finger over my phone and make my second call to the precinct in as many days. Jesus fuck, I'm trying to stay out of trouble, but it keeps finding me. And that shit just pisses me the fuck off.

I pace the street, and those coming and going keep a wide berth, no doubt thinking I'm some nut job as I walk back and forth and curse under my breath. When the black and white finally shows up, I peer into the window and feel a measure of relief that it's not the same officers from last night. I don't want them becoming too familiar with me.

"Hey," I say when the officer climbs from his car. The other officer stays inside and is on the radio. "Thanks for coming so fast."

He steps up to me, and pulls a notepad from his pocket. "So your bike was stolen."

"Yeah, I parked it here last night around ten." He grabs

a pen, takes down my information, then asks for my I.D. I dig my wallet from my back pocket, thankful it hadn't fallen out on Sara's floor again, and hand it over. He goes to the car, and I pace again as he punches in my information. When he comes back he says, "How long you've been back, Tyler?"

"Not long."

"Long enough to have your bike stolen."

I nod.

He looks at me, his eyes hard, all knowing. "My boy is on Collin's football team. He says good things about you."

"Oh yeah. Who's your boy?"

"Jared Holt."

I smile. "Yeah, he's a good kid. Fast. Lots of potential."

I catch a hint of a grin on the man's face, then he's serious again. "You're doing good things with the team." He glances at the curb, to the spot where my bike should have been parked. "I hate to see you getting into any kind of trouble, and getting kicked off the field. It's nice to see you giving back to the community." He stares me straight in the eyes, like he's waiting for a reaction, some giveaway that I'm up to no good.

"I'm not looking for trouble, sir." I scrub my face and keep my eyes locked on his.

After a moment he nods, and looks around again. "Do you have enemies, someone who might be sending you a signal?"

I make a sound, a half snort half laugh. From the way the Phantoms were staring at me, I'm afraid a war might be coming. They did, after all, lose their guns because of me. "I guess it's possible." I shake my head. "I'm not getting my bike back, am I?"

"Hate to say it, but chances are slim to none. There's been a run on Hondas, and Harleys."

"Yeah?"

He tucks his notepad away. "I'm sure your bike has been stripped clean for parts by now."

"Chop shop? Here? In the city?"

"Yeah, but I wouldn't suggest you go digging into it."

"Why's that?"

"A man in your shoes..." He shakes his head. "You don't want to find yourself back on the inside, do you?"

"No."

"Then let this go, and leave us to do our jobs."

Anger seeps through my blood. Fuck, man, I worked and saved hard to get that bike. Justin knew a guy and got me a great deal on it. He'll be as pissed as I am. I have some bucks put away to get a car, but come spring it's my bike I want to drive. "Yeah, okay."

"Need a drive home?"

I give a quick shake of my head. The last thing I need for my mother to see is me being taken home in a cruiser. "No." I gesture with a nod. "It's not to far. I'll walk."

"If we get a lead, we'll let you know, but don't count on it."

He climbs back into the car, and I steal a glance at my watch. Shit, it's getting late and if I'm not on the field in time, Coach Ramsey will have my ass. I walk home with a hurried pace, and shoot a text to Justin to let him know what happened and ask him to keep an eye out over the winter for a replacement. When I approach the house, I notice an old Ford Focus in the driveway. I look it over as I climb the steps to the front door. I try the knob to find it locked, then knock.

Gracie comes rushing to the door. "Who is it?"

"Your favorite brother," I say.

She grins and opens the door. "Did you lose your key?"

"I ah..,"

I step inside and glance at Mom as she sips tea at the table. Her eyes are wary, suspicious when they meet mine.

And why wouldn't they be? I left here last night, and didn't so much as call to explain that I wouldn't be home. Of course her mind is going to race to the worst.

Mom glances at the clock. "Is everything okay?" she asks, but I know what she's really asking. Why am I just getting home now? What kind of trouble have I been into?

I close the door behind me, and sit next to her, figuring the truth is the best thing. Otherwise I risk her kicking me out to protect her other kids.

"Mom, there was an incident at the campus last night." She straightness in her chair, like she's bracing herself for a fleet of cop cars to surround the place. "It's Sara," I say quickly.

"What happened to Sara?" Gracie asks as she takes her seat across from me.

"She was attacked." They both gasp, and I hold my hands up and quickly add, "She's okay. I saw to it that she got home safely last night. She was scared, so I stayed with her." I glance at mom. "That's where I was."

My mom lets loose a breath, and Gracie leans forward. "Oh my God, Tyler. What happened?"

"The details aren't important. Just know the man is in custody, and Sara is okay."

"You called the police?" Mom asks.

"He attacked Sara, Mom. I had to get him off the streets. Who knows what he's capable of, who else he might hurt."

My mom's hand slides across the table and closes over mine. "Thank God you were there, Tyler." She taps my hand, takes another small sip of tea and stands. "I've been meaning to give this to you." She pulls open the junk drawer and produces a house key. The air leaves my lungs when I see it. It's not just a key she's offering me. It's her trust, and I damn will plan to take great care with it. I try to breathe past the knot in my throat, but the air gets caught as my ribcage tightens around my swelling heart.

"Thanks," I manage to get out. "What's with the car is the driveway? Who owns it?"

"You do, bro," Lucas says as he comes into the kitchen, shirtless, his hair mussed from sleep, feet dragging on the floor.

"What?" I ask, and from the other side of the table, Gracie grabs her tablet.

"I'm going to text Sara," she says, opening her special voice transcription device that allows her to text like a normal teenager.

As she busies herself, Lucas looks at me. "You said you needed a car, so I got you one." I study him, note the edginess about him. What's going on with him?

"Where did you get it?"

"I told you, my buddy was selling it. I got you a good deal."

"What do I owe you?"

"Nothing. I got a good deal, let's leave it at that."

I stare at him for a moment and he turns from me and opens the fridge.

"Want me to make you some eggs, Lucas?" Mom asks, and he shakes his head.

"Nah. I need to get going. Busy day."

"You're working too hard," Mom says, a frown marring her forehead. "It was well past two when you got in last night."

Lucas pulls the milk from the fridge, but stiffens at our mother's words. So help me God if he's gotten himself into any kind of trouble. I'm impressed at how quickly he pulls himself together—like he has nothing to hide—but still has his back to me as he grabs the cereal from the cupboard.

"I'm trying to make some extra money." He turns to us,

but the big smile on his face doesn't reach his eyes. "I plan to open my own shop someday. Mr. Johnson is great but I don't want to work for him forever, you know."

"I know," Mom says.

"Ty," he begins, redirecting the focus. "You talked about opening your own sports store, and holding clinics. Ever give any more thought to that?"

As a matter of fact I have. After tutoring Tanner, I grabbed some information on winter courses starting in January. I like working at BSA, but don't want to spend the rest of my life there. But opening my own store without Sara, that just doesn't feel right. I wonder if she has regrets about that, or ever thinks about maybe wanting to give it another go. What the fuck am I thinking? She's not going to give it a go with me, that's for sure.

"I don't know about that," is all I say, and Mom stands, like she can't bear to be a part of the conversation, all the lost years and lost dreams.

She puts her hand on Lucas's cheek. Such a familiar gesture, and one I used to love. She gives him a little pat, then goes about rinsing the dishes. "I must get ready. We're doing inventory down at the store so I need to get in early."

Lucas fills a bowl with cereal and I glare at him until Mom leaves the room.

"What?" he finally asks.

"The car. It's legit?"

"Yeah, it's fucking legit. Can't a guy do his brother a favor?"

I push back in my chair. "My bike was stolen last night."

"Motherfucker," he says under his breath.

"You know of any chop shops around?"

"No," he says quickly.

"You sure about that? I'd think working in the bay you'd have your ear to the ground on those kinds of things."

"Don't know what to tell you, brother."

We stare at each other for a long time, and then I ask, "You good, Lucas?"

He knows what I'm asking. Is he staying out of trouble?

"I'm good," he says and goes back to his cereal. With little time to get to the field, I dart upstairs and jump in the shower. Everyone has left the house by the time I dress and head back down stairs. I pick my two new keys up, one to the house and one to the car, then head outside, locking up behind me.

I make my way to the school and look for signs of Sara as I park. She might not be stopping by to see her father, since he stopped in to see her. I park, grab my backpack from the seat, and make my way to Coach's office.

He's inside when I get there, and I go deadly still when his gaze lifts and collides with mine. "Tyler," he says, in a voice so hard I'm sure he knows what I've been doing with his daughter.

"Coach."

He stands slowly, his joints cracking, and that's when I realize the years have been hard on him too. He used to talk about retiring and moving away from here. My guess is he's long overdue for that, but won't leave the city as long as Sara is here.

"Listen, I want to thank you for being there for Sara last night. She explained everything."

I'm careful not to exhale a huge breath of relief. "She's a tough girl, Coach."

"Yeah, she's had to be."

My throat tightens with at the shit I'd put her through. Fuck, man. I was so stupid. Lucas was my only concern when I loaded my trunk with those guns. I hadn't thought about the future, that I'd do time—what it would do to Sara. I'll never forgive myself for that. There is no sense in telling her I was taking the job for my brother, because when it comes right down to it, *I* committed a crime of my own free will. Now I'm a felon, and will always have that hanging over me.

"She had the situation under control before I ever got there."

"Maybe so, but ah...I'm just glad you got there when you did." I open my mouth to respond, but I'm not sure what to say. I'm not used to compliments. I make a move to grab my bag and get changed when he says. "I know you still care about her."

I straighten. "I'd never do anything to hurt her, Coach."

"You did hurt her, Tyler. A lot."

Fuck.

"Yeah...I know. What I mean is—"

"That you'd never let anyone else hurt her."

I take a deep breath and my hands curl at my sides as the ugly vision of Caleb assaulting her rips through my brain. "I'd kill for her, Coach."

His gaze meets mine and he looks truly worried at that thought. But it's a statement I stand behind. I hate to think what I might have done to Caleb had he finished what he started. Coach opens his mouth, like he's going to say something, hesitates for a second and then says, "I need a favor."

Unease weaves its way through me. The Coach needs something from me. I don't even care what it is. All he has to do is ask, and I'm on it. "Anything," I say.

"Mariam's sister had a stroke. She's in Indiana and doesn't have anyone to look after her. Mariam's pretty upset, so I don't want her driving by herself. I'm taking leave for a few days. I hate the idea of leaving Sara after what happened, but I stopped by her place this morning to tell her the news and check on her, and she assures me she's fine and that I should go."

"If Caleb even thinks about going near her again, he'll have to go through me."

"Which is why I want you to keep an eye on her while I'm gone."

My head comes back with a start. After everything we've been through is he really asking me to keep watch over Sara? Jesus Christ, I must be hearing things wrong, or imagining it. Then again, it could just be wishful thinking.

"Do you think you could do that?" he asks as I stand there dumbfounded.

I pull myself tighter and say, "Consider it done."

"One more thing."

"Name it."

"Would you mind taking over the team while I'm gone?"

Okay, now I'm sure I'm dreaming. "You serious?"

"Yeah, playoffs are coming up in two weeks, and we've got a good shot at winning. I need you to keep working with the guys, get them ready." The corners of his mouth twitch. "This year, Lincoln High is going down." He points to the top of his filing cabinet. "I already dusted off a spot for the trophy." He goes serious again, and says, "I know you're working and if you don't have the time—"

"I'll make the time, and I won't let you down, Coach."

"Sara doesn't need to know about any of this." He looks me square in the eye, and I see the pain in his gaze, a reminder that I let him down in a big way once, and that he's hoping I won't do it again.

After reading the text from Gracie, asking me to stop into BSA tonight to see her—apparently Ty will be reading her book choice at the book club this evening—I tuck my phone into my purse and make my way to the back of the bank to grab a cup of coffee before beginning my shift. My mind races back to this morning, and my Dad at my door. Thankfully, I live on the first floor and Ty could get out my window without any trouble. Still, this running around and hiding isn't good. But I'm glad Dad came by to tell me about Aunt Sandra and that they're going to stay with her for a few days.

I enter the break room and find Kaitlyn, and Rob Fillmore—the bank manager—standing there talking. They both go quiet when I walk in, and I can't help but wonder if I was the topic of conversation.

"Good morning," I say and reach into the cupboard to pull out my mug.

"Morning," they both respond, then Rob turns to me. "Can I see you in my office for a moment, Sara?"

My hand slows as I reach for the freshly brewed coffee,

and my stomach squeezes. Am I in some kind of trouble? "Sure." I briefly look at Kaitlyn, who has a worried look on her face.

Rob runs his hand over a blue tie that protrudes over his bulging stomach, and picks up his coffee mug. "Go ahead and grab your coffee first," he says and exits the room.

"What the hell is going on?" I ask in a hushed voice, as I grab the carafe and fill a mug. The last time I was called in to Rob's office, it was to talk about the big promotion, and the courses I'd need. No way do I think this has anything to do with that, though. The worried look on Kaitlyn's face tells me that much.

"Rob got word that you were associating with a known criminal. That you two were on the campus and police were involved."

"What the hell," I say through gritted teeth. "Jesus, Kaitlyn, who would do something like that?" My mind races to Derek, but I can't imagine he'd do that. He would have been long gone by the time the cops were involved.

"I don't know, Sara. What happened last night?"

"It's nothing like that. Tyler wasn't involved in anything illegal. He actually...Oh, my God I can't believe any of this." Could my life be any more of a shitstorm?

Tyler could go back to jail.

I push that thought out of my mind when Kaitlyn asks, "He actually what?"

I exhale slowly. I'd been hoping to put last night behind me, never wanted to think about it again until the court date, but it doesn't look like that's going to happen now. "Caleb wasn't who we thought he was, Kaitlyn. He attacked me, and Tyler found us."

"Oh, my God, Sara." She grabs my hand. "Are you hurt?"

"Thankfully no. Caleb had me pinned, but I kneed him in the groin. He went down, and then Tyler showed up." I take a deep fueling breath before continuing. "I hate to think what could have happened. Tyler called the police and saw to it that I got home safely."

I let go of her hand, grab the milk from the fridge and pour a splash into my mug. "I guess I'd better go see what Rob is going to say about all this."

I pass a few colleagues in the hall and put on my best smile as we exchange pleasantries. When I reach Rob's office, the door is ajar but I knock anyway.

"Come on in," he says and leans back in his seat. The wheels groan under his weight. He rakes a hand through his balding hair and smiles at me. He's been a good manager, good enough to give me a job when I was going through so much turmoil.

"How are you, Sara?" he asks.

"I'm good. Thanks. How are you?" I say, noting how stiff our conversation seems to be going.

"I'm good. Classes are going well?"

"Very well."

He looks down for a second, and I know he's about to get to the real point of this meeting. "I received some disturbing news this morning."

"Oh?" I say.

"It has been brought to my attention that you're associating with Tyler again." He leans toward me. "Sara, I'm not your father, but your father and I are good friends, and I know what you went through when he was arrested."

"It's not what you think," I say quickly, then rush to tell him what happened last night.

His eyes go wide. "Are you okay?" he asks when I finish.

"Yes, and you see, Tyler was just at the school tutoring. If it wasn't for him..." I let my words fall off.

"Well, thank God he was there. Are you sure you should be at work today?"

I smile at his thoughtfulness. "Perfectly sure," I say.

"Okay, if you need anything, you know where to find me."

I nod and stand. I'm about to leave when he says in a voice reserved for disciplining employees, "I just want you to be careful." He slants me a look that speaks volumes. If I want the job of financial analyst, I probably shouldn't be associated with a criminal.

"I always am," I say, even though it's a lie. Well, it was the truth up until Tyler came home. Now I'm reckless and going against my own best interests. But I'm fighting a losing battle when it comes to Ty, and I have to try to see this thing through, let it burn out.

I make my way to the front of the bank and take my place behind the counter. The rest of the morning went by in a blur. When lunchtime comes around, I grab a salad for lunch with Kaitlyn—since Dad is away with Mom for a few days. I tell her my dilemma, and the wreckage my life has become, and she tells me what she thinks, none of which is good. I know I asked for this affair with Ty, but after this morning's warning from my boss, and hearing Kaitlyn's take on things, I can't help but wonder if I'm risking my entire future for a few stolen hours with the man I'm determined to get over. Maybe I should put a stop to it. Do I even have the strength for that? Then again, this affair *is* about my future, and being able to live a healthy and happy life, right?

When closing time hits, I step outside and make my way home, stopping at the grocery store to grab a few things, including Ty's favorite cereal. I hurry home, and have a strange sense that I'm being watched. I glance over my shoulders, expecting to see Caleb, but he's not there and it's business as usual on the streets. I guess I'm more spooked than I realized.

After making a quick spaghetti and meatballs meal, I send Mom and Dad a text to check on Aunt Sandra. They respond that she's stable and doing okay, and they might need to stay longer than originally planned.

I pace my apartment, flick the TV on and off, and don't want to think too much about how quiet and empty the place feels without Tyler's presence. He asked if he could stay with me, and I said no, but now I'm beginning to rethink that. Then again, I'm rethinking everything and don't know whether to walk away from Ty once and for all, or invite him to stay with me until I know longer feel spooked.

My phone pings and I rush to it, and see that it's from Gracie. I'd debated all day on whether to go or not, whether to shut this affair down with Tyler. But in the end, is it really fair for me to abandon Gracie?

I grab my coat and purse and leave my apartment. I walk to the bus stop and once again feel like I'm being watched. I glance around, but nothing seems out of the ordinary. There are a few other people at the bus stop and it gives me a measure of comfort as I wait. Forty minutes later, I'm dropped off at the Blind Association building, and I hope I'm not too late to catch Ty's reading. The wind bites at me as I hurry inside and make my way to the library. It's been a long time since I've been here and I feel a little guilty about it. I used to read to the kids with Tyler, and continued it for a while after he was incarcerated, but stopped because it always brought back so many memories.

I quietly make my way inside and can't stop the smile pulling at me when I see him sitting cross-legged on the floor with a group of teens, reading to them. His gaze lifts as if sensing me there, and when he smiles, my heart flutters against my ribs. I shrug out of my coat, grab a chair at the back, and scan the crowd. I spot a girl with a vest on, indicating she's an employee. The way she's gazing at Tyler, much the same way I am, rouses something in me. Something dark and ugly. I hate the feeling so I quickly squash it, and suck in a fuelling breath. When I get Ty out of my system, he can be with any woman he wants and I shouldn't hate the idea of it so much.

I lean back in my chair and concentrate on the story he's reading, and when he comes across the kissing parts, and makes a face, his tone changing, the girls in the room all laugh. Tyler rolls his eyes at me and I laugh too. Time ticks by as he reads and soon enough the girl in the vest stands, claps her hands and tells everyone time is up. Tyler closes the book and sets it aside, like it's a lewd object he does not want to touch. That only makes me laugh harder.

As everyone stands, I make my way to Gracie. "Hey Gracie, great choice of books," I say. "I loved it."

"Sara, you came." She turns and I pull her in for a hug. She hugs me back and puts her ear near mine. "Are you okay?" she asks.

Her worry sends my mind racing back to earlier, and how spooked I felt. I ignore the tingle down my spine and brush her hair from her shoulders. "I'm okay, Gracie. No need to worry. Your brother saved the day."

"That's not how he explained it."

I sneak a glance at Tyler, who has a harem of young girls surrounding him. "Oh."

"No, he said you kneed that guy in the nuts so hard, he'll be tasting them for a week."

Unable to help it, I burst out laughing. "He said that?"

"No, I did not say that, exactly," Ty says, coming up beside us. He slides a hand around my waist and my entire body shivers as he rubs his thumb back and forth over the small of my back. He nudges his sister's chin. "My sister here likes to embellish."

"That's why she's going to be a great author."

"If I hear her talking like that again—"

Gracie jabs Tyler in the stomach. "Oh, Tyler. I'm sixteen, not a child."

He rolls his eyes. "Get your things, I'll drive you home."

"Actually, I'm going to get a lift with Brandon."

Tyler glances around the room. "Who the hell is Brandon?"

"A friend," she says. "His mom is driving us." She holds her hand up, palm out. "I don't need another one of your lectures, either." The grin on her face tells me she's half serious. It's so good to see them fall back into a close relationship, with Tyler once again taking the role of father figure. My heart warms at the way they care so much about each other. The way Gracie is pretending to hate it, but secretly likes him worrying about her.

I like him worrying about me too.

"Gracie, I don't like—"

"Ty," I say and touch his face. "I think that's Brandon over there with his mom." He turns to look. "I'd say she's in good hands."

Tyler grumbles, and I stand back as he walks Gracie over to her friend. He exchanges a few words with Brandon, and his mom. I shake my head. Tyler would do anything to protect those he cares about, even if it goes against his own best interests. He makes his way back to me.

"When did she get so grown up?" he asks, but as soon as the words leave his mouth, his brow furrows. I have no doubt he's thinking the same thing as I am. She grew up when he was incarcerated.

He leans toward me and nudges me with his shoulder. "Want to get out of here?"

I nod, and pull on my coat.

"Thanks for coming. I know Gracie appreciated it."

We make our way toward the door when the girl in the

vest hurries our way. "Tyler, you did great tonight," she says. I look at the girl. She's familiar and I try to place her.

"Thanks. I want to be here for Gracie."

She smiles at him, big, genuine, full of admiration. "She's a lucky girl to have a brother like you."

"Cassie, this is Sara." Cassie turns toward me, but her smile is gone. "Cassie and I work together," he explains. "She was a freshman at Collins when we were seniors," he says.

"Nice to meet you, Cassie," I say and hold my hand out.

"Sara is my..." his words fall off, and both Cassie and I glance at him. "...friend," he finishes.

"Oh, just friends," Cassie says, a new hope in her eyes.

"Yeah, just friends," I say, and my stomach cramps because I want more, *everything* with Tyler. But that can never happen and I can't ever forget it.

"I'll see you tomorrow, Cassie," he says and leads me out the door. I head toward the elevator, but Tyler stills.

"What?" I ask.

"Mind if we take the stairs. I...uh..."

He grabs a fistful of hair and that's when understanding dawns. After being locked in a small cell for eight long years, he's not a fan of enclosed spaces.

"Yeah, sure," I say. "I could use the exercise anyway."

We're both quiet as we take the three flights of stairs down. We step outside and the night closes around us. I glance up and down, looking for his bike, and once again the fine hairs on the back of my neck tingle.

"Everything okay?" he asks.

I don't want to tell him I'm spooked. God knows what he'd do to Caleb if he found out the situation bothered me more than I'm letting on. Then again, he handled the situation at Studio Paris in a non-violent way. I grin at him. "I think Cassie has a crush on you."

He frowns. "Yeah?"

"Hey what's wrong?"

"I just...this job is important to me in a lot of ways. I don't want any kind of tension or conflict or anything to mess it up."

As the determined Tyler I once knew stands before me, my heart goes out to him. He really wants to make this work, and I can understand his worry where Cassie is concerned.

"It's just a schoolgirl crush, Ty. I'm sure it will pass." I shrug and say, "Maybe we should have told her I was your girlfriend. That we were committed."

He turns to me, takes me in his arms. "I am committed to you, Sara."

My throat squeezes so hard it's near impossible to talk, let alone breathe. "And I promised a commitment to you while we ride this thing out," I say to remind him what we have here isn't permanent.

He nods and looks up and down the street. His body stiffens, his jaw locks—a man changed.

"Ty?" I ask.

"Let's go."

He guides me toward a car, and opens the door for me. The gesture warms me. He might be a lot of things, but he's still chivalrous, that's for sure. Dad would appreciate that trait in him. As soon as that thought races through my mind, my stomach sinks. Yeah, I'm thinking Dad wouldn't appreciate any of this. As Tyler closes my door, I catch the way he's looking around again. My heart misses a beat, at the worry backlighting his eyes. God, is he spooked too?

"What's wrong?" I ask after he circles the front and climbs in beside me.

He scrubs his chin and I like the sound it makes. "I don't know."

"I think maybe we're both just spooked because of what happened last night."

His head jerks my way. "You're spooked?"

Dammit, I hadn't meant to go down this path, or let him know just how jittery I really am.

"I'm just...I mean..."

"I'm staying with you," he says, his voice hard, adamant as he turns his focus back to the road like it's not open for discussion. "If you don't want me inside the apartment, I'll camp outside on the steps."

"Ty..." I begin, but something inside me softens as his blue eyes move over my face with careful concern. "Okay," I agree, partly because I *am* afraid, and partly because I want to be with Tyler. After seeing him reading to the kids tonight, there's no way I can walk away just yet. But there is that little voice warning me that I won't be able to walk away at all.

How bad would that be?

He gestures with a nod to the building on the corner of the street. "I was thinking about hitting the gym. Want to join me? You did say you wanted some self-defense lessons."

I glance down at my jeans and sweater. "I'm not really dressed for the gym."

"I have some extra clothes in my bag."

"Which will float on me."

"We can go back to your place and you can change if you want."

I shake my head. "No, that's too far. I'll wear your clothes."

"Or you could wear nothing," he says innocently, but the smirk on his handsome face alludes to the dirty things going through his mind. "Your choice, of course."

"I'll choose clothes, thank you very much."

He wags an eyebrow at me. "We'll see about that." I chuckle and whack his stomach, only to meet with a wall of hard muscles.

"Where did you get this car, anyway?" I ask, glancing at the console.

"My bike was stolen last night."

My mouth falls open, a gasp catching in my throat. "You're kidding me?"

"Nope, would never kid about my bike. It wasn't on the street where I parked it last night. Cops said it was probably chopped by now."

I shift in my seat to face him. "You called the cops?"

"Yeah. Lucas knew I needed wheels for the winter, and had this waiting for me when I got home."

"That was timely." I put my hand on his thigh. "I'm sorry about your bike."

"Yeah, it was timely wasn't it?" He places his hand over mine and squeezes. "I have my buddy looking into another one for me. He's the guy who got me a good deal on the stolen one."

"Who's that?"

"A guy I know."

"From around here," I press, noting how secret he's being.

"No, Sara." He exhales harshly. "A guy I knew in prison."

"You still keep in touch with the other inmates."

"There were five of us who grew really close. Justin, Ryder, Jamie, and Christian." There's a hitch in his voice as he rambles off their names. He casts me a quick look and says, "I love those guys like they were my brothers. I'd do anything for them, and vice versa."

"That's nice, Ty," I say quietly, and sink back into my seat, hoping that their bond, their willingness to be there for each other, doesn't lead him down a path to trouble.

He pulls into the gym, quiet this time of night, grabs his bag from the back seat, and he uses his key to let us in.

"I'm surprised you have a key," I tease, trying to lighten the mood.

He ushers me inside, locks the door behind us and presses me against it. "That's a smart mouth you got there. Does it get you into trouble often?"

"Not often," I say, playing along.

His hand goes to the wall and he flicks the lights on. I blink against the brightness as his lips graze mine. "First I thought I'd go over some self-defense moves on the mats with you, then maybe I'll see what we can do about this mouth of yours." He inches back, his gaze dropping to my lips. His lids are heavy, as he gazes at me.

"I thought we were here to work out."

"Yeah, we are. Your safety is important to me, but I know that after rolling around on those mats with you, I'm going to need to spend some time here." He brushes his thumb over my bottom lip. "And then here," he murmurs, his hands sliding to my breasts. "And definitely here," he says, and slips his fingers between my legs. I practically drop to the floor when I catch the hunger in his eyes, the way his hard cock is pressing against my body. He sucks in a fast breath, and grimaces as he inches back. "Okay, let me show you some moves."

I follow him to the doors leading to the locker rooms and take in the mats, ring, punching bags, and exercise equipment. This gym is more for hardcore MMA training than the one I used to go to near the campus. I stand outside the ladies change room and hold my hand out. "Clothes." He smirks, grabs my hand and drags me into the men's locker room. "Hey, what do you think you're doing?"

"We're the only two here."

"And this locker room smells like old socks."

He laughs. "Fine," he says, and we step back out into the hall and he follows me into the girls' room. "Better?"

"Much," I say, even though this space is no better.

He reaches into his bag and pulls out a pair of sweat pants. "These tie at the waist."

I shrug out of my coat, and have a zip-up hoodie on, which will be good enough to work out in, but the tight jeans I'm wearing definitely have to go. I slide the button through the hole, and Ty goes still, his gaze latched on my hand.

"Turn," I say and circle my finger.

He grunts. "I've seen you naked, Sara. I've been inside you, remember?"

"Oh, I remember. But if you keep looking at me like that..." I pause and point to the door. "We'll never make it out there."

He steps closer. "Is that because you want my cock inside you as much as I want to put it there?"

"Yes," I say without hesitation. "Now turn."

"Good to know." He spins, and rolls his broad shoulders to remove his leather coat. "If this training wasn't so important to me, I'd have already had my cock inside you."

My heart squeezes. I like that he worries about my well-being and is putting that over this insane lust we have for each other—a lust I'm hoping I'll soon get out of my damn system.

I tug on his oversized sweats, tie them tight at the waist, then sit on the bench and look over his hard body as he tugs off his shirt and pulls another pair of sweats from his bag. My gaze roams over his hard back and tight ass, and my fingers itch to touch him, to trace the scars that mar his once flawless body.

He turns and I lift my gaze to his, my smile a bit wobbly. He doesn't say anything when he catches my melancholy, the downward turn in my mood. He knows where my thoughts have gone, and he's made it perfectly clear that his time behind bars isn't something he likes to talk about.

He holds his hand out to me. "All set."

I take his hand and stand. "I'll try not to be too hard on you," I tease.

He pulls me to him, and I feel his erection. "I can't say the same."

I laugh and push him away. "Come on, show me your moves."

I pull open the door and his groan curls around me as he follows me out. I hop onto the mat and face him as he grabs a pair of boxing gloves and pulls them on.

He angles his body, his hands out. "Since you seem to have the knee to the groin mastered, why don't we practice some straight punches."

"I learned these when I took the class."

"Doesn't hurt to refresh. Just remember, push from the ball of your foot, and thrust your hip and fist forward at the same time."

I nod, and do exactly what he says, hitting his gloves hard. He jerks back, his expression impressed. "Nice," he says. "If Caleb ever comes near you again, I want you to throat punch him just like that."

"It's different in the situation, though. Luckily my instincts kicked in, but after the adrenaline rush, I was a mess. I wasn't even sure I could get myself out of that room."

"I know," he says, and pulls me to him in such a familiar way that tugs at my heart he drops a kiss onto my head. "I'm going to make sure you're never in that situation again."

"You can't always be there."

He wipes his forehead with his forearm. "Yeah," is all he says. He holds his hands up. "Hit me again."

We practice that move for a good ten minutes, then we move on to front kick to the groin, bear hug defense, and choke defense. After a good hour, I'm breathing pretty damn hard and about ready to collapse.

"Had enough?" he asks.

I lean forward, brace my hands on my knees and take deep gulping breaths. "I think so."

I'm about to straighten when Ty catches me by surprise. In two seconds flat, he has me pinned beneath him. "Are we still practicing?" I ask as his heavy weight pins me in the most delicious way.

"No, what we're about to do, we've perfected," he says, his eyes once again heavy lidded and full of need. "No practice needed." He rolls to the side, and reaches for the strings on my sweats. He tugs them free, and slides a hand inside. A moan rumbles in my throat and I arch my hips, aching for his touch. His finger touches my clit, a barely there touch that fills me with frustration.

"Tyler," I moan.

"Yeah, baby," he says and closes his mouth over mine. His mouth is light at first but his kiss deepens and expands as he applies more pressure to my clit. I move against his finger, and run my hands over his bare back, lightly grazing skin. "You need to come?" he asks after breaking the kiss. He circles my clit, teasing and tormenting me to the point of delirium.

"Yes," I say, and tired of being played with, I grab his shoulders and shove him until he's pinned beneath me.

"Whoa," he says, "What the hell was that?"

I give him a coy look. "I've got moves too, you know."

He puts his arms behind his head. "Show me," he says, looking casual and relaxed, but the way his cock is tenting his sweatpants tells a different story.

I shimmy lower, slowly untie the strings and give a tug until his cock pops free. I grin at him, then bend forward to take him into my mouth.

"Jesus Christ," he growls.

I grin inwardly as I look up at him. "What, you don't like my moves?"

His hips power upward, nudge my chin. "I fucking love your moves, Sara."

I dip my head and take him to the back of my throat. He's practically pulsating in my mouth as I slide him in and out. My pussy is throbbing, aching for something hard to clench around. With need driving me, I straddle him and his hands go around my hips to guide me onto his cock. I sink down, and he fills me so beautifully that tears prick my eyes.

"Hey," he whispers, and I try to blink the water away, but one drop trickles down my cheek. He brushes it with his thumb. "Sara...I..."

I know he's going to tell me he loves me, but I can't hear that from him. Not ever again. I lean forward and close my mouth over his to stop him. We kiss softly, passionately as he moves his hips, bringing me such intense pleasure. His breathing changes, as does mine, and I gasp against his throat.

I sit back up again, brace my hands on his hard chest and ride him. My lids slip shut as I slide into euphoria but Ty's voice pulls me back. "Open your eyes, baby."

My lids flutter open with effort, and the room is haze as I try to focus in on the man beneath me. His gaze is dark, potent as it seeks me out. "Can you see me?" he asks.

"Yes," I say.

"Keep looking at me, Sara. I want you to see me when you come. I want you to know it's me."

"I could never forget," I say quietly. "Whether my eyes are open or closed, it's always been you, Ty."

His hips move faster, pound into me, and I struggle to keep my eyes open, but I want to see Tyler, want to see the pleasure on his face as he comes too. He slides a hand between our bodies, and with each downward thrust, he brushes the rough pad of his thumb over my clit.

"Oh, God, yes," I cry out.

"I'm there, baby. I'm right fucking there." He thrusts hard, creating a mind-numbing kind of friction.

His words, and his heat push me over the edge and I let go, give in to all the pleasure centered between my legs. My hot release drips down his shaft, and wets my thighs. He holds my hips to still me, buries his cock high inside me and his eyes dim as he lets go. I clench, he pulses, and it's the most glorious feeling in the world. One I don't ever want to stop feeling.

When our bodies stop spasming, I cry out, "Ty," and collapse onto this chest, his cock still inside me.

"Come here," he murmurs and peppers soft kisses to my head. I lay there, his strong, fast heart pounding against my cheek, and all I want to do is stay like this forever. Curl up in him, and forget the real world exists, for just a little bit longer. He rolls to his side, and pulls me to him. Our bodies mesh and he gently slides his fingers up and down my arm. I crane my neck to see him, note the way he looks so lost in thought.

"Ty," I whisper, and lightly touch his chin. "You okay?"

A long pause and then, "Do you ever think about the plans we made?"

"You mean of opening our own store, running sports clinics and nutrition classes for athletes?"

He laughs, but it's a hollow sound full of regret. "I guess that's a yes."

He rolls to his back and settles me on his chest. "I'm thinking about taking some classes at the campus. If I'm taking you back and forth in the evenings, I might as well do something with my time, right?"

"Really?" I ask, shocked yet happy to hear that. "Ty, that's wonderful."

He drops a kiss onto my head and says, "Let's go away Thanksgiving weekend."

Taken by surprise by this sudden turn of events, I lift my head to see him. "Ty, we—"

Before I can finish my protest he hurries out with, "Let's get away from this place for a few days. We can hop in the car and take off to New York. We'll watch the parade. Just you and me, forget about everything but us."

Oh, how tempting.

"I can't, Tyler."

"Why not? It's on your bucket list. Remember we talked about all the things we wanted to do."

"I can't believe you remember that."

"I remember everything, Sara," he says so quietly I have to strain to hear. "So what do you say, want to start checking things off?"

I give him a look that suggests he's dense. "I can't, and you can't either. Your brother will be back from school, and you don't want to miss dinner with your family."

"Mom works Thanksgiving Day. She's cooking her turkey on Sunday. The parade is Thursday, and we can spend Friday and early Saturday being tourists. If we leave really early Sunday morning, we can be back for dinner."

"You've given this some thought."

"Say yes."

"No."

He frowns, and runs his thumb over my kiss-swollen bottom lip. He looks so lost, so forlorn my heart squeezes, urging me to agree to anything he asks.

"At least tell me you'll think about it." He climbs on top of me, pinning me with his hard body. "I'm not letting you up until you say you will."

I lift my hips like I'm going to flip him off me, and he groans. It's crazy how much we want each other again so fast. "You're leaving me no choice but to use more moves on you."

"Please do," he whispers as his mouth captures mine.

As we kiss, I envision the life we were supposed to live. I can't deny that I want to go away with him, forget about everything that happened between us and for one blissful weekend pretend the future is ours.

There is a part of me that wonders if a future is possible. Could we make this work?

TYLER

With the season's last football game in full swing, there's so much excitement and anticipation in the air, I can taste it on the tip of my tongue. I examine the guys as they huddle on the field, their captain Jackson going over the last play I'd gave them, a little something special I had up my sleeve so Tanner can find an easier way to get around Lincoln's monster linebacker. He's been giving us hell all night, but that hasn't stopped us from keeping it a tight race, and a three-point spread.

We might be in fourth quarter, fourth down, a do-or-die situation, but we've come so damn far that if we can make the touchdown and get the one point conversion, I know Tanner can kick the ball for the win. I'd been working with him one on one for weeks, honing his raw talent enough that he can do this with his eyes closed. Lincoln might have come here expecting a win, but we sure as hell showed them what we've got.

Standing restlessly beside me, Coach is shifting from one foot to the other, fisting and relaxing his hands. "You think Jared can do this?" he asks, talking about the new play I'd just given them—one where I moved Jared from fullback to tail-back to help with the defense. I glance at him, see the new fire in his eyes, one that was missing when I'd first stepped foot in his school and offered my services.

"He's got this, Coach," I say and check the stands. Scouts are watching and I want our boys to perform at their peak tonight. A few of them have a good chance at getting out of this hellhole and into college to make a better life for themselves and their families. As I scan the crowd, I get a glimpse of my little brother talking to a Phantom, and my blood burns hot. What the ever-loving fuck is he doing? Seeing red, I make a move toward him, but Coach puts his hand on my arm.

"Where you going?"

I scrub my chin. I don't want to walk off the field and disappoint Coach when we're this close to a win, but so help me, if Lucas is up to no good, I'm going to fucking kill him. I look at Coach, then my gaze tracks back to where I spotted Lucas. This time I find him climbing the bleachers with a buddy of his and finding a seat. He gives me a nod and a smile when he sees me, and I exhale, feeling a measure of comfort that he seems to be happy, and not in any sort of trouble. Maybe the exchange with the Phantom had to do with the service bay and needing bike work done.

Sara comes running up to her father. "Hey Dad, good luck," she squeals.

He gives her a hug and a big knot of guilt sits in the pit of my stomach. He's a good man, a good father, and I should have honored my promise to him, but now is not the time to be thinking about that. Not when our team is about to complete the last play of the night—of the season. At least I might be able to do right by Coach by giving him the win he's been after for so long.

"Tyler," Sara says, greeting me politely before taking a seat on the bleachers next to her mother. I smile at Mariam, and she smiles back. It's easy to see where Sara gets her good looks. My mother said all us boys look like our dad, prick that he is. Still though, we all resemble one another, even though I think Lucas is far prettier than Alex or me. But I can't think about that right now because the team is taking up position.

I toss a piece of gum into my mouth and chew hard enough to hurt my jaw as I pace the sideline, Coach tight on my heels. Jesus, I'm more nervous now then when I was playing all those years ago. Parents are cheering from the stands, and I exchange a look with Coach. I catch something in his eyes, something that resembles pride. We both nod, no words needed to say what we're feeling, and I stare back out over the field, my throat a little tighter than it was before.

The QB calls the play and Tanner goes wide. The next thing I know, the ball is in the air. Tanner is running like a son of a bitch to get it, the monster linebacker about to plow him down, when out of nowhere, Jared sacks the guy, clearing the field for Tanner. The crowd goes nuts, but the loudest voice is Jared's father, the cop I talked to after my bike had been stolen. I zero in on him, and when he looks my way, his thumbs up, I nod and smile. I do another quick scan of the crowd. The whole town has come out. I spot Cassie, my coworker, and Kaitlyn, along with some guy I don't know. Even my mom and Gracie are in the crowd. I can't help but think this is my chance to win back the trust of all those I disappointed. With my eyes back on the field, Jared makes a touchdown, then does a little victory dance.

"Yes," I hiss under my breath, and beside me Coach lets out a whoop, then pats me on the back.

"Nice play," he says. "Now Tanner has to make the conversion for the win."

"He's got this." I shove my hands into my jeans. "Tanner,"

I call out. He tugs on his helmet and turns my way. "You good?"

"Good, Coach," he calls back and my heart is racing so goddamn fast I think I might break a rib. Winning this will mean so much. Not just for the kids and Coach, but it will go a long way in rebuilding the relationship between Coach and me. He took a risk by letting me on his team, and when I came back here, it was with the intention of never letting anyone down again.

The crowd goes quiet, a dull hum as the ball is lined up and Tanner prepares to take his kick.

"You got this, kid," I say under my breath as his foot connects with the ball and it easily flies through the goal posts. Beside me, Coach makes a noise and for a minute I think he's crying. I turn to him, but he averts my gaze. The team goes crazy, picking Tanner up and carrying him around. Mariam and Sara run up to us and my knuckles brush Sara's as she waits to hug her dad.

My heart hammers when she sneaks me a look, the pride I see in her eyes taking me back to so long ago. She flicks her long hair back and I catch her sweet vanilla scent. Jesus, I fucking love her so much.

"Congratulations, Tyler," she says.

"Thanks. The boys played great."

"What are you guys doing to celebrate?" she asks, a twinkle in her eye that says she has ideas of her own.

I shrug and make eye contact with her father. He's so excited about the win, he's unaware of the tension between Sara and me. "Grab a beer? Nachos?"

"That sounds like a great plan," Coach says. "How about we head to Lou's?"

"Lou's it is," I say, as the boys rush the field toward us.

"Why don't you both join us?" Coach says to his wife and daughter.

Sara nods. "Sounds like fun."

The next thing I know, I'm being lifted in the air, the team tossing me around and cheering. Coach is laughing and holding his hands up when they try it with him. They shout and chant Collins Cheetahs as they carry me and by the time they let me down, Sara and Miriam have disappeared. I scan the crowd, disappointment taking up residence in my gut. But I do console myself with the knowledge that after our celebration at Lou's, Sara and I will have our own private celebration at home.

Coach and I follow the team into the locker room, and he gives the boys a talk, congratulating them on their win and telling them not to party too hard tonight. They all laugh as he makes his way outside to talk to a few of the scouts. I give out handshakes and hugs to the guys, and slip out to let them continue with their celebration. I can imagine it's going to be one hell of a party tonight.

I make my way to my car, and drive to Lou's. I step inside and find Sara and Miriam at the table, in deep conversation. Sara is frowning, and Miriam looks sad.

"Ah, everything okay?" I ask.

"We just talking about Aunt Sandra," Sara says and gestures to the other side of the booth. "I already ordered."

"Is she okay?"

"She's slowly recovering," Miriam, says, the sadness on her face expanding and I wonder if there is something else going on.

"If I didn't have a big test to study for this weekend, I'd go with you to see her," Sara says.

"No worries, honey," Miriam says, and puts her hand over Sara's. "Your aunt understands, and she wants you to get your degree."

The beers and nachos arrive just as Coach is making his way inside, half the team's parents following along behind him. His smile lights the place up as he saunters over and sits beside me, and across from his wife.

He pats me on the back. "Well done, son."

Son.

The nacho I'm trying to swallow catches in my throat. Coach has not called me son...well, since I was taken away. My gaze collides with Sara, and holds. Clearly she's picked up on the sentiment too.

Coach takes a sip of his beer. "Just like old times," he says, referring to our after-game get together when I played for him and dated his daughter.

Honest to God, sitting here with these three people, laughing and carrying on like the past never happened, is too good to be true.

I remind myself of the old saying: When it's too good to be true...it probably is.

"Except you wouldn't let me have beer back then," I manage to say past a tight throat.

Everyone laughs, then Coach says, "I'm pretty sure it didn't stop you."

We fall into conversation but are interrupted every few minutes as parents and friends want to congratulate us. Before I know it, the night is late and Miriam is covering her yawn with her hand.

"We should get going," she says to Coach.

"I suppose so." He rubs his stomach, and then climbs from the booth. Across from him Miriam scoots out of her seat, leaving Sara and me still sitting across from one another.

"You coming, Sara?" her father asks.

She glances around the room. "No, I think I'll hang out for a bit, play a game of pool." Coach is about to say something when she says, "I'm a big girl, Dad. I can get home safely."

His gaze goes to mine. "I'll be sure she does," I assure

him, a small reminder that he'd asked me to look out for her and have every intention of doing just that.

He stands there a bit longer, like there's a war going on inside him. I suppose there is. Does he leave his daughter with me, or force her to go with him? Like he said, watching over her and touching her are two different things.

"Come on," Miriam says. "It's still early. Let the kids stay and have some fun."

"Yeah, okay."

Mariam blows Sara a kiss and drags a reluctant Coach out the door. I catch Sara's frown as she watches them go.

"What's up?"

"Mom and I were talking about Aunt Sandra when you came in."

"Yeah, what's going on?"

"I didn't want to say anything in front of Mom, but Sandra really isn't doing well. She has a lovely little house in Indiana, a place where you can raise chickens. It's not too far from the city center, either. Dad loves it there, and, since Uncle Leroy died a few years back and Sandra never had any kids of her own, she willed them both the house. They could go there now, after the school year ends if they wanted to. Dad can retire any time."

"But they won't go..." I say and let my voice trail off as my mind races with all the reasons keeping them here. Mainly, Sara.

"No, not if I'm still living here," she says, confirming my suspicions.

I slide my hand across the booth and take hers into mine. I brush my thumb over her soft skin. "Do you love what you do at the bank?"

She snorts. "Not really. But I am finally completing my business degree. It was the push I needed."

"Then what's keeping you here, Sara? Why don't you go

with them, start over?" I say, despite the chaos in my stomach. I hate the thoughts of Sara leaving. Of never seeing her again, but I need her to do what's best for her, which is why I agreed to this affair. Once she gets me out of her system, she can start fresh, and why not do it in a city that isn't plagued with violence? I'd feel much better knowing she was living in a good place—even though it will gut me to watch her go.

"You want me to go?"

I shrug. "It's not that I want you to go, it's just that it sounds like a nice place and you always wanted out of here."

"So did you," she says.

I want to blurt out, *let's go together*, but I bite my tongue. She asked for a bit of time with me, not a future, no matter how much I want that.

"Yeah, but it's not too late for you, Sara. You don't belong here."

"Is it too late for you?" she asks.

I let her hand go and she slowly drags it back and places it on her lap, her big brown eyes latched on mine, searching, seeking answers. "You need to do what's best for you. I'm a convicted felon and don't factor in to that."

Her face goes pale at that reminder, and she glances down at her hands in her lap. A slow second later, her head lifts.

"Ty."

"Yeah?"

"I want to go home."

So do I. Except there is no place I'll ever be able to call home, not without Sara in it.

SARA

Sara

The end of November, and Thanksgiving weekend is upon us, which means I have no choice but to break out my winter jacket. I reach into my closet, and reluctantly grab my white down-filled parka. As I shrug into it, I glance at my clock, and the overnight bag I have packed on my living room floor.

There is a part of me that can't believe Ty and I are driving to New York tonight to play tourist for the next few days before we return Sunday for dinner at his mother's house. Yet there is another part of me that can totally understand my last minute decision to take him up on the offer. He's an addiction I can't seem to shake, but after this weekend, I'm hoping I'll be able to do just that.

The truth is, up until yesterday, I hadn't planned to go. No, I had every intention of having dinner with Mom and Dad tomorrow, and discussing Aunt Sandra's house in Indiana and how we should proceed. But Aunt Sandra took a bad spell and they decided to spend the holidays with her. They'd wanted me to come, of course, but I politely declined. I begged off with the excuse that I had too much schoolwork to do. Not a total lie, I do have my books packed, although I have no idea when I'll find the time to open them. Next weekend I'll be past a few hard exams and can make the trip to Indiana to spend some alone time with my aunt.

When Gracie found out my folks would be out of town and I'd be spending Thanksgiving alone, she insisted I have dinner with her family come Sunday. It was just last month I said I wouldn't be able to make it—had zero intentions of ever trying. Yet so much has changed since I began this journey of healing with Tyler. Which is why I'm gifting myself with this one last intimate escape with him, hoping deep in my gut that I manage to overdose on him and come Monday morning, I'll have the strength to walk away without the need to look back.

My door opens and I turn to see Tyler walk in like he owns the place. He's grinning as he shoves the key I'd finally given him into the front pocket of his low slung jeans. The smile that curls his beautiful, kissable lips when his gaze lands on me, damn near shatters me.

"You look beautiful," he says, his eyes bright and alive like he's five again and Santa just arrived. I put that look on his face last night when I finally agreed to this trip. But I sense that he knows this is a turning point for us too, that this weekend is about closure. After all, he was the one who suggested I leave with my folks.

He crosses the room, and his familiar scent of man and leather fills my senses. His head dips and he brushes his lips over mine, light enough to make me want more, but firm enough to let me know he's ravenous for me.

"All set?" he asks, when he breaks the kiss.

I stifle a yawn, and groan. "I'm ready, but not looking forward to a long night of driving."

"I can drive the whole way and you can get some sleep. I don't mind."

"No," I say. "I don't want to sleep. I want to be awake when you are." He nods in understanding. "What did you tell your mom?"

"That I was going away with a friend." A shrug and then, "Not a lie."

My heart beats a little faster. This affair was supposed to be kept under wraps. The last thing I want is for anyone to get hurt. "She knows, doesn't she?"

"Hard not to, I guess."

I give a slow shake of my head, and pray to God we all come out of this unscathed. "At least we've been able to keep this from my Dad."

"I'm not sure we have, Sara," he says, and touches my cheek. "One look at us and...you know."

"Yeah, I know."

He bends and grabs my bag, and I scoop my purse off my table. "We better hit the road if we want to grab a few hours sleep before the parade starts." We step into the hall, and I lock up tight behind us. "I've never been to the Macy's Thanksgiving Day parade before," I say as I follow him outside. The wind bites at me, and he drags me to him and puts his arm around my body to warm me as we make our way to his car.

"Same."

"I think it's going to be fun."

"You're still up for the skating on the rink at Rockefeller?" he teases as he opens my car door for me.

I roll my eyes at him. "I fell once, Ty. Once!" I shoot back, my mind racing to the time we both went skating when we were at Penn State and I landed, with an undignified thud I might add, on my ass. "What about you, you still up for a tour of the Empire State Building?"

He cringes at the reminder of his fear of heights. "Touché," he says and closes the door.

He puts my bag into the trunk and climbs in beside me. I look at him, waiting for him to start the car, but he goes quiet for a moment, and stares straight ahead at the dark road like he's lost in thought. I'm about to ask if he's okay, when he turns to me, slides his hand around my head and drags my mouth to his for a deep, yet tender kiss.

I have no idea what's going through his head, but when he breaks the contact, my heart nearly breaks right along with it. He turns the ignition over and I try to settle in for the long night ahead. Ty turns the radio down as I nestle into the seat beside him, but I have no intention of drifting off to sleep. I need to make these last days with him count.

We fall into an easy conversation for the ride, and watch the signs fly by as we cut across states. My lids grow heavy, but I suck in a few deep breaths and force myself to stay awake. The hours tick by, and I unfortunately find myself dozing off. A car horn wakes me fully, and when I blink and look around at the increasingly heavier traffic, it's clear we're approaching Manhattan. We're well into the wee hours of the morning, and the city is still alive around us as he pulls his car up to our hotel. Ty wanted to make all the arrangements for the trip, and I certainly didn't think we'd be staying at such a posh place. I read the sign. Hilton Midtown.

"Tyler, this place is amazing."

"I thought you'd like it."

"How did you get it? These places book up years in advance."

He averts my gaze. "I had a friend help me out. He has many connections."

I can tell he doesn't want me to push, so I say, "You didn't need to get a place so upscale."

He gives a casual shrug, but I can't fight the unease in my stomach. He makes minimum wage at the BSA, and he's been buying groceries for his family, and paying some of Gracie's expenses. He can't afford this. Unless he's making money some other way, a way that has to do with the connections he just mentioned. I give a hard shake of my head. I hate myself for those ugly thoughts, but sometimes it's hard to forget the past.

"Don't worry about it, Sara," he counters, obviously reading between the lines.

"Ty," I say. "I want to go splits on it with you."

"No. It's covered."

"But—"

"Sara, really, it's covered. I had some money put away for a new bike. It's no big deal."

My stomach tightens. No big deal? Of course it's a big deal. He was pretty upset when his bike was stolen. It meant a lot to him. "You didn't have to do this. Not for me."

"That's where you're wrong. You're way more important than any bike." He looks down and the muscles along his jaw clench. When his gaze seeks mine out again, I get the sense that he wants to tell me something.

I put my hand on his arm and his muscles tighten. "Ty?"

"We should get showered, and grab a quick nap before the parade." He checks the dashboard on his car. "It passes by here around nine thirty, so we should be on the sidewalk by seven if we want to get a good spot."

"That's in four hours," I groan.

A man comes from the hotel and makes his way to Ty's side of the vehicle. We both climb out and Ty hands his keys to the valet and gives him a tip. The valet pops the trunk, and hands us our luggage. Ty takes both pieces and we make out way inside the grand entrance with the spectacular statue in the middle of the lobby.

People are bustling about, some checking in, some checking out, and some lounging at the on-site bar. "This place is amazing," I whisper.

"Come on."

I follow him to the counter, and a very nice man named Seymour checks us in and points to the bank of elevators we need to take to the fifteenth floor.

"Ah, wait," I say, understanding Ty isn't a fan of enclosed spaces. "Do you have anything on a lower level?"

"I'm not sure I do," Seymour says, as he presses buttons on his keyboard.

Ty puts his hand on my back and I turn to him. "It's okay," he says quietly, then glances at Seymour. "The fifteenth floor is fine."

Tyler captures my hand, and we step onto the elevator together. I give him a reassuring smile, and he squeezes my hand. It's nice to see him relaxed like this, working to put the past behind him. We ride up along with another couple and I stifle a yawn as we make our way down the hall. Ty passes the keycard over the lock and we step inside.

I flick the light on and catalogue the gorgeous room. "This is so nice, Tyler."

He drops the bag, comes up behind me and presses a kiss to my neck. "We have it for three nights."

I eye the big queen-sized bed. "I can't believe we have to get up in a few hours."

He gives me a playful whack on the ass. "Maybe it's not worth sleeping at all. I'm sure I can find another way to pass the hours."

"As fun as that sounds," I say, desperate to enjoy every moment of the weekend, "if we want to play tourist, we need rest."

"True enough." He yawns and I say, "Come on, let's have a quick shower and get to bed. You're exhausted."

We both jump into the shower for a quick rinse, and I set my phone to go off at six before we climb into bed. Tyler pulls me in close and I let my eyes fall shut as his warmth and strength wrap around me. Honest to God, it feels so good to be held by him like this, to pretend nothing exists in this world but the two of us. He's not the same man he was when he left all those years ago, but deep inside, I still see so many glimpses of my Ty. I swallow against the tightness in my throat, and strive to enjoy this while it lasts.

Before I know it, my damn alarm is going off.

"Fuck," Tyler says from the other side of the bed.

I turn to face him and laugh. "This was your idea, pal."

"Yeah, I know, let's go," he says, his mood changing quickly, his childlike enthusiasm back in place. I smile. I love when he's like this. He jumps from the bed, and stark naked, he makes his way to the window and pulls back the curtains.

"Ah, that might be considered public indecency."

"If I'm going to get in trouble, why don't you come over here with me and we'll really put on a show."

"I'm not into exhibitionism, Tyler."

"No? Just voyeurism?"

"Nope, not that either," I shoot back.

His grin is playful, mischievous. "You could have fooled me."

I rub my eyes. "What are you talking about?"

"You haven't taken your eyes off my cock since I turned around."

I groan, grab a pillow and toss it at him. "Time to wake up, Ty. I think you're still dreaming."

He catches it and tosses it back onto the bed beside me. "If you want my cock, then come and get it."

"I don't want it," I shoot back. A lie. I *had* been staring at his early morning erection.

He crosses the room, falls over me, and pins my arms above my head. His grin is deliciously dirty as he pushes his cock between my legs. I open for him, instantly and readily. It's futile to pretend I don't want him.

"What about the parade?" I ask as his mouth seeks mine.

"I'll be fast."

"When aren't you?" I tease.

He pushes my hair from my face and my heart nearly stops when I see the tenderness in his gaze as he stares down at me. "Hey, watch that smart mouth of yours, or I'll put it to better use."

I wet my lips as I slide my legs around his back. "I like the idea of that, and if we didn't have a parade to get to, I'd push you on your back and take you into my mouth."

His cock throbs between my legs. "Fuck, girl, I'm going to hold you to that."

"It's a plan. Now inside me. Hurry," I say and in one quick thrust he enters me. He pumps deep and it doesn't take long to take me to the edge. "You're not the only one who's going to be fast," I say breathlessly, as I run my hands over his body and cup his ass.

"Fuck, Sara," he murmurs, changing position to seat himself in deeper. He slides a hand between our bodies and the second he touches my clit, I tumble into an orgasm. I squeeze around him, and two seconds later he's flying with me, our breaths coming in ragged bursts as we give another little piece of ourselves to each other.

He collapses on top of me and we just hold on to one another, neither wanting to be the one to break the contact, but when we hear a lot of noise on the street below, he groans and rolls off me. "Tonight," he says, sliding out of me. "More of that."

"And my mouth," I tease, rubbing my hand along his cock.

"That is the plan," he says. He stands and drags me up with him. "Come on. Let's shower, grab a bite to eat downstairs, and get outside."

Thirty minutes later we're scarfing down mufins and coffee, and hurrying outside to get a good spot on the sidewalk. We could see the parade from our room, but it wouldn't be the same experience as standing in the cold with the crowd. I hug myself, and Ty takes up position behind me. He pulls me to his chest and links his arm in front of me, warming me with his body. The street fills up, and people close in on us. Normally I would hate the claustrophobic feeling, but I feel so safe in Tyler's arms. I could stand here with him holding me for the rest of my life.

Oh, God.

I shouldn't be having thoughts like that. I should be thinking about my future, of looking for another job in Indiana, so I can finally get my dad to retire. But I don't want to go to Indiana without Tyler.

"You okay?" Tyler asks, like he can sense the battle going on inside me.

"Yup," I say, and then point to a couple across the street, to the girl with her hand over her protruding stomach. "What do you think they're saying?" I ask, my mind tripping back to the time I tried to play the game with Caleb. But thoughts of Caleb, and having to go to court in a few weeks to testify, bring on a shiver.

Tyler must mistake it for me being cold. He runs his hands up and down my arms to create friction and puts his mouth next to my ear. "I think she just told him they were having twins."

"Yeah?"

"Yeah, look at his face. It's like he doesn't know whether to laugh or cry."

I chuckle. "I think I'd cry."

"Not me," he says.

I turn in his arms until I'm facing him. When our eyes meet and I see the 'little boy lost' look on his face, it's all I can do not to sob. I bite the inside of my mouth to keep the tears at bay, but don't miss the sound his throat makes when he swallows, like he too is remembering more things on our bucket list—like having our own family.

"Twins do run in my family, remember," he says, his voice hitching slightly.

"Yeah, your grandmother was a twin, I remember." I turn from him, unable to take the sadness on his face as he looks at the couple across the street. "I think she's saying she's a bit afraid."

"I think he's saying she has nothing to fear, that he'll make sure nothing ever happens to her or the babies."

At this point I can no longer talk, so I just stand there, a few tears slipping down my face as I really hear what Tyler is saying to *me*.

I glance around, looking for a distraction, anything to help keep a big ugly cry at bay, when cheers erupt. I swallow. Hard. Then I say, "Look, the parade is coming!" Floats rise up over the city. "It's Snoopy," I say and Tyler's soft chuckle in my ear curls through my blood, warming me from the inside out.

I clap as the floats go by, and wave to the people hanging off the sides or riding inside the vehicles. Balloons fill the air, and I grab my phone and take a few pictures so I can savor the memories later. The truth is, I still can't quite believe I'm here.

"Look," Ty says and points to the marching band coming. The crowd grows louder, and it's hard to hear over the music. Bedside me a man lifts his daughter and sets her onto his shoulders, and when I turn to see Tyler, take in the way he's looking at the family, my lungs squeeze. The look on his face says it all.

He wants that.

Then why oh why did he run guns and rob us both of a future, a family?

"Angry Birds," the little girl shouts, and Ty's gaze jerks

away. "It's Scrat from Ice Age," she squeals, and her father pats her knee and laughs.

"Look Katy, Elf on the Shelf is coming," the father says.

Little Katy claps, and I turn from them to watch the parade. Laughter and clapping surrounds us, as I concentrate on the parade and remind myself what this weekend is really about.

"Having fun?" Ty asks, his mouth close to my ear. His warmth sizzles through me.

"Big fun," I say. "You?"

"Oh yeah."

I focus back in on the street, and Ty continues to warm me from behind until Santa in his sleigh goes by, waving to the crowd and signaling the end of the parade.

I turn, and wrap my hands around Tyler's shoulders, go up on my toes and kiss him.

"What was that for?" he asks, taking his bottom lip between his teeth, like he's tasting me.

"For coming up with this idea."

"I can't wait to see how I'm rewarded after Rockefeller." He tugs my hand. "Come on, let's get a hot cup of coffee and go skating."

"Let's do it."

Fighting our way through the crowd, we go back into the hotel, grab a hot coffee, and make our way to the rink. My eyes go wide by the time we get there. "God, that line. We'll be in it for hours."

He shrugs. "I'm okay with that if you are."

I think for a minute. "Sure, why not?" We take our place in line, and Ty glances around.

"Hot dog?"

"Mmm, New York street food. Another thing on my bucket list," I tease.

He takes my empty coffee cup, and says, "Wait here."

He disappears into the crowd, and I look around, watching all the people, and wondering what their story is and what conversations they might be having with each other. When Ty finally comes back, he's carrying two big hotdogs.

"Ketchup and mustard, hold the onions," he says as he hands it to me.

"You remembered."

"I don't forget anything, Sara," he says and takes a big bite. He chews and his eyes roll. "Jesus, this is the best hot dog I've ever had."

"You get that from Drew's truck?" a male voice asks from behind us.

We both turn, and I take in the guy and the girl standing there holding hands. "Yeah," Ty says.

"We had them yesterday, they were awesome."

With that I bite into mine, and much like Ty, I roll my eyes as I chew. "Ohmigod, you're right."

The girl chuckles. "Good, eh?" she says.

"Delicious."

"I'm Peter, by the way," the guy says and holds his hand out. We both shake it then he introduces his wife, Cheryl.

"I'm Tyler, and this is Sara my...wife." My gaze darts to his and when I find him looking at me, warmth in his gaze, I smile back and play along.

"Where you from?" Peter asks.

"Chicago. We drove through last night. How about you?"

"Nova Scotia. We're actually on our honeymoon."

"Oh, how nice," I say, and smile at Cheryl.

"It is, but now I'm rethinking my decision not to go to Jamaica." she says hugging herself to ward off the chill. Peter drags her to him and the loving way he holds her is identical to the way Ty holds me. We eat our hotdogs and fall into conversation with our new Canadian friends. I love they way they talk and sometimes add 'eh' to the end of their sentences.

The rest of the morning slips by as we get to know each other and it's early afternoon by the time we finally make it to the rink. We get into our skates, and I feel a bit wobbly in them as Ty helps me onto the ice.

"Should we see if they have helmet rentals," he teases.

"Not funny." I whack at him, but he skates backward out of my reach.

"A little funny," he says.

"Come here. I'll show you just how funny I think you are."

"Nope. You'll have to catch me first." He skates away and I push off the boards to go after him. He's so damn graceful as he moves in between the other people, I can't help but want to just stare at him. For a big, tough guy, he moves with a grace few men have. I'm not the only one noticing him, either. He's caught the eye of a few other women, who seem to be following him around, closing the distance.

Oh, hell no!

I take a few glides until I'm a little more stable, then cut across the rink. I skate right into him and nearly knock us both to our asses. Tyler laughs and grabs me to help right us both. When we're finally stable, I go up on my picks and kiss him again.

"If I had known you were going to show me how funny I was with a kiss, I wouldn't have fled."

I angle my head and the girls scowl at me as they skate by. "Come on," I say. I hold his hand and we skate together, the cool afternoon air in our faces, and my skates are a bit too tight, but I'm having too much fun to care. We laugh and touch as we skate, and Ty shifts to skate backwards, while holding both of my hands. Lost to everything but this man and the fun I'm having, our half hour flies by.

"That went way too fast," I say, breathless but exhilarated.

"I didn't make any plans for the rest of the day. Tomorrow, though, we should hit the Empire State building first thing, so we can avoid the long line."

"You made plans for later," I remind him.

We pull our skates off, and slide back into our boots. "I did?" he asks, as a bubble of excitement wells up inside me. Honest to God, I'm having so much fun here I feel like a giddy schoolgirl.

He keeps eyeing in me as we move through the crowd and return our skates. When we're finally away from the rink, he says. "You going to remind me or do I have to guess?"

"Well, there was something you said about my mouth?"

His grin turns wicked. "Now how the hell could I ever forget a plan like that?"

Hand in hand we maneuver through the busy crowd and make our way back to our hotel. When we finally enter our room, we're both practically vibrating with need. It's insane how happy I am, how much I want him right now.

I sit on the edge of the bed and crook my finger. "Come here, big boy."

We fall into bed together, our bodies tired after such little sleep and an early morning, but neither wants to give up making love for rest. We come together as one, our love-making less hurried than this morning, but ever bit as touching and powerful. After a glorious round of sex, we fall asleep, only to wake up sometime in the early evening.

"Hey, babe," he says quietly, the bed dipping beside me as he shifts.

"Hey," I say and roll toward him.

"Hungry?"

"Starving."

"Do you want to go out or just get room service?"

My eyes widen. I never considered room service. "Eating

here sounds better than getting dressed and going back out into the cold."

He runs his finger down my arm, and I quiver. "I thought you had fun today."

"I did, but I had fun inside too."

He grins, slides from the bed and reaches for the phone. He puts in our order, knowing exactly what I like to eat. My mind races. I know when this weekend started, it was about overdosing on him so come Monday morning I could walk away. But I've been a fool. A total and utter fool for thinking this weekend would tear us apart. All it did was bring us closer together, make things better.

Why can't Tyler move to Indiana with me?

He said he wanted to go back to school, finish his degree. Maybe we can put the past behind us, and start doing all the things we've talked and dreamed about. If this weekend has taught me anything, it was that we're good together, and that he's the only man I want beside me as I check things off my bucket list.

He'd called me his wife today, and I damn well liked it. I want that. I want everything with him. Here I said I'd never give him my trust, but along the way, intentional or not, I'd gone and done just that. But the past is the past and this Tyler has been nothing but caring, attentive, taking care of me, his family, and even the guys on Dad's football team as he walks the straight and narrow, no sign of trouble in his future. Once this weekend is over, we need to carve out some time to talk, sooner rather than later.

I just pray to God I'm not making a mistake in trusting this new version of Tyler, otherwise...well, I can't go there.

TYLER

"I was not afraid," I say as Sara teases me about our trip to the Empire State building from the passenger seat.

She pokes me in the side and chuckles. "I thought you were going to pee your pants."

"Stop it," I say, laughing, and grab her hand. I take it in mine, bring it to my mouth and pretend to bite her finger.

"Seriously, Tyler, it was amazing," she says on a sigh, and lays her head against the seat, her smile so big and wide my heart fills with the love I feel for her. I gaze at her for a second longer, then turn my concentration to the dark road ahead of us. After getting up early this morning and visiting the Empire State Building—yeah, it was fucking scary—we spent our last day in New York roaming the streets, drinking coffee and browsing the shops. Now here we are, driving before sunrise to make it back for Mom's Thanksgiving dinner.

As I put on my signal light and pass a car, Sara lets loose a long, contented breath, and I can't help but smile. We've come to a new place, Sara and me. I can feel it deep in my bones. I'm smart enough to know this weekend was about closure, but it had the opposite effect. Everything in the way she looks at me, touches me, alludes to something deeper, something even better than we had before. But what now? Where do we go from here? She has her folks and her work to consider, and I made a promise to her father and urged her to move away, start fresh without me.

Her lids fall shut, no matter how hard she tried to keep them open. I lower the radio so she can sleep. I take a pull from my water bottle and concentrate on getting us home safely, despite the fact that I'm tired, too.

Many, many hours later as the sun rises on the horizon, I pull up in front of Sara's apartment. She stirs beside me.

"What time is it?" she asks quietly.

"We're here?"

She sits up, blinks and looks around. "Already."

"Time goes fast when you're sleeping."

She frowns. "I'm sorry, Ty, I would have done some of the driving."

"It's fine, and your snoring kept me wide awake anyway."

She whacks me playfully, and reaches for the door handle. "Come on in. I'll make you something to eat, then you can sleep for a bit."

I release my seat belt, and climb from the car. Hand in hand, we make our way to her apartment. Once inside, I strip to my boxers, make a quick trip to the bathroom, and come back to find her pouring me a bowl of cereal.

"Cereal?" I tease, my heart so full as I watch her pour milk into the bowl. Being with her like this, playing house, feels so right. "I drive all night and all you give me is cereal."

"But it's Captain Crunch," she says.

"Well then...I'll let you get away with it this time."

She puts it on her table, and pours herself a bowl. We sit

quietly together and eat, and she shakes her head at me. "I don't know how you can eat this stuff. It's pure sugar."

"Mmm, sugar," I say and take another spoonful.

I scarf it down, put my bowl in the sink and stretch out. "Come to bed with me?" I say, needing to hold her in my arms.

"Just for a bit. I told Gracie I'd make dessert for dinner."

She stands, holds my hand and we make our way to her room, and that's when it occurs to me that I hadn't had a nightmare in a very long time. Sleeping with Sara in my arms has kept the demons at bay. The fresh scent of her sheets surrounds me as we slide in together. I pull her to me, spoon her from behind. Her hair tickles my nose as my body relaxes and I drift off to sleep.

Hours later, a phone chirping in the other room wakes me, and I stretch out and check the clock. Damn, I must have been really tired. We're due at Mom's in less than an hour.

I kick the blankets off and pad quietly down the hall. I round the corner and find Sara in the kitchen, talking quietly on the phone. From the conversation, it sounds like she's talking to her parents. I watch her for a moment, take in the sway of her body, her graceful movements as she puts the dishes in the sink, keeping her voice low as to not wake me.

When she finally sets her phone down, I whisper, "Hey."

Startled, she turns, her hand to her chest. "Tyler, you scared me." Alarm turns to a scowl. "How long have you been standing there?"

"Long enough to know."

"Know what?"

I push off the doorframe. "How much I want to be inside you."

Her scowl changes to arousal as her gaze drops to take in my tenting boxers. I pull her to me, claim her mouth with mine, and the soft, sexy mewl rising in her throat turns me on even more. I break the kiss and she puts her warm hands on my chest, fingers splayed.

"I want that too, Ty. But we have to be at your mom's in less than an hour and look at me."

I step back, take in her upswept hair, the pieces falling against her face. My gaze rakes over yoga pants that hug her curves, and an old tattered T-shirt that showcases her beautiful breasts. She has chocolate smeared on her cheek. I swipe it with my thumb, and bring it to my mouth. "Mmm, sweet."

"Chocolate cake," she says.

"No, you. You're beautiful, Sara."

Her eyes glaze at the compliment. "I need a shower."

"Me too."

"Oh, no," she says laughing as she gives me a push. "If you climb in there with me, we'll be late, and I'm not going to be late for Thanksgiving dinner with sex written all over me. Besides, I need you to put the icing on the cake. It should be cool enough now."

I groan. "I'd rather put icing on you."

"Tyler," she warns, pointing a knife at me before handing it over. "I'll shower first, then you."

"You're kind of mean," I say as I take the cake from the fridge. "And if I make a mess of this, it's your fault." I go to work slapping the icing on the cooled cake, then smoothing it out. I honestly have no idea what I'm doing, but as long as it tastes good who cares. I shake my head. Who'd have ever thought that I'd find myself in Sara's kitchen icing a damn cake, thinking about her naked in the shower as she gets cleaned up for a family dinner.

Family dinner.

My heart takes that moment to hitch. I want a family with Sara. I want everything with her and for the first time in a long time, I feel like we can have that. A lifetime has passed since things were this good between us, and I'm almost afraid this is too good to be true.

By the time she comes back into the kitchen, wearing a soft blue dress that falls just above her knees, I'm finished making a mess of the cake. She looks at it and smiles.

"Good job." She takes the knife from me and gestures with a nod. "Go shower." She proceeds to do little swirls with the knife, creating a design. I hurry to the shower, rinse off, then shrug into my jeans and T-shirt. Since I don't have anything dressy at Sara's, I'll change when I get home.

Thirty minutes later, I park the car in Mom's driveway. The front door swings open and Alex comes running out barefoot and without a coat on. I jump from the car, throw my arms around him and hold him tight.

"Hey little brother," I say, and struggle to keep my voice even. "I'm so fucking proud of you."

His fingers curl in my jacket, tugging on me hard, and his breath is uneven as we hold each other. As hard as I try, I can't keep the memories of him at bay the day they took me away.

"Thanks," he finally says. "I'm so glad you're home."

Working to keep my shit together, I inch back to see his pretty face and don't miss the water in his eyes. Fuck, mine are wet too. I missed my baby brother so fucking much. "I want to hear all about Penn State, and your scholarship," I say, keeping one hand on his shoulder, needing the connection with him.

The car door closes and I turn at the sound. Sara is leaning against the door, a warm smile on her face as she takes in our brotherly show of love.

"Alex," she says. "It's so good to see you."

Arms wide—Alex is obviously a hugger—he runs to Sara, scoops her up and spins her around. "Sara, I missed you."

She laughs out loud and my throat clogs at the sight of

them. I stand there, grinning like the village idiot as they reacquaint, then grab the cake from the back seat.

"Get in here before you catch your death of cold," Mom says from the doorway. She's scowling, but beneath it, there is so much joy on her face. She's happy to have her family all together again, Sara included.

We all rush inside and Mom hugs herself as she shuts the door. "Sara, I'm so glad you could come," she says, no hint of worry on her face today. It seems like everyone is now accepting the fact that Sara and I are together again. That things are right in the world once again.

"Same, Viola."

Mom smiles. "You didn't have to bring anything."

"I think Gracie might have something to say about that. This is her favorite."

"Sara," Gracie says from the door and the two hug as Lucas comes racing down the stairs, looking good in his dress shirt and pants. We exchange nods, and he says hello to Sara before making his way to the fridge despite the big turkey on the counter. I swear all that boy does is eat.

Sara stands back and takes in my sister. "You've been experimenting with that make-up kit haven't you. You look amazing."

Gracie beams up at the older sister she always wanted, and my heart pounds in my too-tight chest.

"After dinner, maybe we can go over some of the strokes I've learned," Gracie says.

"I'd like that a lot," Sara says.

"I should get changed," I say, and dart upstairs. I pass my bedroom, and see that it's still empty. Alex must be in his own bed, which means I have to go back to my room. Oddly enough, it doesn't quite seem so painful anymore. I grab my clothes from the other bedroom, including the box that Justin sent with my clothes, and take them all to my room.

Soon enough I have to start thinking about getting my own place—a place with Sara far away from here. I plop down onto my bed, my heart tumbling around in my chest. A noise at the door has my head lifting.

"I didn't mean to interrupt," Sara says quietly. "Your mom sent me to find you. Dinner is ready."

I stand, my gaze going from Sara, to my trophies, back to Sara. Her eyes are full of questions as she looks at me. She walks into the room, lightly runs her fingers over the base of my trophies. Tears prick her eyes as she turns back to me, and leans against my dresser. A strange, strangled noise catches in her throat, and I brace myself.

"Why, Tyler? Why did you do it?" she asks, the question that has no doubt been plaguing her for nine long years but until now, never had the courage to ask.

"Sara," I say and take her into my arms. I bury my face in her hair, wanting to tell her everything but I can't. "I'm so fucking sorry I hurt you."

"Ty," she says and wraps her arms around me. "Is it going to be different this time?"

"Yes," I say. "I made a mistake. It won't happen again."

"I need to believe that."

"I know."

"I can't..."

"I know, Sara." The sounds of the plates hitting the dinner table prompt me into action. I inch back, wipe the tears from her face, and capture her hand. "You okay?"

"I am," she says. "You?"

I nod, and we make our way to the kitchen, and take our seats.

"Mom this looks amazing," I say as I look at the feast before me. The shit they fed us in prison still haunts me.

Lucas reaches for a drumstick, and Mom slaps his hand away. "Grace first, you know that."

Everyone chuckles, then we all lower our heads as mom says a prayer and we all give thanks for the meal in front of us. I lift my head, look around the table. I take in my family, and lace my fingers through Sara's beneath the table, knowing I have so much to be thankful for.

Soon we're lost in conversation, Alex telling us all about football and school. When I mention I'm going back to school too, a huge smile splits Mom's mouth, and Alex pats me on the back.

"You and Sara going to finally open that sports store you always talked about?"

"Maybe," I say and steal a glance at Sara, who is watching me carefully. My gaze slides to Lucas, who is checking his phone. He frowns, shoves it back into his pocket, and shakes his head.

What the fuck is going on with him?

I plan to find out, but now is not the time or place. We finish our meals, and after we all help with the dishes, Alex and I plunk down to watch the game while Mom, Sara and Gracie pull out Gracie's make up kit.

Lucas disappears upstairs, and comes back dressed in his jeans and an old shirt. "Gotta go out for a bit," he calls from the kitchen.

"Hey," I say. "What's going on?"

"Just a friend with car trouble," he says and I'm about to stand, but the door slams shut behind him. I look at Alex, who just shrugs and goes back to watching the game. But something is off with Lucas. I feel it deep in my bones, and I'm not about to ignore it. Tomorrow I'm going to hunt him down and get to the bottom of the matter.

After a while, Sara pokes her head into the living room. "I should get going. I'm tired and have an early morning tomorrow."

I jump from my chair, and Alex stands with me. We exchange another hug.

"See you at Christmas," I say.

"Can't wait. See you, Sara," he says.

"Proud of you kid," I respond and give him a nudge on the chin with my fist.

I say goodbye to Mom and Gracie and walk Sara around to the passenger side of my car. She slides in and I scan the streets as I walk around the front and climb in. Something is off tonight, a strange ripple in the wind. The hairs on my neck stand, and I can't help but feel there is a storm coming. Only this storm isn't weather related. Maybe it's because right now life is going too good. I can't ever forget my motto: when it's too good to be true...it probably is.

I slide my hand across the seat and hold Sara's as we make our way home.

Home.

Jesus I like the sounds of that. I park, and scan the streets again as we walk to the front security door. My boots thud as we move down the hall to her apartment. She lets us in, and I lock up behind us. She turns to me, her eyes dark, serious. She looks like she's about to say something important. Her mouth opens, but then she seems to hesitate. Her cold hand lands on my chest and I put my palm over hers to warm her.

"The weekend was perfect, Tyler, just perfect."

"You think it's over?" I tease as I shrug out of my coat and unzip hers. I know we need to have a long talk, but first I need to make love to her, then the two of us can figure out where we go from here.

She touches my face. "I love you," she whispers.

"I love you too," I say and scoop her up. "I've never stopped." I carry her to the bedroom, ready to show her just how much I love her, when my damn phone goes off.

"Shit," I say.

"Do you have to answer?"

I hesitate for a second, but my mind races to Lucas and his behavior tonight. "Yeah," I say and fish the phone from my front pocket. Every muscle in my body clenches and red-hot rage goes through me as I read the message. I take a minute to compose myself even though all I want to do is hit something, but I glance at Sara, who's looking up at me with nervous eyes. Jesus Christ, we were just getting our footing again. I can't involve her in any of this. I won't.

"Ty," she says, looking at me like she's never going to see me again. But that's not going to happen. I'll go help my brother, and then when I come back, I'm going to talk to her about our future.

"I have to go."

18

SARA

After a very restless night, I wake to find the other side of the bed empty, and the minute I do, my throat tightens. When Ty left here last night, his eyes murderous, every instinct in my body went on high alert. I waited hours for him to come back, to hear him put his key in my lock, but ended up falling into a fitful sleep.

What the hell is going on with him?

It's a question I'm not sure I want the answers to. Last night he said this time it would be different, and I have to cling to that. I have to believe he's living a crime-free life, otherwise... Well, there can't be an otherwise. There just can't be.

I pull the twisted sheets off my body, and my grab my phone from my nightstand. But there are no missed calls, no texts to let me know he's okay. I run my fingers over the screen, then climb from my bed. Hopefully he's at the school with my Dad this morning, and I can find a minute to talk to him. With that last thought in mind, I take a fast shower, dress, pack a lunch, and head out the door.

The sky is dark, overcast, and I'm pretty sure I spotted a snowflake or two as I rush to the bus stop. Twenty minutes later, as I climb off the bus, and see a police car in front of the school, the bottom drops out of my world. I do a quick scan and glimpse Tyler's car parked on the street near the front doors.

My breath comes quicker and turns to fog in front of my face as I hug my oversized purse to my body, my legs shaky beneath me. As I convince myself this has nothing to do with Tyler, I force my legs to move, and hurry inside the school, unable to deny that I terrified at what I might find when I get there. The halls are empty at this time of the morning, and my heart is pounding so hard in my chest, I'm breathless by the time I round the corner and find Tyler, my Dad, and two police officers inside my father's office. My gaze flickers to the broken window, but I don't enter. Instead I step back and press against the hallway wall, my vision fuzzy around the edges as the officers question Tyler on his whereabouts last night, and if he took the petty cash.

"I told you, I was with a friend, then my brother called," he says, as breathing becomes more difficult for me. I make a wheezing sound, like air being let out of a balloon. "I picked him up, took him home, and stayed the night at my mother's house."

I lean forward, and brace my hands on my thighs, thankful he has an alibi, because no way would he break into my father's office and take money. Someone has to be setting him up. I'm sure of it.

"Your brother and mother can corroborate this?"

"Yes."

"What about this friend? Can he or she corroborate this as well?"

A pause and then Tyler says, "Look Coach, you know I wouldn't do this."

"Will this friend corroborate your story or not?" the officer asks again before my father can say anything.

Ty goes silent and I know it's because he's protecting me, but I'll have no part of that. No way is he going to take the rap for this, because I made him promise to keep our affair a secret. This isn't an affair anymore. Tyler and I love each other deeply, and want a future together. I didn't want Dad to find out this way, but what choice do I have now?

I push off the wall and walk into the office. All eyes turn to me.

"He was with me," I say, as Tyler's gaze sweeps to me. From my peripheral vision I catch the way my father is staring at me. I slowly turn and when I glimpse the deep-seated disappointment on his face, worry lines tightening around his eyes, I grab the back of the chair to stabilize myself.

"Sara—" my father begins.

"We spent the weekend together," I say. "He left last night around ten when he got a text from his brother." Truthfully, I didn't see or read the text, but since it's what Tyler confessed to the cop, I can only assume it had been Lucas texting him because he was in some kind of trouble.

My father drops into his chair, the wheels rolling over broken glass as it slides it backward, stopping with a thump against the wall, near the busted-out window.

"And you are?" the balding cop asks me.

"Sara Ramsey," I say and the cop makes a note on the pad he's writing on.

"We have a witness who says your motorcycle was spotted outside, around eleven last night," the heavy cop says.

Tyler grabs a fistful of hair and defends himself. "I reported my bike stolen over a month ago. Sara, you know that." I nod in agreement as the heavier officer grabs his radio, and steps out of the room, no doubt to check out Tyler's story.

"Someone must setting me up," Tyler says, and starts pacing, his heavy boots echoing through me. "But none of this makes sense. I help the Coach out, but I haven't been here since last week."

"Then why was your bike registration found on the floor?" The officer holds it out for Tyler to see.

"I keep that with my bike. Do you really think I'd leave it behind if I did this? What kind of idiot do you think I am?"

"Maybe it fell out of your coat."

Tyler rakes his hand through his hair. "I just said it was with my bike."

"You have enemies?" the balding cop asks.

Tyler goes still. "If you're asking if I've been staying out of trouble, the answer is yes. Look, I didn't do this. I didn't break anything or take anything. My car is outside, you can check it if you want."

"Take me to it."

Tyler walks toward me, and our gazes meet. "I didn't do this, Sara," he says quietly. "You have to believe me."

"I believe you," I say, and catch a measure of relief in his eyes before he leaves with the officer. Dad stands, his eyes questioning as they focus in on me.

"I'm sorry, Dad," I say.

"Sara, I just..." he begins. "I know you love him, that you never stopped loving him. But after everything you've been through..."

"I know." My gaze flitters around the room to take in the trophy they'd won last week, broken on the floor. I point to it. "That meant the world to Tyler. He didn't do this."

"Then who did?"

"I don't know. Maybe he's being set up, like he said."

"Tyler has a history..." he says

He didn't do this. He couldn't have.

Right?

"I need air," I say.

My father puts his arm around me and leads me outside. He continues to hold me, keep me on my feet as my legs wobble. Students are now standing around, talking in hushed voices and forming tight circles as they watch the action unfold before them. Some have their phones out and are recording the event. No doubt this will be all over the six o'clock news tonight. My mind flashes back to nine years ago, and a cry catches in my throat as the milk I'd had at breakfast curdles in my stomach.

Tyler's standing on the sidewalk as the balding officer puts on a pair of gloves and searches his car. I don't expect them to find anything. Tyler didn't do this, I'm sure of it. I believe wholeheartedly that he left last night because his brother needed him, not to break into the school and take cash.

I can't be wrong about this. I just can't be.

Chatter from the crowd gets louder, until the officer pulls a gun out from beneath the passenger seat. I freeze on boneless legs, my heart thudding hard against my chest as the students all back up a bit. I blink through the puddle blurring my eyes, and take in Tyler's murderous expression. When another black and white comes to the scene, lights flashing, my lungs seize and I lean into my father for support.

"A Glock 19 9mm. As a convicted felon, it's against the law for you to own, or have a gun in your possession," the officer says.

"It's not mine," Tyler shoots back quickly, his voice hard, deadly.

"As the owner of the vehicle, you're responsible for all property and belongings in it. Looks like you have some explaining to do," the balding cop says as he examines the weapon.

"It's not my gun."

"A lot more explaining than you think," the heavy cop says as he pulls his handcuffs free.

"What is that supposed to mean?" Tyler asks, his throat working as he swallows, his gaze latched on those silver cuffs like they're a machete about to take his head off.

The cop stands before Tyler, legs wide. "You know a man named Caleb Douglas?"

Tyler goes stiff, his jaw clenching as his gaze jerks to mine, like he's guilty of something. "Yeah, what about him?"

"He was jumped last night, and he just identified you as the man who pulled a gun on him, then beat him badly. What makes me think it was this gun?"

"It's not mine," he says through clenched teeth, his body hard, lethal as he stares at the cop.

"We're taking you in and you've got a whole lot of questions to answer."

Tyler's eyes darken, and he looks past my shoulders. I know his tics, his body language, and it's clear that he's remembering something. But what?

"Son of a bitch," he says, his fingers curling at his side. That's when I see the blood on the sleeve of his coat. A little gasp catches in my throat, because I'm not the only one who's noticed it.

"I'm going to need that coat for evidence," the cop says.

"Tyler," I squeak out, disoriented, my mind racing, struggling to sort through everything.

He was going to kill Caleb?

I breathe deep, but it feels like I've inhaled razors.

"You went after Caleb for what he did to Sara," my father says, speaking my thoughts out loud. He gives a slow shake of his head, like he's putting the pieces of the puzzle together.

"You told me you'd kill for her," he says quietly, incredulous. His grip on my arm tightens, and his eyes go wide. "Tyler, what have you done—?"

"I..." Tyler begins, but then his well-carved lips pinch tight.

Why isn't he defending himself? Why isn't he telling the officers he didn't beat up Caleb, that the blood on his sleeve is from something else? I want to scream. I want to jump up and down. I want to hit something as he stands there, shoulders sagging, staring at the ground—mouth shut tight.

The officer turns to Dad. "I'd like to take your statement," he says.

Bile punches into my throat, and I put my hand over my sick stomach. Is this really happening?

Tyler turns toward me, his jaw locked, his muscles clenched so tight I fear they might snap, as he makes a move to come my way. "Sara, go stay with your aunt in Indiana for a few days."

"Tyler, no," I whisper, dazed, disappointed, hollowed out inside. "Don't push me away. You didn't do any of this."

"Sara, I need you to leave." Intense eyes lock on mine, burning as he searches my face. "Now."

Paralyzed at the scene playing out before me, the darkness returns, pulls me under, and I choke out, "No, Tyler." I stare at him, and right before my eyes he transforms—bigger, harder, far more dangerous—the Tyler from prison. Stone cold convict.

The officer bags the gun, and my knees crumble. I sink to the ground, and bury my hands in my face as I cry uncontrollably, inconsolably.

"Let's go," the officer says, and I put my hands over my ears, the clang of the handcuffs ugly and deafening.

I peer up in time to see Tyler with his big battered hands shackled behind his back. His face is dark and grim—unrecognizable to me. I let loose another big hiccupping cry as I try to breathe through the pain, the betrayal. I can't believe what is happening, that he's being arrested again and pushing me away, leaving me here to circle the drain, with nowhere to go but down.

19

TYLER

What the ever-loving fuck is going on?

Rage builds inside me as I pace inside the small interrogation room, tethered like a wild animal on display. I roll my tongue around my dry mouth as the walls close in on me, squeezing air from my lungs. I kick my chair and run shaky hands through my hair as I glance at the two-way mirror. A goddamn bug under a microscope. I'm intelligent enough to know I'm in real fucking trouble here, trouble that could end with me behind bars again—taken away from all those I love. My mind drifts to Sara.

I told her to leave. Needed her to leave. If someone was setting me up, they've obviously been watching me, and that meant they could be watching Sara, too. With me behind bars, no way to protect her I needed her gone until I could figure out what was going on, and guarantee that she was safe.

I have no idea where it came from. But I can't deny the possibility that Lucas dropped it in my car last night. Before I say a word, I need to know exactly what's going on. I need to fucking talk to him is what I need, but they won't let me speak with anyone except my lawyer.

I go over the events from the second I received Lucas' text message, telling me he was hurt bad and needed a lift home. I picked him up near the college campus, his hands bloodied and aching. He'd been in a fight, told me he'd gotten jumped. By who, he didn't know. But it was bad enough that he couldn't drive. By the time I got to him, his breathing was labored, and raspy. I wanted to take him to the hospital but he refused, saying it was just a cracked rib and there was nothing anyone could do about it. I took him home, and spent the rest of the night at his side, keeping him under my surveillance, with an inquisition planned for the morning. Except I drifted off to sleep and come morning, he was gone, and I found myself chained and locked up, facing my own interrogation.

Was it Caleb he'd gotten into a fight with? If so, who jumped who? The part that doesn't make sense to me is they didn't even know each other. There was no way that Lucas knew about Sara and Caleb's history, right? He couldn't have, which means he'd have no reason to go after him.

Unless...

A sick, heavy feeling closes in on me and my lungs seize. Motherfucker. Cold fury grips my throat, and I shove my hands into my pockets before I start to pound on something.

"Lucas, what the fuck have you done?" I say under my breath. I pace as my mind races and a long while later, the door opens and the officer who'd been questioning me steps in. "Your lawyer will be by later," he says, and puts the hand-cuffs back on me.

I stand to my full height, an intimidating bastard when I want to be, but it's lost on the man with a gun in his holster. "Are you charging me?"

"The investigation is ongoing, but we have the right to hold you for seventy-two hours, so let's get you comfortable."

Comfortable?

My entire body breaks out in a sweat as he leads me down a hall and into one of the holding cells. Air leaves my lungs in a heavy rasp as he places me inside and removes my cuffs. The metal on metal clang rattles my teeth as he slams the door shut, locking me in and the world out.

I grip the bars, squeeze my fingers around them until my knuckles turn white. Someone is setting me up, and that someone can only be a Phantom. They don't want one of Deacon's men in their territory. That has to be it. I saw the way the gang's leader studied Caleb that night he'd been taken in.

I let go of the bars, and drop down onto the bed, throwing my arm over my eyes. I try to breathe past the panic. Going back to prison will fucking kill me—kill Sara, and everyone else I care about.

This can't fucking be happening.

Seeing the look of misery on her face when I told her to leave completely gutted me. Trouble follows me and she was trying to get on with her life. I never should have started up with her again. I should have come right out and said no when she asked for this affair. But I fucking love her, would die for her. I had to give her what she needed, but now...well, now everything is fucked up.

Maybe I never should have come home.

A sound I have no control over rises in my throat as I think about my mother, and sister. How can I ever face them again? See the disappointment on their faces? I have to prove I'm innocent in all this, but if I do, what does that mean for Lucas? Was the gun his? If so, where the fuck did he get that? Only one place I know.

Phantoms.

As questions race through my head, the time slowly ticks by. I can only imagine I'm all over the news tonight. I scoff, and pound the mattress beneath me.

I toss and turn on the nasty, stained pad they pass off as a bed as I wait for my lawyer. My stomach grumbles, but hunger is the least of my problems. The lights dim, indicating it's nighttime, but I'm too ramped up to sleep. I continue to toss and turn and many hours later, the lights brighten. I can only guess that it's nearing morning when footsteps finally herald someone's approach. I jump from the bed and grab the bars.

An officer approaches, and I back up. What the fuck is going on? Is he here to practice his batting swing? Wouldn't be the first time I was abused by a man of authority while locked up.

"Where's my lawyer?" I ask.

"You're out."

My heart stalls. "Out? I'm not being charged?"

"No charges."

"What's going on?" I ask hesitantly. How could the charges just be dropped? A gun was found in my car, and I'm a convicted gun-runner, plus Caleb identified me in the battery. Not to mention all fingers point at me for breaking into Coach's office, and taking the money.

The cop leads me through the hall, and I'm given back my things. Next thing I know I'm walking toward the exit doors. I step out into the morning light, and when I see who is waiting for me, I suck in a fast breath.

No. Fucking. Way.

"You okay, buddy?" Justin asks, as I take in my brother-hood, the four rock-hard and lethal guys I banded with in prison, and might not have made it through without. Their fierce loyalty touches me on a whole new level.

"How did you know?" I ask, and let my head drop forward, a little weight off my shoulders with my brothers here to help me carry it.

"You were all over the news," Ryder says, and pulls me in

for a hug. "What the fuck is going on?" He rests one hand on my shoulder as we part.

"From what I gather," I begin as I look up and down the street, the hairs on my nape tingling, and I know better than to ignore them. "Someone is setting me up."

Christian cracks his knuckles. "Then let's go find them and give them a motherfucking beatdown."

I hesitate. "I need to find my brother first. He's involved in this somehow."

"Lead the way," Jamie says, his jaws clenching.

Just then I spot my mother walking toward the station, and my blood pumps faster. How can I face her? See the disappointment in her eyes?

"Can you guys give me a minute?"

The guys back off, and my boots slap the pavement as I hurry to my mother. Her head lifts as I close the distance, and sorrow for everything she's been through burns through my blood when I see how red and swollen her eyes are from crying.

"Mom," I say and she practically collapses in my arm. "I didn't do the things they're saying."

"I know," she says quietly, so quiet I have to strain to hear.

"You do?"

She blinks up at me, a new kind of sadness in her eyes.

"What?" I ask, fear slithering through my blood. "What's going on?"

"It's...Lucas."

I hold her shoulders and inch back. My throat tightens, and I have to push my words out. "What about him?"

She makes a soft, broken sound as she goes on to explain, "Last night, after we saw the news...he broke down and told me things."

"Jesus," I say under my breath. "What has he done? What kind of trouble is he in?"

"He's in a lot of trouble. He turned himself in this morning, and this time there is nothing you can do to get him out of it."

Air evacuates my lungs in a rush as I absorb her words. "Mom?"

A cold breeze blows the lapels on her jacket and she tugs them together, holding them to her chest. "He told me things last night. Lots of things, Tyler."

I step back, the world spinning around me. I stare at the people walking by, their expressions blank as they hurry to work. My pulse thuds, beats steadily behind my burning eyes, and I struggle to get my words out.

"I...he..."

"I'm sorry for everything you've been through." Mom reaches up and cups my face and it's all I can do not to fucking sob. "I'm sorry that you ran guns for your brother."

"I didn't want him to do it. I didn't want to see him get himself into any kind of trouble." I shift to face the courthouse, partly so my mother can't see my pain.

"The Phantoms," she says. "They took your bike and brought it to the chop shop. Lucas recognized it. That's why he had that car waiting for you. He thought they were going to strip it, not use it to frame you. He couldn't say anything. The gang..." she lets her words fall off, unable to vocalize what the gang would have done to Lucas—my family—if he betrayed them.

"Fuck..." I curse under my breath.

"They wanted him to kill Caleb," she says on a cry. "He didn't know who Caleb was, or that you knew him. He only pieced it together after the news. The Phantoms wanted to pin you with his murder, but luckily Lucas couldn't pull the trigger." By now tears are spilling down her face, her heart no doubt broken into a million fucking pieces. "He couldn't do it, and instead they ended up getting into a fight. You and

Lucas look so much alike, and it was dark. Caleb must have thought he was you. Lucas said that had to be why the Phantoms sent him to do the job in the first place. The gun...he dropped it in your car by mistake. He said it was the gun that would put you behind bars again, and he couldn't let that happen."

"He won't make it in prison," I say quietly.

A keening, wailing noise catches in my mother's throat as she dabs her tears with a tissue. "He said he's going to make a plea. He's been working in the chop shop at nights, and he can give up the gang and the location in exchange for a lighter sentence."

I step back, dizzy, incredulous. "If he does that, he's a dead man." If the Phantoms get to him first... Oh fuck, I can't even let my thoughts go there.

"Tyler, this has to work. If it doesn't..."

I look past her shoulder and see my band of brothers standing on the curb, waiting for me. "Go home, Mom. Get some rest. I'm going to take care of things. Everything will be fine. I promise."

"Tyler, please don't do anything—"

"I won't." I hesitate for a second, and then ask, "Have you talked to Sara?"

She looks down, and stares at her feet, unable to meet my gaze.

Oh, this is bad, so fucking bad.

"Mom," I say as my stomach twists, knots up. Bile punches into my throat. I swallow and try not to vomit. "Where is Sara? Did she go to her aunt's?"

"Yes, she's gone, Tyler. She left to go stay with her aunt in Indiana like you told her too. Lucas said the Phantoms were probably following her, and they trashed the office to really dig that knife in deep. According to Lucas, they didn't want you around, and wanted to rob you of everyone, including your girl and her family. They couldn't take you out themselves, not without consequences from Deacon. At least that's Lucas's theory."

I curse under my breath. The thoughts of those fuckers following Sara, of something happening to her because of me, fills me with white-hot rage. Messing with me is one thing, but messing with those I love is another fucking thing entirely, and it's time they damn well knew it.

I briefly pinch my eyes shut, but can't dispel the way her haunted brown eyes looked at me when I told her to leave, like I was admitting guilt—again. That look had more power than a bullet to the head, a baton to the kidneys. Sara is my world, but I had to push her away for her own safety.

"I need to talk to her," I say, as heartache sets my chest on fire, making it nearly impossible to breathe let alone speak.

"She came to say goodbye last night. She's been hurt, Tyler. She doesn't want you to try to contact her."

Fear of losing Sara again fills that scraped out hole inside of me. "But—"

"Even if you're not responsible for any of this, trouble follows you now, Tyler. You can't bring Sara into this world." A long pause and then, "It nearly killed her last time...It nearly killed us all."

Anger pulses hard and deep inside of me, and it's a good thing Lucas is currently behind bars. The truth is, I'm now one of Deacon's men. I'll always be one of his men, which means I'm the one responsible for putting Sara's life at risk with the Phantoms. My fingers curl into fists. I'm a convicted criminal who attracts trouble. As long as I'm around her, will she ever be safe? Will my family ever be safe?

They're better off without you, dude.

Mom touches my arm. "It's what she wants, Tyler."

What Sara wants, Sara gets...no matter what it will do to me.

As those words play over and over in my head, I turn my

mother around, and tell her to go home. Head down and shoulders slumped, she walks away. I fucking hate how broken she looks, how much she's been through.

I step up to my brothers, working to keep my shit together as my heart explodes in my chest. Emotions play no role in what I need to do. If the Phantoms catch a hint of weakness in me, it'll be all over before it starts. Deacon is bound to get wind of how they set me up. Once he does, he'll send in an army, and those fuckers will be lucky to live to talk about it. But this is personal and I want my chance at leveling those bastards, and showing them they fucked with the wrong guy.

Will this shit land me back in jail? Probably. Get me killed? Possibly. But I'll do whatever it takes to protect those I fucking love. And when it comes right down to it, how the fuck can I go on without Sara in my life, anyway?

"Anyone know where the Phantoms chop shop is located? I need to pay them a visit."

Justin, the toughest guy I know, eyes me carefully as Ryder pulls out his phone to make some calls.

"You're not alone." Justin holds his finger up and circles it. "We're with you, brother," he says and steps up to me, shoulders square as we stand eye to eye—a force united—like we've done so many times before.

I shake my head. "I'm not about to drag you guys into my trouble."

"Your trouble is our trouble," Christian says and cracks his knuckles again. I look over my four friends. Big strong, scary motherfuckers, tough and unintimidated, who are all under the umbrella of Deacon. We fought some hard-ass lifers behind bars, and came out alive. If we can't stop the Phantoms with a straight-up beatdown, then Deacon can have his turn. One way or another, they won't be going near my family again, and if I get caught in the crossfire, so be it.

Many hours later, walking the streets under the cover of darkness, we make our way to the chop shop—Ryder having gotten the location from a contact. We cut down a long narrow street, and see a rundown laundromat at the back of a cracked and pitted driveway. The front for the gang's illegal activities.

Breathing hard, I'm about to go in and take down the toughest bastard, when the wails of sirens fill the air. We all jump back, hiding in the shadows as numerous black and whites flood the streets, the vehicles closing in on the laundromat. Lucas' plea must have worked. Doors bang as they're being kicked in, and curses fill the air. Gunshots ring out, the sound splitting the quiet of the night.

"Let's get the fuck out of here," Justin says and grabs the back of my shirt to tug me away. We bolt down the street until we reach Justin's car parked in an alleyway. We jump in, and Justin peels away.

"Fuck, looks like we dodged a bullet there," Ryder says.

Jamie grins. "Yeah, too bad. I was itching for a fight."

From the passenger seat, I turn to Justin. "I need to go back to the courthouse. As soon as my brother is out on bond, I'm going to beat the shit out of him, then I'm getting out of this place."

For good.

20

SARA

With my one week vacation coming to close, I toss my clothes into a suitcase and pad quietly down the hall to see Aunt Sandra before I head back to Middletown with Mom and Dad. I left like Tyler told me to—just like he did last time after he committed a crime—but now I need to get back to my life.

There is still a part of me that can't believe he had a gun, and had beat the living hell out of Caleb, considering the non-violent way he handled the situation after Caleb had attacked me. I know there is violence in him. He needed it for survival, but he's not shown that side since he'd been home. Not even when he came to my rescue at Studio Paris. He de-escalated the situation by pretending to be my boyfriend. Is it possible that he's innocent—that I didn't believe him because of past hurts?

Or is that just wishful thinking on my part?

I'm not sure, but one thing I do know is after everything we'd been through this last month, after getting to know this version of Tyler, I never in a million years thought he'd do anything that would land him behind bars again.

I take the stairs to the main floor, and my stomach cramps as I look at the framed pictures littering Aunt Sandra's walls. Tyler and I talked about having a house like this some day, but sadly, that day will never materialize. At least while I was here hiding from reality, I was able to shut the world out and turn off my phone, concentrating only on my studies and mending my broken heart. But I'd come to the conclusion that there is no getting over Tyler. I was a fool to try. There is only moving forward, one day at a time.

"There you are," Mom says as she lingers at the doorway waiting for me, her eyes full of motherly concern. Outside, Dad starts the car, the sound of the roaring engine cutting the tension in the room. "All set?"

I plaster on a smile and nod. "I just want to give Sandra a kiss goodbye. I'll be right back." I set my bag down, and step into Sandra's bedroom off the main hallway to find her napping, a nurse fluttering about. She's doing better after the stroke, but she still has a long way to go. It will be good when Mom and Dad move in at the end of the school year so they can keep a better eye on her.

"See you soon, Aunt Sandra," I say quietly and bend to give her a kiss on the cheek.

Her eyes flicker open. "Sara, is that you?"

"It's me. We're heading back."

Her hand closes over mine and squeezes. "So soon. You just got here."

I've been here a week, but I don't tell her that. Her memory has been affected by the stroke. "I have to get back to work," I say.

A small smile pulls at her mouth. "And to that man of yours."

Aunt Sandra never knew I'd gotten back together with Tyler. She must be pulling memories from a time long gone.

"Yes, for sure," I say.

"When are you finally going to make me a great aunt?"

Never.

I force a chuckle, and say, "Oh there is plenty of time for that."

"For you maybe, but not for me," she says, and the reminder that life is short fills me with longing and heartache.

"You get some rest," I say, and pat her hand.

Her eyes close and I think she's drifted off, but then she says quietly, "Always trust your heart, Sara."

I glance at the nurse who just shrugs and I assume she's speaking gibberish. "Take care, Sandra," I say and meet my parents in the driveway.

I climb into the back seat, and stare blindly at the trees as we drive back home. Many hours later, Dad drops me off outside my apartment, and grabs my bag from the trunk. I give Mom a hug and meet my father on the sidewalk.

His brows furrow as his gaze moves over my face, searching for the girl he once knew. But I'll never be that girl again. "Are you sure you don't want to stay with us tonight?"

"Positive," I say. I relied heavily on my folks to get me through the dark days when Tyler left us. I can't do that to them again—never thought I'd ever have to. But at least a decision has been made, and once I complete my degree, we'll all make the move to Indiana, where I won't see the ghost of Tyler on every street, the school...in my bed.

I choke back a tear, refusing to shed any more, and let myself into my building. I walk quietly down the hall, and open my door. The second I enter, my chest squeezes tight.

"Oh, God," I cry, and close the door behind me so I can lean on it. My gaze darts from Tyler's sweater, which is tossed haphazardly on my sofa, to his workout bag sitting near the front door. I press my palms to my eyes, desperate to block him from my life, and my heart.

I draw in a deep fueling breath, pick myself back up, and

step into my kitchen. The little bit of wine left in my bottle isn't going to cut it. A trip to the market is definitely in order. I turn and a sense of loneliness envelopes me. It's so quiet and sad here without Tyler—all the more reason I need to move.

My phone pings and I dig it from my purse to read Kaitlyn's message.

You home.

Just got here.

Want to go for a drink.

I'm not in the mood to go out but I get the sense that Kaitlyn will drag me out anyway.

Sure.

I'll swing by and pick you up.

I walk into the other room, and when I see the red light on my phone flashing—a landline Dad insisted I install in case...in case of what I'll never know. I stare at it for a minute and my heart does a little flip, but I quickly shut that shit down. I don't care if Tyler is trying to reach me.

Yes, you do.

No, I don't. Which is why I am not going to check those messages. I'm about to turn when some part of my brain urges me to press the damn button already. I pinch the bridge of my nose, and after a hard debate with myself, I decide to check—after all, it could be work.

I press the button, and disappointment I really don't want to feel, takes up residency in my gut when Lucas' voice comes through.

Sara, we need to talk.

What the hell? What could Lucas and I have to talk about? I listen to a few more messages, and they're all from Lucas. If he's trying to convince me to go visit Tyler, he can forget it. I'm done with his brother. Completely and utterly finished. I grab my coat, and head outside to wait for Kaitlyn on the curb, locking the ghosts of Tyler inside my apartment, unable to face them right now.

A car slowly drives by like someone is casing the place, then the wheels come to a screeching halt. What the hell? I back up as fight or flight instincts kick in. Lucas jumps from the passenger seat, looking like he hadn't slept in a week.

"Sara, thank God. I've been trying to get a hold of you. Do you know where Tyler is?" he asks quickly, as he approaches.

I stand there dumbfounded. Why would he be asking me about Tyler's whereabouts?

He tugs on his hair, such a familiar gesture, and my heart aches with loss. "Sara, please, do you have any idea?"

"He's in lockup, isn't he?" Oh, God, please don't tell me he escaped. I know I haven't had the news on, but surely someone would have told me. Then again, I've had my phone off, but I would have heard about a manhunt on the national news stations right?

I glance at Lucas' eyes, the yellow ring around one—the last remnants of a bad bruise. "What happened to your eye?"

"Tyler happened. He punched me in the face."

I gasp. If he punched his own brother in the face, a guy he loves with his whole heart, then it really is possible he was the one who'd beaten Caleb. Why did I even, for one second, question that?

Because something isn't right about all this. Your heart knows it.

"Then he took off, and I don't know where he is."

"What do you mean he took off?"

"You haven't been talking to him?"

I exhale slowly. "No, he's in prison."

Lucas gives me a look that suggests I'm dense. "Do you have any idea what's going on?"

"Obviously not, Lucas. I've been away."

He glances left, then right, and steps up to me, his look

conspiratorial. "I'm the one who beat up Caleb and accidentally dropped my gun in Tyler's car when I asked him to come pick the pieces of me off the street. I didn't want to call him, but I had no choice. The Phantoms wanted me to kill Caleb. I knew I could never do it, so I attacked him from behind instead, and showed my gun, hoping to scare him out of town."

I gasp and step back, nearly falling on my ass, when Lucas grabs my arm to keep me upright. "What the hell..."

"I'm sorry, Sara. He didn't do any of this. I was working in the chop shop, but I wasn't part of the gang. I didn't want to do it, but then they said I either do what they told me to, or they'd go after my brother. They didn't like one of Deacon's men in their territory. He was framed, Sara. They set him up." He shakes his head. "You were his alibi until I texted him. I'm guessing those bastards knew I would. They were probably following me. It's all my fault."

Sick deep in my heart, I stand there completely flabbergasted, my blood pounding in my ears. A choked cry escapes my lips.

Lucas' brow tightens. "I turned myself in, and made a deal. The Phantoms were arrested."

A tightness grips my chest, and I fight to catch my breath, the knot in my stomach growing tighter and tighter." "I can't...I don't even know..."

"There's more, Sara," he says. "Nine years ago I was the one running the guns. It was a one-time deal for a shit load of money. But Tyler did it for me. He was scared I'd get myself killed, and he was so fucking angry with me, I couldn't stop him. He put the guns in his car, and..."

The world goes woozy around me, and I grab hold of the stop sign beside me and struggle to breathe.

A big ugly cry wells up inside me and I shake my head violently. "Why...why didn't he ever tell me any of this?"

"That's something you'll have to ask him. But I guess he figured the reason didn't matter. He chose to do the job. I tried to fight him on that, but he did it to protect me."

"Oh, my God."

"He's fucking gone, Sara. Gone. I have no idea how to find him. He was so angry with me. I'd only ever seen him like that once before, and look how that ended. He looked like he wanted to murder someone. I broke his fucking heart, Sara."

Me, too.

I went to his mother's, told her I never wanted to see him again.

"I trusted my head, not my heart," I whisper, Aunt Sandra's words coming back to haunt me.

Ty committed a crime, but he was protecting those he loved. In his head he thought the reason didn't matter, but it did. Now he's gone.

"He said goodbye to Mom and Gracie," Lucas says, real panic in his voice. "I'm afraid we'll never see him again. I'm afraid for him, afraid of what he might do."

I open my mouth but no words come. Just then, Kaitlyn pulls up. She hops from the car and when she sees my face she rushes to me. "What's wrong?"

"Everything."

I take a long swig from my beer bottle and glance around the room, cataloging Justin's favorite pub as he racks the balls and takes a shot. Justin had been good enough to let me stay with him this last week, but he's going through so much shit himself as he tries to integrate back into society, he doesn't need my sorry ass around. I need to find work and figure my life out now that it's been totally fucked over. Again.

Although, it could have been a hell of a lot worse had the cops not arrived when they did and taken the Phantoms into custody. The last thing I wanted was to drag the brotherhood into my problems, but no way were they going to allow me to face off against those ruthless bastards alone. In the end it worked out for the best, I suppose. My stupid fucking kid brother is facing a lesser charge, and will likely only get house arrest or community service, and my family is safer without me around.

"Are you going to stand there and fucking mope all night or are you going to take a shot?" Justin asks.

I set my beer down and bend over the table. "I'm not fucking moping," I say as I take the shot and sink my ball.

"Yeah, could have fooled me."

I line up the next ball. "Want to take this outside?" I say. Justin knows I'm not serious—a fight will land us both behind bars—but he also knows I've been itching to punch someone or something, since I'd been unable to take my frustration out on one of the Phantoms.

"I wouldn't want to mess up that pretty face of yours," he counters, laughing.

I touch my scar, and glance at my friend. "It's already messed up."

I shoot again, but miss the pocket. Justin chalks his cue and slowly walks around the table. "If I were you, I'd put her over your shoulder caveman-style, and take her somewhere where you can tie her up and keep her there until she believes you."

I exhale slowly. Yeah, I can't hide anything from Justin. He knows the shitstorm going on inside of me, every bit as much as I know what's going on inside of him. And yeah, I've been fucking moping.

"I don't think your caveman tactics will work with Sara."

Christian comes up to us, a beer dangling from his hand. He slaps a five-dollar bill onto the table. "I play the winner," he says, then looks at me. "What's up your ass?"

"Fuck you two," I grumble and finish my beer. I catch the attention of the waitress and gesture for another round.

"It's like this. You have two choices. Do nothing and forget about her once and for all. Or go find her and make this shit right," Justin says.

Easier said than done.

"She said she never wanted to see me again," I respond. While that might be true, it's not the real reason I left town.

She's a good girl who doesn't need my kind of trouble. She's safer this way. Everyone I care about is.

"When have you ever not fought for what you wanted, Tyler?" Justin asks, his brow pulled together tight.

"Never."

"Then why are you starting now?"

"Because she's better off without me in her life," I blurt out.

"Yeah, I hear ya," Christian says with an understanding nod. He's clearly going through his own shit, too. "She should be with a guy who'd treat her right. A guy who'd keep her safe."

I'm that fucking guy.

"She's obviously not worth the trouble," Ryder pipes in, joining us.

I'm practically snarling, frothing at the mouth when I say, "You're fucking wrong."

"Yeah, that's what I thought," Justin says with a slap to my shoulder. "Look, no guy is going to love her the way you do. Your troubles are behind you. You need to go make this right, buddy. Go find her, get the fuck out of Dodge like you guys talked about nine years ago. Don't waste this second chance. After everything you've done, you deserve this."

Maybe Justin is right. Maybe I do deserve this, but what if trouble finds me again and Sara gets hurt? "I....fuck."

The waitress comes with another round and when I glance up to see her, see who's standing in the doorway, glancing around the room like a deer in the headlights, my heart jumps into my throat.

"No. Fucking. Way."

Our eyes lock, and she gives me a wobbly smile. I blink, sure I'm hallucinating, but when I open my eyes again, and find Sara still standing in the open door, I nearly fucking sob.

I suck in a fast breath, shove my cue into Ryder's hands

and push through the crowd, until I'm standing inches from the girl I love more than life itself.

"Sara," I say, sounding as breathless as I feel. Is she here for me, us? Do I dare hope? Then again, how can we be together, when I'm trouble? "What are you doing here? How did you find me?" I rake my hands through my hair, trying to make sense of this.

"Justin's return address was on the box of clothes he sent you," she says. "I went to the address and was told I could probably find him here."

"You found him," I say and point to the pool table.

"It's not him I'm looking for. It's you, because you left with something of mine."

My heart sinks. She's not here to give me a second chance. She's here to collect something. I wrack my brain and give a hard shake of my head. I left home with nothing but the clothes on my back. "Sara—"

She puts trembling fingers to my lips to stop me, and the softness in her touch fills me with so many emotions, ranging from rage that someone could have hurt her, to all the love rattling around my ribcage like a damn pinball.

"You left with my heart, Tyler," she says as tears spill down her face.

"Sara," I say again, and wonder if it sounds as tinny to her as it does to me.

"I thought I could get you out of my system, Tyler, but I—"

"I can't do that again, Sara. I can't. You know I'd never say no to you, but if we start things up again, it'll fucking kill me when you're done."

"I don't want to be done."

I pinch the bridge of my nose, my heart crashing so hard, I'm sure she can hear it over the music. "What are you saying?"

"I want you, Tyler. I've never stopped wanting you."

"Sara...we can't."

"Lucas told me everything," she says, and for a moment my heart stops beating.

"Everything?"

Tears fill her eyes again, and I'm about to pull her to me when she starts sobbing hard. She lifts her hands, and pounds on my chest. "Tyler..." she cries. "So many lost years. I understand why you did what you did, but our dreams, our hopes... we lost so much."

I hold my breath and let her beat on me for a minute. When her frustrated pounding slows, I capture her wrists in my hands. "I'm sorry, Sara," I say, the pain in my chest intensifying, and it's not from her pounding.

"No, Tyler. I'm the one who's sorry," she whispers, her voice catching in her throat. "You are the best guy I know, and I never for one second should I have questioned that."

"I never meant to hurt you, ever. All I ever wanted to do was love you."

"Then love me, Tyler, please. Love me hard and fierce. We have so many years to make up for." She goes up on her toes, and unable to help myself, I press my lips to hers, for a breath-robbing kiss that leaves us both shaking when I break it. I look at the woman I love, have always loved, and then harden myself.

"Sara, I can't."

Her look is stricken, her big eyes, wide and stark against her white skin. "Don't, Tyler, don't do this to us."

She pounds on my chest again, her tears falling hard.

"I can't put your life in danger. I can't do that."

"Tyler, don't you get it? As long as I'm with you, no one will ever hurt me."

"Is this asshole bothering you?" some mouth-breathing douchebag asks. My gaze flies to the man standing over Sara.

I take in his cut, his gang colors, and rage builds inside me. He puts a beefy hand on Sara's body, and takes a menacing step toward me. In that instant, the world around me fades and all I see is red. Motherfucker is messing with the wrong guy on the wrong day. Nobody touches Sara and gets away with it. Nobody. Years of pent up fury boil my blood and before I can stop myself, I pull my fist back.

EPILOGUE

Tyler

Four years later:

Wailing sounds come from down the hall, and I blink in the black of the night, trying to get my bearings and figure out where I am and what the hell is going on. I wipe my damp hair from my forehead and stand, wobbly on my bare feet, the floor cool beneath me as I fumble around in the dark.

With my lids only half open, I walk toward the sound and grope the air until I feel the solid bars before me. I grip them tight, the keening cry growing louder and louder, piercing the quiet and rousing me even more.

I blink again, almost fully awake now, as I tug on the bars. They release with a soft click and I lower them. "Shh, little one," I whisper in a soothing voice, and I reach into the crib and pull little Avery from her blankets. "Are you hungry again already?"

Avery screams harder, and a night-light flicks on in the

hall, filling the room with a soft golden glow. Sara quietly enters the room and puts her hand on my back, touching me lovingly as I cradle little Avery, holding her to my bare chest...my heart.

"You didn't need to get up," I whisper and turn to give Sara a light kiss. I catch her smile in the light pouring in from the hallway.

She stifles a yawn. "It's my turn. You got up last night, remember?"

"I don't mind."

Her warm sleepy smile draws my attention, her mouth begging to be claimed by me a second time tonight. "I know, which is why I love you," she says.

I never get tired of hearing her say that. "I love you too." I lean into her, breathe in her vanilla scent, let it swirl through my blood and fill me with hunger.

"I know," she says, warmth in her eyes as she brushes Avery's soft cheek. "I think little miss is going through a growth spurt."

I rock Avery, and Sara's hairs tickle my face as she leans forward and kisses our ten-month-old daughter. "Do you want me to heat a bottle, or do you want to feed her?" I ask.

"I'll feed her."

I hand Avery over, and my heart fills with love as Sara drops into her nursing chair. Avery's cries are hushed as Sara releases the flap on her nursing bra and feeds our sweet baby girl. I drop down onto the floor in front of them, and yawn as I hug Sara's legs.

"Why don't you go back to sleep," Sara says. "You have to get up early for the clinics."

"Sleep is overrated," I say, not wanting to miss a moment of my wife and our beautiful baby together like this. As I take them in, absorb the love in the room, I can't help but think I've used my second chance to the fullest. It could have gone down a whole lot worse, had Justin not stepped in and stopped me from pummeling that mouth-breather who dared to touch Sara.

In the end, Sara was right when she said as long as she was with me, nothing or no one would ever hurt her. The Phantoms aren't part of my world anymore, and with Sara in my life permanently, as well as our beautiful daughter, all living in late Aunt Sandra's house in Indiana, the pent up anger and frustration had dissipated, and the nightmares had subsided.

A noise in the hall gains my attention and I turn to see Mom and Gracie enter the nursery. "What are you two doing up?" I ask.

"We heard Avery." Mom sits in the rocking chair next to Sara and my heart swells as she smiles at her daughter-in-law, and first grandchild.

"You didn't have to get up," I say.

She waves her hand at me. "Oh, hush. When my grandbaby cries, I get up."

Sara chuckles, and Gracie comes and sits next to me on the floor. Just then Alex and Lucas come stumbling in. Any second now I expect Sara's parents to come barreling in through the front door, to see what the ruckus in the Barrett household is all about. They left Aunt Sandra's house to Sara, and moved into a smaller place less than a mile down the road. I can't help but think how lucky we are to be surrounded by such a loving family.

"What's going on?" Alex asks as he rubs his eyes. Alex had recently graduated from Penn State after getting his degree in education. He's staying with us until he starts his new job at the local high school next week. Who would have thought my kid brother would grow up to actually follow in Coach Ramsey's footsteps. He's going to be a fine coach and teacher, and when he's not on the field or in the classroom, he helps me out with the clinics at the sports store Sara and I built from the ground up. Mom works there too, even though she's past retirement, but she enjoys getting out of the house, and spending time with me. Honest to God, it's hard to believe that Sara and I have checked so much off our bucket lists, our education included.

I shake my head. "What are you two doing up?"

"We heard the crying and then you all talking," Lucas answers as he drops down onto the floor next to Gracie. He throws his arm around her shoulder and she leans into him. During their free time, Gracie and Lucas both help out at the store, too. When Gracie isn't working with me, she's another page deep into her latest novel. I've been working closely with her on it, considering it's all about a golden boy who went to prison, and how he got back on his feet again. I think it's going to be a bestseller. Yeah, I'm proud as fuck of her.

And then there's Lucas. He ended up with house arrest for a few months. Since he moved in with us after we took over Sandra's old homestead, he's been able to save some money, and is in the process of opening his own garage bay nearby. We left our troubles behind us, in the past where they belong, and Lucas and I are good.

If I could change the past, would I? Probably not. Yeah, Sara and I had to climb through hell before we found our footing, but that footing is rock solid and unbreakable. If I had done anything differently maybe we wouldn't all be where we are today.

I scan the room. God, we've all come so far. The truth is we didn't plan for things to turn out this way, but sometimes plans change. Sara and I are stronger now, and while we never did get back what we had, what we have now feels more real, sharp, and far deeper and more intimate than anything we'd ever had. Simply put...everything is better.

Everything is exactly as it should be.

AFTERWORD

Thank You!

Thank you so much for reading Betting Bad, book one in my Reform series. I hope you enjoyed the story as much as I loved writing it. Please read on for an excerpt of The Playmaker.

Interested in leaving a review? Please do! Reviews help readers connect with books that work for them. I appreciate all reviews, whether positive or negative.

Happy Reading,
   Cathryn

THE PLAYMAKER

Fat drops of spring rain pummel my head, wilting my curls as I dart through Seattle's busy traffic to the café on the other side of the street. My best friend, Jess, is inside waiting for me, undoubtedly hyped up on her third latté by now.

I step over a pothole and search for an opening in the traffic. I hate being late, I really do. I totally value other people's time, but when the email came through from my editor, asking me to write a hot hockey series, my priorities took a curve. I've worked with Tara for a couple years now, and I know her like—pardon the pun—a well-worn book. To her, hesitation equals disinterest. She's a mover, a tree-shaker, and it wouldn't have taken long for her to offer the opportunity to another author. She wanted a quick reply and I had to give it to her.

I got this!

Yeah, that was my response, but what did I have to lose? I've been in such a rut lately, thanks to my fickle muse, deserting me when I needed her most. I swear to God, sometimes she acts like a hormonal teenager. I need to whip her into shape so I don't lose this gig. The royalties from a series will help make a sizeable dent in the bills that are piling up high and deep.

High and deep.

I laugh. One of those self-derisive snorts that crawls out when you'd really rather cry. Yeah, that pretty much sums up the *I got this* response I emailed back. High and deep, like a big steaming pile of—

A car horn blares, jolting me from my pity party. With my heart pounding in my chest, I step in front of the Tesla and flip the guy off. I safely reach the sidewalk and once again my mind is back on my job, and off the impatient jerk in the overpriced car.

I step up on the sidewalk and lift my face to the rain, the cool water a pleasant break from this unusual spring heat wave we're having. Pressure fills my throat. The hum of traffic behind me dulls, leaving only the sound of my pulse pounding in my ears. Panic.

Why the hell did my editor think I, former figure skater turned romance novelist, would want to write a series about hot hockey players? Yeah, sure my brother is an NHL player, but that doesn't mean I'm into the game. I hate hockey. No, hate is too mild a word for what I feel. I loathe it entirely. But you know what I don't loathe? Eating. Yeah, I like eating. Oh, and a roof over my head. I really like that, too.

I draw in a semi self-satisfied breath at having rationalized my fast response.

Except my reply was total and utter bullshit. I don't *got this*. In fact, I...wait, what's the antonym of *got this*? All that comes to mind is, *you're screwed*. Yep, that pretty much describes my predicament.

Why didn't I just stick to figure skating?

Because you took a bad spill that ended your career.

Oh right. But seriously, a hockey series... Ugh. Kill me. Freaking. Now.

I reach the café, pull the glass door open and slick my rain-soaked hair from my face. I quickly catalogue the place to find Jess hitting on the barista. Ahh, now I get why she picked a place so far from home. I take in the guy behind the counter. Damn, he's hotter than the steaming latté in Jess's hand, and from the way she's flirting, it's clear he'll be in her bed later today.

I sigh inwardly. It's always so easy for her. Me? Not so much. Men rarely pay me attention. Unlike Jess, I'm plain, have the body of a twelve-year-old boy, and most times I blend into the woodwork.

I pick up a napkin from the side counter and mop the rain off my face. Doesn't matter. I'm not interested anyway. From my puck-bunny-chasing brother to all his cocky friends, I know what guys are really like, and when it comes to women, they're only after one thing, and it isn't scoring the slot. I roll my eyes. Then again, maybe it is.

And of course, I can't forget the last guy I was set up with. What he did to me was totally abusive, but I don't want to dredge up those painful memories right now.

I shake, and water beads fall right off my brand-new rain-resistance coat. At least something is going right for me today. Semi-dry, I cross the room and stand beside Jess.

"Hey, sorry I'm late."

Jess turns to me, smiles, and holds a finger up. "I'll forgive you only if you're late because you were knees deep into some nasty sex, 'cause girlfriend, it's been far too long since you've been laid."

Jesus, what ever happened to this girl's filters?

Thoroughly embarrassed, my gaze darts to the barista, who is grinning, his eyes still locked on my friend, looking at her like she's today's hot lunch special and ignoring me like I'm yesterday's cold, lumpy oatmeal.

Ugh, really?

"Non-fat latté," I say, and scowl at him until he puts his eyes back in his head. I might be an English major but I have a PhD in the death glare. Truthfully, I'm so sick of guys like him, one thing on their minds. Then again, Jess only wants one thing from him, so I really shouldn't have a problem with it. Why do I? Oh, maybe because Mr. Right, my battery-operated companion, isn't quite cutting it anymore, and it's left me a little jittery and a whole lot cranky.

Jess is right. I *do* need to get laid.

Jess's lips flatline when she takes me in, her gaze carefully accessing me. "What?" she asks, her mocha eyes narrowing.

God, sometimes I really hate how well she can read me. "Nothing."

She straightens to her full height, and I try to do the same, but she dwarfs me, even without her beloved two-inch heels. I square my shoulders, but it's always hard to pull off a high-power pose when you're only five foot two, and teased relentlessly about it.

"Come on," she says, and guides me to a corner table. I peel off my coat and plunk down. Jess sits across from me. "Spill."

I point to my forehead. "Do I have 'idiot' written here?"

She looks me over, and cautiously asks, "No, why?"

My phone chirps in my purse, and I reach for it. Great, it's my editor wanting to set turn-in dates. "How about never?" I say under my breath.

"Uh, Nina. You're talking to your phone. You better tell me what's going on."

"You're not going to believe what I just agreed to."

"Do tell," she says and leans forward, like I'm about to spill some dirty little sex secret. If only that were the case.

I grab my phone and hold it up, showing her Tara's message. "I just agreed to write a hockey series," I say, and toss my phone back into my purse, mic-drop style—without the bold confidence.

Jess pushes back in her chair, clearly disappointed. She lifts her cup, and over the rim, asks, "I don't see how that makes you an idiot."

My mouth drops open. Jess and I have been friends since childhood. She of all people knows how much I hate hockey. "Are you serious?"

She shrugs. "You're a writer."

Mr. Sexy Barista brings me my coffee and he shares a secret, let's-hook-up-later smile with Jess. "And...?" I ask when he leaves.

"Writer's write and make things up. I know you hate hockey, but what does that have to do with anything?"

"I can't come up with a plot, or write about the game, if I don't know anything about it."

She shakes her head. "And I can't believe your brother is a professional player and you never once paid attention to the game."

"I was busy pursuing a professional skating career, remember?"

She reaches across the table and gives my hand a little squeeze. "I know. I'm sorry."

My tailbone and neck take that moment to throb, a constant reminder of a career lost.

I didn't just lose my dream of skating professionally the day my feet went out from underneath me, I lost my confidence, too. A concussion will do that to you.

Good thing I majored in English in college. Once I hung up my skates, I began to blog about the sport and sold a few articles. I joined a local writers group, and after talking to a group of romance writers, I tried my hand at one. Much to my surprise, it actually sold. I went from non-fiction to fiction, in every sense of the word. Happily ever after might exist between the pages, but it certainly doesn't in real life. At least not for me.

I take a sip of my latté, and give an exaggerated huff as I set it down. Jess instantly goes into problem-solving mode when she sees that I'm really stressed about this. As a brand-new high school guidance counselor, she can't help but want to fix me.

"Okay, it's simple," she begins. "You have to learn the game."

"How am I supposed to do that?"

"Turn on the TV and watch."

"I can watch a bunch of guys chase a stupid puck around a rink all I want, I still won't be able to understand the rules."

"How dare you call my favorite sport stupid."

"Jessss..." I plead. "What am I going to do?"

She crinkles her nose. Then her eyes go wide. "I've got it. Shadow your brother."

I give a quick shake of my head. "No, he's on the road, and he won't want me hanging around."

Jess goes quiet again, and that hollowed-out spot inside me aches as I think about Luke. I miss my brother so much and wish we were closer. Luke and I grew up in a family where there were no hugs or words of affirmation. I know Mom and Dad loved us, but as busy investment bankers, work consumed their lives. Sure, they put me in figure skating, and Luke in hockey when we were young, but they never shared in our passions, or really supported our pursuits.

I guess I can't expect my brother to display love, when none was ever displayed to him.

"Why don't you teach me?"

"It might be my favorite sport to watch, but I don't really know all the rules. I think you'd be better off getting your brother or…" She straightens. "Wait. I got this," she says, and I cringe when she tosses my three-word email response back at me. A warning shiver skips along my spine, and I get the sense that whatever she's about suggest, is going to take me right down the rabbit hole.

"What about Cole Cannon?"

I groan, plant my elbows on the table, and cover my face with my hands. "Never," I mumble through my fingers. "Not in a million freaking years."

Jess removes my hands from my face. "Why not? He's your brother's best friend. I'm sure he'll help you."

"Cocky Cole Cannon, aka, The Playmaker. Do I need to say any more?" I reach for my latté and take a huge gulp, burning the roof of my mouth. Damn.

"I know you hate him, Nina, but—"

"Of course I hate him. You remember the nickname he used to use when we were kids—Pretty BallerNina. I was a figure skater, not a ballerina," I could only assume he was mocking me about being pretty too, but I keep that to myself.

"At least he worked your name into the moniker, and hey, it could have been worse. He could have called you Neaner Neaner, like Luke did."

I glare at her and she holds her hands up. "Okay, okay. I get it. But Cole's been home for a month, recovering from a concussion, and his team—the Seattle Shooters, in case you don't know the league's name," she adds with a wink, "are probably going to make it to the playoffs, so you know he's watching all the games. You don't have to like him to ask him to explain a few of the plays, right?"

"I suppose."

Wait! What? Am I really thinking about asking The Playmaker to help me? I reach for my latté and blow on it before I take another big gulp.

"And if you ask me, while he's helping you learn the plays, I think you two should hate fuck."

I choke on my drink, spitting most of it on my friend as the rest dribbles down my chin.

OMFG, how embarrassing. All eyes turn to me. Mortified, I grab a napkin and start wiping my face, but Jess is laughing so hard, I start laughing with her.

"Couldn't you have waited until I swallowed?" I ask.

"That's what she said."

"Ohmigod, Jess. How are we friends?"

She waves a dismissive hand. "You know you love me because I'm hellacioulsy funny."

"I do, just stop cracking jokes when I'm drinking."

She leans towards me conspiratorially, and I brace myself. "I wasn't joking. You and Cocky Cole Cannon should hate fuck. He's as sexy today as he was when he used to hang out with Luke at your house when we were teens." I give her a look that suggests she's insane. She ignores it and wags her brows. "He's explosive on the ice, but do you know why they really call him the Cannon?"

"Because it's his last name."

"Yeah, but that's not the only reason."

Don't ask. Don't ask.

"Okay, then why?" I ask.

"'Cause he's loaded between his legs."

Yeah, okay, I totally set myself up for that.

"You don't know that," I shoot back. My mind races to my brother's best friend, and I mentally go over his form. He's athletic, tall and—as much as I hate to admit it—hot as hell. The perfect trifecta. Could he be packing too? Working with some top-notch equipment?

Jesus, what am I doing? The last thing I should be thinking about is Cole's 'cannon'.

"Come on." Jess grabs her purse. "I'll drive you there."

I flatten my hands on the table. "I'm not going to his house, especially not unannounced."

"Give him a call then."

"No."

She sits back in her chair and folds her arms, a sign she's changing tactics. "And here I thought you liked your condo and food in your cupboards."

I groan at the direct hit.

Her voice softens and she touches my hand. "But you know you always have—"

"Fine." I stop her before she brings up my trust fund. Yeah, sure, Mom and Dad set money aside for me, but I don't want to use it. I want to live by my own means, make it on my own merit. Besides it wasn't their money I wanted, then or now, it was their attention, their love. I moved out years ago and only ever hear from them on my birthday or at Christmas.

I pull my phone from my purse. "I'll text him. If he doesn't answer, we don't talk about this again." I go through my contacts and find his number, having stored it years ago when he called to check on me after my injury. The call had taken me by surprise; so did his concern. Maybe my brother put him up to it. I don't know. Nor do I know why I kept his number.

My fingers fly across the screen, but in no way do I expect him to respond. At least I hope he doesn't. I read over the text. *Sorry to hear about your concussion. I was wondering if you could help me with something.* Then hit send.

I set my phone down and look at Jess. "Happy?"

"Hey, I'm not the one who's going to be homeless."

Point taken. Maybe I should be hoping he *does* text back.

My phone pings, and we both reach for it. Jess gets it first, and from her smirk, I guess my wish just came true—Colin responded.

Careful what you wish for.

"What does it say?" I ask, afraid of the answer.

"It says, sure what's up?" Jess's fingers dance over the screen as she responds for me.

"What are you saying?" I ask, panic welling up inside me. "So help me, if you're telling him I need to get laid..."

The phone pings again and she holds it out for me to read.

"I asked—I mean *you* asked if you could stop by his place, and he said sure."

"I don't know whether to kiss you or choke you," I say.

Jess laughs. "I think you'll be thanking me." She stands. "Come on."

We make our way outside, and the rain has slowed to a light mist as I follow her down the street to her parked car. I hop in and question my sanity. Am I really going to ask Cocky Cannon to teach me the game?

Jess starts the car and the locks click as she pulls into traffic. Guess so.

"You remember where he lives?" I ask. I think back to when he bought the house. He had a big party to celebrate. I was invited but didn't go. Why would I? Watching the hockey players with their bunnies was not my idea of a good time.

"Of course." She jacks the tunes and sings along off-key as she drives. Twenty minutes later, she pulls up in front of his mansion. It's a ridiculously big house for one person. I stare at it, and once again question my sanity.

"Go," Jess says.

"I'm going," I shoot back. I open the door, and smooth my hand over my mess of curls. Why the hell did I do that? It's not like I'm trying to make myself presentable or impress him. We don't even like each other.

I force my legs to carry me to his door, and I'm about to knock when it opens. My breath catches as I take in Cole, standing before me shirtless and barefoot, dressed only in a pair of faded jeans that hug him so nicely.

God, he is so freaking hot—and I never, ever should have come here.

As we stare at each other, like we're in some goddamn Mexican standoff, I can't stop thinking about his 'cannon'. My gaze drops to the lovely bulge between his legs, and a moan I have no control over catches in my throat as Jess's words come back to haunt me.

You two should hate fuck.

Thank you, Jess, for planting that idea in my brain. Christ, I should have choked her when I had the chance.

ABOUT CATHRYN

New York Times and *USA today* Bestselling author, Cathryn is a wife, mom, sister, daughter, and friend. She loves dogs, sunny weather, anything chocolate (she never says no to a brownie) pizza and red wine. She has two teenagers who keep her busy with their never ending activities, and a husband who is convinced he can turn her into a mixed martial arts fan. Cathryn can never find balance in her life, is always trying to find time to go to the gym, can never keep up with emails, Facebook or Twitter and tries to write page-turning books that her readers will love.

Connect with Cathryn:
Newsletter
https://app.mailerlite.com/webforms/landing/c1f8n1
Twitter: https://twitter.com/writercatfox
Facebook:
https://www.facebook.com/AuthorCathrynFox?ref=hl
Blog: http://cathrynfox.com/blog/

Goodreads:
https://www.goodreads.com/author/show/91799.Cathryn_Fox
Pinterest http://www.pinterest.com/catkalen/

Instinctive

Impulsive

Indulgent

Sun Stroked Series

Seaside Seduction

Deep Desire

Private Pleasure

Captured and Claimed Series:

Yours to Take

Yours to Teach

Yours to Keep

Firefighter Heat Series

Fever

Siren

Flash Fire

Playing For Keeps Series

Slow Ride

Wild Ride

Sweet Ride

Breaking the Rules:

Hold Me Down Hard

Pin Me Up Proper

Tie Me Down Tight

Take Me Down Tender

Stand Alone Title:

Hands on with the CEO

Torn Between Two Brothers

Holiday Spirit

Unleashed

Knocking on Demon's Door

Web of Desire